THE SAMURAI CIPHER

ERNEST DEMPSEY

JOIN THE ADVENTURE

Visit ernestdempsey.net to get a free copy of the not-sold-in-stores short story, RED GOLD.

You'll also get access to exclusive content not available anywhere else.

While you're at it, swing by the official Ernest Dempsey fan page on Facebook at https://facebook.com/ErnestDempsey to join the community of travelers, adventurers, historians, and dreamers. There are exclusive contests, giveaways, and more!

Lastly, if you enjoy pictures of exotic locations, food, and travel adventures, check out my feed @ernestdempsey on the Instagram app.

What are you waiting for? Join the adventure today!

PROLOGUE

TOKYO, JAPAN

Shibuya Ward 1946

Iemasa heard the knock on the door. The sudden harsh noise interrupted his meditation. He knew the sound was coming soon, just not that soon.

They must be in a hurry, he thought. *Always rushing, the West.*

Things were much simpler when he was younger. But the Industrial Revolution had changed all that. The world was speeding up at an incredible pace. The old ways were a thing of the past. Soon, they would be all but forgotten.

He smoothed out his ceremonial robe and floated over to the door. Iemasa drew in a deep breath, straightened the glasses on his nose, and twisted the doorknob. He greeted the men in the atrium with a stoic nod. Everything he did for the rest of the day would stand on tradition and ceremony. There would be no display of emotion, no actions that would cause trouble.

The American officer gave a polite but short nod. Two other US soldiers and a representative of the Japanese military escorted him. The latter, a man named Reiko, Iemasa knew well. He'd served as a personal escort of Iemasa on several occasions. Not that he felt he needed an escort. Being part of the Tokugawa Clan brought a certain respectability with it. They were the remnant of a golden age in the country's history. Being part of that group had its privileges, though being called a prince was something that Iemasa felt a little heavy for his tastes. He'd worked hard his entire life, going to university to study law and moving up through the ranks of Japanese government with the idea of creating a better world.

Then the war happened and everything changed. He'd served his emperor loyally, never questioning the decisions that were made or the actions taken. In the end, Japan lost. The toll had been severe, in both lives and resources. And now, the final price was being being paid.

The disarmament of Japan was part of a master plan put together by the Allied generals, with Douglas MacArthur leading the way. All Japanese citizens and military personnel were to hand over all weapons, even antiques, items of historical significance, and worst of all, family heirlooms.

Many Japanese protested the extremes of the disarmament protocols. Giving up ancestral swords or bow and arrows in a world where wars were fought with tanks, planes, and automatic weapons seemed beyond excessive. What harm would those weapons bring? Some had suggested that taking away items with personal or historic value was the Americans' way of totally breaking their spirit. That had mostly happened when the two atomic bombs had dropped on Hiroshima and Nagasaki. Iemasa was still hearing the horror stories from those two areas.

But this? This was ridiculous and unnecessary, yet there was nothing he could do to stop it. The law was clear and could not be broken.

Of course, there was the other possibility behind the detailed disarmament procedures. The Allies wanted trophies. A sick and primitive way to end the war; taking trophies of their victory was not only a slap in the face, it was an atrocity against historical and familial preservation. But what could be done? The only exception to the rule was that religious institutions were off limits to Allied troops.

"Tokugawa Iemasa?" the American officer asked to make sure he was speaking to the right person.

Iemasa nodded, leaving his thoughts to the ether.

"You ready to go?"

Iemasa nodded again. "Yes, I was just finishing my morning meditation. But the required items are ready for transport."

"Good. That's good. These two boys will be accompanying us to the collection facility. I figured we'd need a few extra hands seein' that you have quite a few weapons to turn in."

The thought sent a needle through Iemasa's heart, but he wouldn't let them see any anger or sadness. To them, he would remain strong. For his family and for his people.

"Right this way," he stepped aside, motioning with his right hand for the men to enter.

With a show of disrespect, the Americans stomped their way inside without bothering to take their boots off. Their Japanese escort didn't make the same mistake. Out of a lifetime of habit, he removed his boots carefully at the door.

The officer turned and looked around the elegant, minimalistic home, its plain white walls separated by cherry wood beams. The room was like most other traditional Japanese interiors he had seen during his short time there, and he was unimpressed by the lack of what he considered to be modern amenities. But he wasn't there to judge the décor. He was there to do a job.

"Right this way, gentlemen," Iemasa said, pointing to a sliding paper and wood door on the other side of the room.

Once the visitors were inside, the host closed the door and stepped around in front of them, leading the way down a narrow corridor. The walls were decorated with pictures of family and framed Japanese characters the American's couldn't read. Light poured through the windows of the rooms they passed, doing more to illuminate the hallway than the dim lights above.

At the end of the corridor, Iemasa turned left and led the group into a massive room. In the center of the far right wall, an ornate set of armor stood on a stand. Its black, gold, and red accents were exquisite. Even without a body inside it, the Samurai armor was imposing.

"That all of it?" The American officer pointed at a collection of open boxes on the floor.

At least a dozen sheathed katana swords, three sets of bows and arrows, and a few spears were stacked neatly inside. Despair filled Iemasa's eyes as he gazed upon the collection. His ancestors would be disappointed. Some of those weapons had been handed down through half a dozen generations. One or two pieces were even older.

The officer motioned to his two subordinates, and they immediately started sifting through the boxes, tossing the weapons aside like they would pieces of trash. Iemasa winced with each object thrown onto the floor.

When they were done, the men put the weapons back in the boxes, not nearly as neatly as they'd originally been packed, and stood by waiting for further orders. The officer stared at a box that was separate from the others. There was only one sword in it, which was odd.

"Why is that one packed by itself?" the officer asked.

The Japanese escort started to respond, but Iemasa cut him off. "It is a weapon that has been in the Tokugawa family for centuries. It's older than all the others and is our most prized possession. That blade must be kept separate because it is different. It deserves that honor."

The officer snorted. "Honor? Were your people thinking about honor when they pulled that sneak attack on Pearl Harbor and killed men while they slept? You all sure do talk a lot about honor, but I don't see a lot of it in the way you fight. I guess you won't be doing much fightin' for a while, though." He waved his hand at the boxes. "Get this crap out of here, boys. We have several other stops to make today after we get these to the collection depot."

The other men started hefting boxes off the floor and headed for the exit. The officer noticed the two Japanese men were still standing there and raised his eyebrows. "That means you two need to help too."

The men nodded respectfully, stepped over to the remaining boxes, and gently picked them up with the greatest of care.

Iemasa followed the Japanese escort out of the room and down the hall. They heard the front door open, signaling that the two soldiers had stepped out. Satisfied the Americans were out of earshot, he spoke in a whisper to Iemasa.

"You cannot do this. You cannot let them have it."

When Iemasa responded, there was a distant sadness in his voice. "It is the law."

"Whose law? The Americans'? It isn't right."

"It is done, my friend. Perhaps someday it will return to its rightful owners."

The escort shook his head in disgust as they passed through the door. "I've heard they have been melting down the old weapons. If this happens, it will be lost forever."

Iemasa's jaw set firm. "They will not destroy it. I am certain of this."

"How can you be so sure?"

Just before they arrived at the military truck on the street where the two soldiers were sliding the boxes into the back, Iemasa answered in a way that gave Reiko pause. "Things aren't always what they seem."

1

TOKYO

Shinji stared out the empty wall frame of the newly built high-rise. The lower floors had already received walls but this one – at the top level – had yet to be protected from the elements. Shinji had never been bothered by heights, and he wasn't now, even though he knew he was about to die.

Wind plowed through the fortieth-story construction platform, blowing his hair around like leaves in a cyclone. He winced as debris and dust washed over his face. But Shinji remained calm. Internally, his mind retreated to a meditative state, just as he'd learned to do so long ago when he was a child. He ignored the external elements—the wind, the sounds and smells of the city—and stood silent against their request. The men wanted information—, information he would never give them.

He'd been taken from his home in the middle of the night, his house torn apart in their search for something he knew they wouldn't find. Not there, anyway. Shinji was cleverer than that. He knew what the man standing behind him wanted. There was no way Shinji was going to let him have it. Death didn't frighten him. His only concern was for his niece. If these men believed she knew something about what he was working on, they might go after her. Once he was dead, Shinji could no longer protect her.

"This is the last time I'm going to ask you, old man. Where is it?" The voice came from behind Shinji. It was younger, though only by a decade or so. His name was Taka, and his reputation darker than most in the city's sprawling criminal underworld.

Shinji allowed himself to laugh, which was rewarded with a swift chop to his kidneys. The laughing turned to coughs as he dropped to his knees, catching himself with his right hand on the dirty concrete floor. He winced but picked himself up quickly.

"Not so funny now, is it old man?"

Shinji nodded a few times, still coughing under his breath. "How do you know? You don't even realize what I'm laughing at, young man."

"Perhaps you could enlighten me; all of us." Taka waved his hand to encompass the other four men in the construction zone. They all wore black button-up shirts. Of course, the top two or three buttons were undone to reveal the tops of their gang's signature tattoos. The ink was standard issue for anyone who swore allegiance. While there were variations in the designs, the overarching pattern remained similar. The only thing Shinji could liken it to was a zip-up suit that remained unzipped at the top like a pair of open tattooed wings. It was one way people could identify them, and stay out of their path. That, or do whatever they said.

Taka had risen to power quickly within the Yakuza. He controlled a vast segment of the city. And no one defied him. To do so was to be at the wrong end of a horrible death. Shinji knew all of that. In his mind, it didn't change a thing.

When he spoke, Shinji did so with staunch resolve. He would never bend to these animals, no matter what the threat. "Even if you had the cipher, you wouldn't be able to understand it. Someone who spent their life trying to cheat, steal, and murder their way to success only looks for the easy path. It is not the path of the Samurai and, therefore, will never be yours to walk."

Taka pursed his lips and nodded. "You're not wrong, old man. I've done all those things. I wasn't born into a life of privilege like you. But I've built something for myself the best way I could."

"And once you have the cipher, then what? You'll have everything you have always wanted? You'll repent of your sins and become a good person?" He chortled. "I don't think so."

"Repent? No, I have no intention of repenting. I have loftier goals. Once I have the cipher, I will find the treasure it leads to. And when that happens, I will be the unquestioned leader of all Yakuza. No one will stand in my way. I will be an emperor. And my reach will be limitless."

Shinji frowned at the younger man, and he cast a disapproving gaze as he would to a child trying to steal another cookie from the jar. "Do you really believe it will bring you such power?"

"Of course it will. Why wouldn't it? It is a symbol of our national heritage. It will command respect from all."

"No," Shinji shook his head. "It will make you a target. And those who seek the cipher's treasure must possess honor. When I look at you, I see no honor. You are a coward and a fool, bent on material gain and whatever pleasures life can offer you. The treasure will not be yours. It can only be found by a hero, not a villain."

Taka listened to his captive's rant, but he would hear no more. He held up a finger for silence. Looking down at the ground for a moment, he sniffled and wiped his nose with the back of his hand. When he looked up, the frustration was gone. His eyes were filled with a terrible resolution.

"You're really not going to tell us what we want to know, are you, Shinji?"

The old man drew in a long, deep breath and tilted his chin back. He said nothing, which was all Taka needed to hear.

"That's fine. We'll find the cipher without you. Even if we have to tear your ancestral home apart, we will find it. We will scour the earth for every person you know. And when we are done, we will have the cipher. You have my word on that."

Shinji stared out across the bright lights of the big city. It cast a pale glow into the darkness above, drowning out all but the brightest stars. "The word of a coward is no better than the word of a pig," he said.

Taka grabbed his prisoner by the back of the shirt and shoved him over to the edge. The wind picked up and blew across their faces. Taka's wavy black hair whipped around with each gust. He held Shinji's upper body over the edge, leaning him over so he could see the sidewalk and street below. A few cars rolled by, but most of the sidewalks were clear, save for the random late partygoers. Shinji's eyes widened. Even he wasn't totally immune to fear.

"Last chance, old man. Tell me where the cipher is, and I will let you go."

Shinji couldn't help but notice the odd choice of words the younger man used. Either way, he was a dead man. Whether he told Taka the location of the cipher or not, he was going to end up on the pavement below. There was no stopping that now. The only thing he could do was slow them down and hope.

He turned his head to face his captor and looked him in the eyes. "The blade doesn't belong to you, Taka. And it never will."

Taka's right eye twitched. He took in a short, angry breath. "Very well."

His fingers let loose of Shinji's shirt, and gravity did the rest, pulling the old man down, slowly at first. By the time he'd passed the floor three stories down, he was speeding toward the street.

To Taka's surprise, Shinji screamed, the piercing sound quickly absorbed by the sounds of the city. Taka watched the man's entire fall until it came to a silent end on the asphalt forty stories below. His nostrils flared as he stared at the body. He stepped back from the edge and addressed one of his men.

"Hideo, take your men, and search his house again." Before Hideo could protest, Taka raised his hand. "I know you searched it thoroughly before. Perhaps there is something we missed the first time."

Hideo nodded. He was obedient, a good soldier. Always quick to do Taka's bidding and extremely persistent, Hideo had ridden Taka's coattails into the stratosphere of the criminal underworld. The two had joined the organization at almost the same time. The main difference between the two, other than Hideo's shaved head and stout physique, was that Taka possessed great ambition. Hideo preferred to stay in the shadows, taking care of business from behind the scenes.

"Go," Taka ordered. "And let me know what you find."

The men scurried away, disappearing down the unfinished stairwell. Taka looked out over the city: his city. The old man had hidden the cipher somewhere. It would be found. Perhaps there was a place he hadn't checked, someone he hadn't spoken to yet. No stone could be left unturned. Nothing could stand in his way of his goal of becoming a new kind of emperor, a Yakuza emperor. It all hinged on finding that cipher. If he failed, his life could hang in the balance.

2

CHATTANOOGA, TENNESSEE

Sean couldn't believe what he was seeing. The room still hadn't come into total focus. His mind was groggy, numbed by something. Was it lack of sleep or something more sinister? He shook his head to try to clear the cobwebs.

The scene cleared, and with that clarity a terrible feeling crept into his stomach.

He was standing in the kitchen of his Southside condo. A burning, acrid smell filled the air and seeped into his nostrils, causing him to wrinkle his nose. Dark liquid pooled on the floor at his feet. He'd not realized it at first because of his flip-flops, but he was standing in a small puddle.

The liquid oozed off the counter and dripped freely down to the floor. Sean tried to remember if, in all his years, he'd ever seen anything like this. Nothing came to mind, and as he exhausted his memories the heavy reality set in.

Questions riddled his mind like bullets from a machine gun. *How did this happen? Why did it happen? What did I do to deserve this? How am I going to clean this up?*

Anger boiled up inside him, but he pushed it away, forcing it back down into the depths whence it came. Getting angry wouldn't solve anything. Right now, he had to clean up the mess. There would be plenty of time to work through emotions later.

He lifted a foot out of the pool of liquid and stepped over to the counter. There it sat, staring at him with an uncaring and innocent glow. Something was missing. And he knew what it was.

Sean shook his head, now remembering how it had all happened. He flashed back to the night before. It had been a crazy evening. Monday Night Football was on, and he'd had a few friends over to watch the game. When they left, he'd decided to run the dishwasher. After a quick look at the coffee pot, he figured he might as well throw it in there to give it a good cleaning.

The coffee pot was still in the dishwasher that morning when the coffee maker automatically started running. Without the pot to collect the fresh brew, the filter overflowed and spilled the hot liquid all over the counter and, subsequently, the floor.

He put one hand on his hip while the other scratched his head. A quick check of the paper towel rack didn't fill him with reassurance. He might have enough to clean up the mess. Maybe. If not, he'd have to use towels from the bathroom.

One thing was certain: He'd have to walk up the street to get this morning's coffee, which wasn't a big deal. He lived two blocks away from the city's best coffee shop, a little place on Main Street adjacent to one of his favorite nighttime hangouts. Chattanooga's south side was sprouting new places to eat, drink, and hang out with friends. At almost any time of the day, there was something to do or somewhere to go. It was a far cry from the place he remembered as a child.

Sean shook off some of the liquid still clinging to a flip-flop and reached over for a paper towel. He ripped off a generous handful and started soaking up the coffee on the counter as he shut off the machine and removed the filter. After throwing the steaming filter away, he was returning to the paper towels to get reinforcements when the phone in his pajama pocket started ringing. He took a glance at the clock on the oven and frowned. Who would be calling at 7:12 in the morning?

He fished the device out of his pants and looked at the screen.

Of course. There were only a couple people he could think of who were even up at that time. One of those was his former boss, Emily Starks. She was the director of the government agency known as Axis. They did the things other agencies didn't want to mess with or didn't consider viable. After four years of service, Sean had called it quits, leaving her and the agency behind to work for his friend Tommy, head of the International Archaeological Agency. It was the latter whose name was displayed on the phone's screen.

Sean hit the green answer button and put the device to his ear. "I'm kind of in the middle of something right now. And I've asked you before not to call me before eight."

The voice on the other end sounded wide awake. "What's the matter, haven't had your coffee yet?"

Sean's head turned slowly from one shoulder to the next as he examined the mess. "Not exactly. I had sort of a complication."

"I'm not even going to ask what that means."

"I'd rather you not. By the way, you sound spritely for such an early hour."

Sean knew his friend was an early riser. Tommy Schultz was always up at the crack of dawn. Ever since they'd known each other, Tommy was the early bird trying to get the proverbial worm. Sean, on the other hand, preferred to sleep in until at least 7 a.m. And if he could hit the snooze button beyond that, it was a bonus.

"You know me," Tommy said. "Not enough hours in the day, so I try to get as many in as possible."

It wasn't the first time Sean had heard that mantra from his friend. And he knew it wouldn't be the last. He decided to get to the point of the call since he was still standing in the middle of a catastrophic mess. "I assume you have something interesting to talk about other than last night's game?"

"What game? Oh right, football was on."

Tommy's love of sports was hit or miss. When more important things were pressing, he barely stayed aware of what was going on.

"Yes," he answered. "I do have something interesting. Do you remember a few years ago when we checked out that lead down in Pitts, Georgia?"

Sean frowned. He'd been a lot of places and done a lot of things since then. "Vaguely. Refresh me."

There was a sense of eagerness—maybe anxiety—to Tommy's voice now. "I thought you'd say that. During World War II, Japan's citizens and military were completely disarmed. I mean any and all weapons were taken from them, including ancestral ones like swords and bows, that sort of thing. Even some knives."

"Right. I remember reading about all that."

"Yeah, well, we found a lead in Pitts that was supposedly linked to one of the most famous swords of all time."

Now it clicked in Sean's mind what his friend was talking about. "Oh yeah, the sword. That lead turned out to be cold. We couldn't get the family in Georgia to even talk to us. As I recall, they put out a restraining order on you." He had to chuckle at that memory.

"Yes, I am aware of the legal issues. And not just any sword. The Honjo Masamune. It's the single greatest sword ever made by the single greatest sword maker to ever live."

Sean derailed from his point. "You're not thinking about bothering them again, are you? Because I gotta be honest, I got the impression they aren't your biggest fans."

Tommy let out a heavy sigh, exasperated. "No, I'm not going to bother them. Would you just listen?"

"Sorry. You did ask me if I remembered that whole scenario."

"Well, forget the family in Pitts. Although I am still fairly certain they have something they're not supposed to have in the way of illegally obtained artifacts. The point of all this is that I think we may have another lead on the Honjo Masamune."

Sean took a deep breath. "OK, just to be clear, when you say 'we' you actually mean *you,* right? You remember I don't work for IAA anymore, right?"

"Yes, I'm well aware. And thanks for the reminder. For the record, I think you should come back. Just a thought."

"Seems like I've heard this song before."

"I know. I know. But listen, this is unfinished business, man. I mean, this is something we spent a lot of time on and never got to see through."

Sean shook his head. He hoped the coffee wouldn't stain the wood floor in his kitchen. Holding off on responding to his friend, he grabbed another handful of paper towels and tossed them on the floor.

"You. You spent a lot of time on it. I was just along for the ride, which was a long one, I might add. Pitts isn't a hop skip and a jump away from Atlanta."

Tommy scoffed. "It's not that bad."

"It's south of Macon and Warner Robins!"

"OK, maybe it's a little out of the way, and I'm sorry about that. But I don't ask you for many favors."

Sean laughed, booming his voice through the entire condo. "Seriously? You ask me for favors all the time!"

"Not all the time. Just hear me out. Can you do that?"

"Sure. Why not?"

"Exactly. Why not! It's not like you have anything else going on."

"I'm hanging up now, Tommy."

Sean put the phone down on the counter for a second and picked up the stained paper towels. He could hear his friend's voice through the earpiece, saying Sean's name and asking if he was still there. Sean smirked. Giving his best friend a hard time was one of his favorite things to do. And Tommy was easy to aggravate.

He picked up the device and put it back to his ear. "Hello? Who is it?"

"Oh come on! Stop screwing with me. I'm serious."

"OK, Tommy. I'll stop. What is it you want to do?"

Tommy was obviously frustrated. "Thank you!" He calmed down for a second before continuing. "Like I was saying, we...I...may have a new lead in the Masamune case. I got an email from a woman in Japan requesting our...my...help. After I read the email, I gave her a call. She said her uncle had spent years looking for the missing sword but never found it."

"Let me guess, he found *something*, though. Right?"

"Exactly. She claims he found a cipher that supposedly leads to the sword."

Sean thought about what his friend was saying. A key component of it didn't make sense. "So if he's the one that found the cipher, why is she the one contacting you? Does the guy not speak English?"

"The guy is dead, Sean. She said he was murdered yesterday, thrown off a building in the middle of Tokyo."

"Oh..."

"Yeah, pretty gruesome. I checked it out just to make sure she was on the up and up. Sure enough, a man named Shinji fell forty stories out of a building under construction. The police are calling it a suicide."

Forty stories. Sean shuddered at the thought. He'd been afraid of heights his whole life, the fear of falling the primary driver of the phobia. "That's pretty terrible. And the cops are calling it a suicide?"

"Yep. The niece is convinced it was murder, though—that the people who did it want the cipher."

"Where is the cipher now?" Sean took the bait. He knew that Tommy knew he would, which irritated him a little. But he couldn't resist.

"She doesn't know for sure. All she has is some cryptic clue that he sent her via email the day before he was killed."

So the uncle sent the email on Saturday. That was only two days ago. He must have known someone was coming for him. The gears started turning in Sean's mind. It was an involuntary response, part of being a curious student of history. He remembered the research Tommy put into trying to recover the Honjo Masamune. He'd spent months tracking the thing down, leaning on decades of research from other people. When it resulted in failure, Sean knew his friend never truly let it go. Now the legendary sword had reared its head again. And Sean knew the only way his friend would stop was to see it through.

"So he sent the email on Saturday. Did anyone see him meeting with someone suspicious that day or maybe the day before?"

"No idea. But we can ask her all that stuff when we get there."

Sean's voice turned suspicious. "When we get where? Tommy, Japan isn't just around the corner."

He heard a noise outside in the dark morning. Instantly, his ears pricked, and his eyes shot to the window. Someone was probably just going to work. The noises of the city were prevalent at this time of day as compared to the relative quiet of night.

"Well, that's where we're going."

Sean resisted. "Buddy, I'd love to help you, but I can't. Adriana is supposed to be coming into town early next week, and I haven't seen her in a while."

"We'll be back by then. I promise. And besides..."

The phone went dead. "And besides what?" Sean looked at the screen. The call had ended.

A second later, three knocks came from the front door. Sean twisted his head and looked over. Frowning, he waded through the remaining few puddles of coffee, kicked off his dripping flip-flops and padded barefoot to the entrance. He cracked the door and saw his friend standing outside in a gray winter coat. Tommy's thick, curly brown hair was tucked into a beanie. His brown glasses sat atop flushed cheeks. Sean's friend was about the same height, maybe an inch or so shorter, and about twenty pounds heavier, a fact that Sean continually encouraged his friend to change with diet and exercise.

Sean shook his head. "You're unreal. You know that?"

He opened the door wide, letting Tommy in out of the cold.

"Yeah, I know."

"What time did you get up this morning?"

Tommy unzipped his coat, quickly acclimating to the warmth of the condo. "You're really hung up on that, aren't you? Look, I know it's sudden, but I really feel like we can help this girl."

Sean shook his head and meandered back toward the kitchen. "Help her or help yourself find that sword you missed out on?"

"Both," Tommy shrugged and followed behind. "And besides, what's wrong with helping find a national treasure. It's not just about helping the girl. We're helping a whole nation." He paused and looked around at the mess. "What happened in here?"

Sean waved off the question. "I had a little coffee accident."

"Little? So I guess that means we're going out for a cup before we leave for Japan?"

"Buddy, I can't just up and go to Japan on a moment's notice. That sort of thing takes planning and packing and...I can't go to Japan with you!"

Tommy ignored his best friend. He sat down at the bistro table nearby and crossed a leg over his knee. "Sure you can. I'll wait while you pack. The plane is waiting at the local airport. It's not leaving without me."

He was right. Sean didn't really have anything pressing he had to get to. And he had to admit, finding one of the most coveted relics of Japan's past did arouse his interest. He sighed and put his hands on his hips.

"Fine. But first, you have to do something for me."

Tommy clapped his hands together in excitement. "Sure. Name it."

"Help me clean up this mess."

3

TOKYO

"He must have hidden it somewhere else," Taka said. He scratched his chin slowly, staring out at the rest of the men in the room with fiery eyes.

He'd sent out a team to find Shinji's cipher, but after a long day of taking apart everything in the dead man's home, they still came up empty-handed. His men had looked everywhere, even tearing up sections of flooring they thought sounded hollow and could be a secret hiding place. They'd broken vases—some of them probably valuable—and shattered picture frames. Drawers were removed and tossed aside. Every piece of furniture was ripped apart. And still, they found nothing.

Hideo and his men stood around the long boardroom table, staring at their boss with regret.

Taka sat in a chair made from maroon leather and trimmed with bronze-colored rivets. He blinked slowly as he stared down at the table. His brain worked hard to figure out where Shinji could have placed the cipher.

"Any deposit boxes? Storage facilities he used?"

Hideo shook his head. "No. He was a man of simple means. Everything he owned was in that house."

"He was a retired historian!" Taka raged. "Surely he had bank accounts or something."

"Accounts yes, but his finances were meager at best. And there were no safety deposit boxes in any of the accounts. Our man who deals with the banks checked that thoroughly."

Taka put a hand to his mouth and grazed the knuckle on the index finger with his teeth. "There has to be something we aren't seeing. Anything on his niece?"

"We have a man watching her. So far, nothing suspicious. She's been going to work as usual, other than helping with the funerary arrangements. She did receive two visitors. Americans."

This was new information, and Taka's curiosity spiked. "Friends?"

"One is an archaeologist. He runs an agency in Atlanta that helps facilitate discovery and transportation of rare artifacts. From what we know, the other worked with the same agency, but information on him before that is scarce. In my experience, that usually means government work of some kind."

Taka slammed his fist on the table. His voice was an erupting volcano. "Those men are here to find the cipher! Get over there, and find out what it is she's using them for!"

Hideo nodded. "Yes, sir. Right away."

He stood up and left the room, followed by three other men, leaving two bodyguards sitting to the right and left of Taka. "You two, wait outside," he ordered.

Both men gave a nod and obeyed, disappearing from view. The last one out closed the door behind him, leaving Taka alone in the room with his thoughts.

"What is it you were up to, Shinji?" he said to himself.

Taka stared at a piece of paper with Japanese characters on it. The lines didn't make sense to him, although he'd never been any good at deciphering riddles. This one was particularly troubling to him in its simplicity. He hated things he couldn't figure out or understand. It infuriated him and drove him to the point of madness, which is why he put other people on such tasks.

What troubled him now was that Shinji's niece had brought in two Americans to help. If one was an expert in history, the cipher had to be why they were here.

He stood up, taking the paper with him, and walked out the side door. He rubbed his head to massage away the stress. Heading down a long corridor, Taka made a sharp right turn and stalked by three closed paper doors until he reached the one he was looking for. He slid the door open and stepped into his study, a lavishly decorated room. Moving around behind the heavy black desk, he opened the main drawer and removed a little pill bottle. His fingers made quick work of the cap, and he dumped two pills into an open palm. After popping them into his mouth, he grabbed a nearby bottle of water, unscrewed the lid, took a drink, and swallowed.

None of his subordinates dared question his use of the painkillers. They knew better.

The pills—a high-octane version of Percocet—relaxed him when he felt the onset of too much stress. He was plagued by headaches, something that he'd experienced since childhood, and the pills helped prevent them.

Taka had discovered painkillers when he was fifteen. His father had come home from work drunk one night, as he did so many other nights. But this night was different. He'd lost his job at the mill and decided it would be a good idea to have a few extra drinks to drown his sorrows. Taka had grown accustomed to the beatings. He'd developed a sort of numbness to the pain. Deep down, he was certain his headaches were a result of being hit in the head so much as a child. At fifteen, though, he could take a punch. But throwing one took more courage. He knew once he did that, things would escalate. And if that was going to happen, Taka had to be ready.

He'd been secretly training in a local dojo after school since he was fourteen. He didn't have the money to pay the teacher, so he worked an hour every day after their sessions, cleaning the floors and bathrooms. His teacher was the only person who had ever taken pity on him, had ever shown him kindness. And he was the only one who ever taught Taka discipline.

When his father came home in a drunken rage that night, he'd started hitting Taka's mother much harder than usual. Taka watched from the corner like a cobra. His father started by smacking her across the face a few times. Then he changed to fists, punching her harder and harder. She wailed and screamed for him to stop, but he wouldn't. He kept saying something about how his life was awful because of her and their bastard son in the corner. When she was almost unconscious, her face swollen, bloodied, and bruised, he turned his attention to Taka.

He strode across the floor with a raised fist, swearing and cursing the day Taka was born. The young man had clenched his teeth. *Today is the day,* a voice in his mind had said. *It ends now.*

Standing in his study, Taka twitched his nose and sniffled. The memory wasn't one of sadness. It didn't hang a banner of grief over his heart. It was his ultimate moment of triumph. He turned to the bar in the corner, picked up a glass, and poured himself a short round of sake. After the warm liquid burned through his throat, he thought once more about that fateful day.

His father had lashed out, clumsily, foolishly. It was the first time Taka had ever fought back, ever dodged a blow. He did it easily, ducking to the side and grabbing his father's forearm with more strength than the older man could have ever anticipated. Taka pulled on the arm and slung his attacker into the nearest wall with a thud. The sudden impact shook a picture frame from its housing, sending it crashing to the floor. His father's surprised frown turned into something far stranger. It was almost as if he was glad Taka had defended himself, like a hunter glad to finally have met his match with a forest quarry.

He charged. It was a reckless attack. Taka snapped a quick jab squarely into his father's nose. He fired another and another, his knuckles only stopping when they'd reached his full arms' reach, two inches behind the target. With each blow, his father's head rocked back and then forward again, as if it was on a spring. Taka drove him back until he finished the round of six jabs with a straight on kick to the abdomen.

The kick sent his father crashing into the wall again. Taka waited in the mantis position he'd learned from his teacher. The older man was stunned and suddenly less drunk. He shook his head to rid himself of the shell-shock. His hand felt the blood trickling out of his nose, and a look of fury washed over his face—an expression Taka had never seen before. He knew then that his father was out of control. And he was.

The older man stood next to the kitchen counter where a rack of knives was kept. His left hand stretched out and grasped the handle of the largest one. He yanked it out and held it in front of him menacingly. Taka wasn't afraid, not anymore. His teacher at the dojo had taught him all about fighting people who had weapons.

His father lunged, swinging wildly with the blade. The tip went back and forth, swiping through the air but missing his target as Taka ducked, dipped, and weaved around. He dove forward under the knife and popped up behind his father before the old man could spin around. When he tried, Taka swung his right leg around, clipping the older man's heels. The sweep sent his father sprawling. His legs flew out from under him, and for a second, everything happened in slow motion. His father's eyes went wide as he fell to the floor; his body shuddered from the jarring impact.

The only mistake Taka made during the fight was letting down his guard for a split second after his father fell. He hesitated, uncertain what to do. It was the first time he'd ever had the old man in a vulnerable position. During that lapse, his father, the man who'd raised him from birth, took the knife and shoved it between the bones in Taka's shin.

He yelled out, feeling more pain than he'd ever felt before.

Taka set down the sake glass and peered out the window. He could still feel the stiff soreness in his leg, even though more than two decades had passed. But he didn't complain. He didn't feel like a victim. Taka knew that at that moment, the second his father stabbed him, he'd been set free.

Young Taka hobbled backward, letting rage overcome the pain, and yanked the knife from his leg. His father was still stunned from the previous assault and struggled to get off the floor.

Taka surged forward, pouncing on him with all the momentum his thin body would carry. It was enough to drive the old man back to the floor. Taka raised the knife high and brought the tip down hard into the old man's chest. He pulled it out and repeated the thrust even as his father's hands attempted to block the onslaught. Taka wouldn't be stopped, though. He kept driving the knife deep into the old man's chest and neck. Blood spurted and gushed from the wounds, and soon young Taka's face, hands, and torso were covered in it. He howled like a wild beast as he kept stabbing, up and down. Even when his father's hands fell limp to his sides and his body became still, Taka didn't stop. He kept thrusting the blade until his muscles grew weak and he couldn't do it anymore.

Tears had streaked the blood on the young man's face. He breathed in deep, heavy gasps. His eyes stared down at the mangled mess between his legs. Then he glanced at the knife and tossed it aside. His hands started shaking, and he somehow managed to stand. He looked over into the corner at his quivering mother. She was alive, somehow. Her feeble moans echoed in the small apartment that was otherwise eerily silent. She'd not seen a thing.

Pouring another glass of sake, Taka remembered everything that had followed. He'd done some weekend work as a courier for a local businessman, a man who had way more money than he should have for the business he was in. He sold seafood out the front of his store and cocaine out the back. Of course, when he met him, Taka hadn't known that. He'd only known of his associations from the tattoos on his chest and back. It was this man that Taka called when he murdered his father.

The seafood seller had been happy to help, with only one condition. Taka would become his loyal shatei, or little brother, in the Yakuza. With nowhere else to go and a helpless mother, Taka accepted the offer of the man who, as it turned out, was a waka gashira, a first lieutenant in the organization.

It was the best thing that ever happened to Taka, and he would be forever grateful to the man who gave him the opportunity. From it, he quickly became one of the most feared members of his gang. He dealt out justice swiftly and mercilessly. Taka's reputation for ruthlessness impressed even the highest bosses in the organization. All the while, Taka had something pushing him from deep inside. It was more than ambition. His difficult upbringing had given him a thirst for what he believed was justice. It was beyond vengeance. It was a desire for control. In the back of his mind, Taka believed that if he had enough power, he could make Tokyo a better place. Sure, his empire would be financed with drug money, but his Yakuza would be the new underground police. They would clean up the city and end the corruption. Killing some people along the way was a small price to pay to create a better Japan. Anyone who interfered would also have to be eliminated.

Something occurred to him as he thought about his grand plans for the future. He picked up his phone, found the name he was looking for, and dialed. A moment later, Hideo answered.

"Yes, sir."

"On second thought, Hideo. Bring the Americans to me. I want to speak with them."

"Yes, sir. Right away."

4

TOKYO

Keiko Kimura stared at Sean and Tommy as they gazed at her computer screen. Their brains were a little groggy from the long flight, in spite of having their own company jet provided by the IAA.

The boys packed light for the trip, only carrying one gear bag each and small backpacks· for their clothes. On the plane, Sean observed Tommy retrieving something from his rucksack. It was a tangled ball of climbing rope, which caused him to laugh.

"What's with the rope?" Sean had asked.

Tommy was defensive. "You never know when you might need some rope."

Sean shook his head. "I guess. But we're not going rock climbing. We'll be in the city."

"You never know," Tommy repeated. "Don't worry about my bag."

The conversation ended there and wandered into a variety of topics for the rest of the flight.

They'd had a car pick them up at the airport and take them through the overwhelming traffic into the heart of the city. Keiko had opened the door with a polite smile and introduced herself to the two men, then promptly brought them back into her home. She, too, looked weary. It was easy to tell she had beautiful eyes in spite of her fatigue. Sean and Tommy assumed it was from dealing with the stress and grief of losing a family member, especially the way her uncle had died. Gruesome.

Her short, messy black bangs hung seductively above her eyebrows. Loose strands of hair framed the creamy skin on her cheeks, chin, and forehead. Lush pink lips were firmly pressed together underneath a gently sloping nose. Her white, sleeveless blouse and black pants gave the impression she intended to go to work at some point—that or at least to look professional.

For Tommy it was love at first sight, and he had to fight to keep his focus on the task at hand. He'd gone strangely silent the moment Keiko had opened the door, a fact Sean was more than happy to point out since he knew the exact cause. He'd been aware of Tommy's penchant for Asian women ever since they were in the ninth grade together. Sean halted his teasing after a few minutes, not wanting to make his friend feel too awkward. The second he walked into the young woman's home, Tommy wanted to compliment the interior with its paper doors and traditional décor. But he was too bashful.

Now they were in a realm both men were comfortable with: solving riddles. Only problem was, they didn't have any context for the one they were staring at on the screen.

Tommy read it out loud, keeping his eyes locked on the computer monitor, too afraid to make contact with the pretty woman across from him. "Stand on the threshold of those whose possession is right. Rise to find the way." He shook his head. "Those whose possession is right? What threshold?"

"I'm not sure," she said in perfect English.

Sean sat up straight and looked across at the young woman. "I don't mean to be callous to your circumstances, but this was sent on Saturday, yes?"

She nodded. "Yes. My uncle, he sent that the day before he died."

"It also says that whoever solves this riddle will discover the path to the great sword, the Honjo Masamune."

Keiko nodded again.

Tommy finally found his guts, probably on the floor. Even so, when he spoke, his voice trembled, and he stuttered. "So why the riddle? If your uncle wanted you to find this treasure map or whatever, why didn't he just tell you where it was?"

"That is a good question. And I'm not entirely certain. Uncle had a funny way of doing things. When I was a little girl, he used to give me riddles and puzzles. There would always be a treat or a toy at the end of his quests. Sometimes I enjoyed them. Other times they frustrated me. I think he liked them more than I did. It was his way of interacting with me. Now I wish I'd put more time into his games. Perhaps figuring out this one wouldn't be so difficult."

Sean stood up and walked over to the living room window. He peered out at the sprawling city. "I'd say he was probably also protecting you...and the location of the cipher itself. If he believed that you, your email, or anything else could be compromised, he'd have to put the location of the map into a riddle that only a savvy person could figure out."

Tommy nodded, following his friend's chain of thought. "That also means he doesn't believe whoever killed him...sorry." He blushed. "Whoever he was worried about wouldn't be smart enough to decipher the riddle for themselves."

Sean stepped away from the window and crossed his arms. His face scrunched into a frown. "And you don't have any idea who could be behind this or why they'd want to kill your uncle?"

She shook her head. They were questions the police had already asked her. Sean knew that. But he still had to ask. It was part of his process, a systematic procedure of questions and answers that had been ingrained in him during his years working for the government.

"I wish I did. The fact is that my uncle and I weren't that close. I suspect the only reason he sent this email to me is that I'm his only living relative he still spoke to. Most of the family stopped associating with him because they thought he was crazy."

Tommy's eyebrows lowered. "Crazy? Why would they think that?"

Keiko shrugged. "Probably because he was always on some wild treasure hunt, always trying to find the next ancient relic or artifact. It was all he talked about. His search for the Honjo Masamune pushed them over the edge. He kept mentioning new clues he'd discovered, or how he was so close to finding it. Eventually, everyone grew tired of his tall tales. They figured he was lying. Maybe he wasn't. But I have no idea what this riddle means. I'm a business person, not a historian."

"Really?" Tommy was intrigued. "What kind of business?"

She smiled and looked down at the floor, somewhat embarrassed. "I run a small sushi bar six blocks from here."

"Sushi!" Tommy exclaimed. "I love sushi."

Sean interrupted. "I'm sorry, but can we get back on track here?"

"Sorry."

"When it comes to figuring out riddles like this one, it helps to have context. In this case, the Honjo Masamune is our context."

"It's all we have." Tommy added.

"Right. But is it?" Sean pointed his finger at the screen and tapped on one of the words. "Maybe it's telling us exactly where to go."

Tommy read the words out loud again. "Those whose possession is right." He thought for a few seconds and then it hit him. "You think that means the original owners of the sword?"

Sean nodded. "Could be."

"The Tokugawa clan," Keiko blurted. She immediately apologized. "I'm sorry."

Tommy shook his head and smiled. "Don't be. That's right. It's the Tokugawas. The last known person to have the sword was Iemasa Tokugawa. It was reported he was the one who handed it over, along with many other weapons, to the American forces after the war. And you said you're not a historian."

It was her turn to blush. "Most of us here in Tokyo know that part of the story."

While he was entertained with Tommy's terrible attempt at flirting, Sean steered the conversation back to the point at hand. "A threshold is an entrance, or the base of an entrance. It must mean we have to stand in some kind of doorway."

Tommy knew better than to worry about the last sentence of the riddle. There was no point in even considering it until they'd determined the location mentioned in the first half. He turned from his friend back to Keiko. "The Edo Castle," he said, "where the Japanese Imperial Palace is now. How far away is that?"

She thought for a moment then shook her head. "Not far. Twenty minutes. Why?"

Sean answered. "Because the Edo Castle was the original shogunate for the Tokugawa family. It was where they called home for centuries. Since they're the rightful owners of the sword, it would make sense that your uncle meant the threshold to that castle would be the place."

Tommy pecked at the keys on the computer and pulled up several images of the historic location. He bit the corner of his thumb as he scrolled through the pictures. "Only problem is, which threshold? Was he talking about a door? Or was it one of these big gates?" He tapped the screen.

Sean leaned over to get a better look. Curious, Keiko stood up and moved around behind Tommy, bending over his shoulder to see what they were talking about.

The scent of lavender and vanilla filled his nostrils, doing more to distract him than he needed.

She reached a toned bare arm around in front of him and pointed at one of the images of a large, wooden gate surrounded by stone. "That is the main entrance to the grounds. It's the Tayasu Gate. I've been there before, with my uncle. He explained its significance to me."

The two Americans stared at the image with narrowed eyes.

"It definitely looks like it has hiding places for something small like a map or a codex," Sean said.

"Worth a look," Tommy added. "Worst-case scenario: we'll get to check out a historic Japanese landmark."

"Saddle up," Sean said and then turned his attention to Keiko. "You coming with us? If so, you'll need a coat. It's pretty chilly out there."

Winter was knocking on the door, and the temperature had plummeted to the point where going outside in short sleeves—or in Keiko's case, no sleeves—was out of the question.

She nodded. "I may as well come along. It's what my uncle would have wanted."

"That's the spirit," Tommy chimed.

Sean lifted his rucksack off the floor by the door and slung it over his shoulder. Tommy grabbed his gear bag as well and waited on their host. Keiko disappeared into a room down an adjacent hallway to put on a jacket and collect her small black clutch. She reappeared a few minutes later, sliding her phone into the little bag.

Before she reached the entryway, Sean heard something outside and immediately held up a hand, signaling her to stop. A look of concern washed over his face. He put a finger to his lips, leaned to his right, and looked through the peephole in the center of the door. Outside, a man with a shaved head, black jacket, and a loosely buttoned black shirt stood close by. He was surrounded by two others, but Sean got the distinct impression there might be a few more. Shaved Head didn't move. Why wasn't he knocking?

Sean didn't have to ask. He already knew the answer. The guy and the other goons were waiting for them to leave. But were they there for Keiko or he and Tommy? It had to be Keiko. No one outside the IAA even knew they were here.

He stepped away from the door, retreating stealthily like a cat who'd come across a bigger predator.

Tommy put his hands out to his side and mouthed, "What's the problem?"

Sean's response was only one word, and he didn't even whisper it. His lips moved enough for his friend and their host to understand. "Trouble."

5

TOKYO

Sean motioned to the sliding door on the far side of the room. It led onto a small balcony. He'd noticed it when they arrived. Being aware of his environment was something that came second nature to him. And it was a skill that had saved his skin on more than one occasion.

He'd seen the fire escape ladder attached to the side of the balcony and had the fleeting thought that it would be unfortunate to have to use it. Now it seemed they had no choice.

When the group of three arrived at the balcony door, Tommy grabbed his shoulder and hissed. "What's wrong with you?"

He should have known better than to ask. They'd been through enough narrow escapes and hairy incidents together. Maybe he was just asking for Keiko's sake. The Japanese woman stood just behind Tommy, a confused expression on her face.

Sean pointed at the front door. "There are three guys standing out there waiting for us to leave. From the bulge in their jackets, I'd say they're armed, which means they aren't part of the tourism welcoming committee."

"What?" Tommy spun around and cast a questioning glare at Keiko. "Friends of yours?"

She was as surprised as they were. Keiko shook her head slowly. "No." There was worry in her voice. "Do you think it's the men who killed my uncle?"

Sean sighed. "No way to know for sure. But one thing is certain, they're Yakuza."

Tommy whirled back around. "What? Are you serious? Yakuza? How do you know that?"

Sean calmed him down. "I saw the edge of one of the guy's tattoos peeking out from under his shirt. Their tats all have a uniform look to them. He's definitely Yakuza."

"Why is the Yakuza here?"

Sean ignored his friend's increasingly panicked reaction, unzipped his rucksack, and pulled out his Springfield XD .40 caliber.

Tommy's eyes went wide. "Oh come on," he whispered. "Really? We just got here."

Keiko's expression was equally troubled by the sudden appearance of the weapon. "Where did you get that?"

Tommy calmed for a moment, digging his own gun out of his bag. "Oh, we brought these with us."

She looked mortified. "How?"

Sean answered. "It's a long story. We have a plane. Look, you two go ahead. I'll wait until you're on the next level before I come down."

Tommy nodded then asked, "You gonna be OK, buddy? That's a long drop to the street."

"Thank you," Sean said. "I'm fully aware."

Tommy smiled devilishly.

Sean's fear of heights was well known among his circle of friends. He claimed it traced back to when he was a small child and had fallen at a playground, but there was no real way of knowing. All Sean knew was that whenever he even got close to the edge of a tall building or cliff or anything else high above ground level, he had to fight from freezing up.

Tommy led the way out onto the landing. A cold wind blasted over him. Keiko pulled her jacket tight around her arms. She had a worried look on her face but followed nonetheless. Under normal circumstances, she might have questioned Sean's assessment of the situation with the men outside her door. In light of what happened to her uncle only days before and the mysterious message she'd received from him, she decided to trust the American's instincts.

Outside, Tommy lowered the ladder down to the next level as quietly as he could. The metal creaked a little but otherwise didn't make much sound.

"My neighbor downstairs," Keiko whispered, "she's a nice woman. I think she's home right now. I'll knock on the door when we get down there, and maybe she'll let us in."

"Perfect," Sean said. "I'd rather not have to climb down the entire fifteen stories on a bunch of ladders. Now hurry."

She nodded and descended the ladder as Tommy moved aside to let her go first. He went down right behind her as Sean stood by the door, waiting with his weapon at the ready. At any second, he anticipated the men outside the entrance would burst through and enter the condo, but they didn't. For some reason, they kept waiting. Why? Were they thinking it would be easier to grab the occupants on their way out? Sean wasn't about to wait around and find out. Reluctantly, he slid his foot out onto the balcony. A sickening feeling filled his gut, and he felt his body go stiff. Slowly, he moved his other foot out onto the landing, clutching the edge of the door frame with a death grip that turned his knuckles white.

Below, Tommy and Keiko had already made it to the neighbor's balcony. She was hurriedly rapping on the glass door, trying to get the attention of the woman inside.

Sean stuffed his gun into his belt and reached over to the door, pulling it shut while still trying to grip the outer edge of the doorsill. He stared at the wall, desperately trying not to look down, but it was a vain effort. His left hand stretched over to the railing and grasped it tightly, followed shortly by his right. Now there was nowhere to look but down or out. And neither made him feel any better. The fifteen-story drop to the street sent a shiver through his body.

"It's OK, buddy," Tommy encouraged from below. "You can do this. You've done worse." The downstairs door opened, and an older woman with a pleasant and wrinkled face stepped into view. She smiled at Keiko as the younger woman explained that the building supervisor was doing some construction in her hall and they needed to leave before the crew was finished.

The older neighbor accepted the lie and motioned for them to come in. Tommy waited for his friend, watching as Sean hesitantly inched his way over to the ladder. Sean swallowed hard and closed his eyes as he swung his first leg out and planted his foot onto the first rung. He grabbed the side of the ladder tightly and repeated the process with his other foot.

One step down. Then another. Then another. The entire time, Sean kept his eyes glued to a skyscraper off in the distance. He didn't want to look off to the right or down for fear he'd faint and fall. In truth, the fall would only be a few feet to the next landing, but there was no rationalizing with a phobia like that. Suddenly, he felt his foot touch the downstairs balcony and he let go of the ladder and nearly fell into the older woman's condo, desperate to get away from the ledge.

He didn't pay any attention to the décor of the room. Paper lanterns hung in the corner. A little bamboo plant stood by the window next to a television. The rest was a blur. Sean was just happy to be back in a safe place, and he recovered almost immediately. He righted himself and headed for the door.

"Tell her we said thank you," Sean said as he reached the entrance.

Keiko nodded and did as he said, smiling politely at the neighbor who mirrored the gesture and nodded. Tommy gave her a short bow and also said thank you in English before following the other two out the door.

They didn't notice the woman's eyes go wide at the sight of the weapons tucked in the back of their pants.

Out in the hall, Tommy closed the door behind him and then looked to Sean. "What next? We go out the front door?"

"Unless there's a rear entrance." He looked to Keiko.

She nodded and bit her lower lip. "Yes. It's this way." She started to head toward one of the elevators, but Sean stopped her.

"We should take the stairs. Elevators box you in. No way to get out if someone is waiting on the other side."

She swallowed and nodded her understanding. "OK, stairs are this way."

The three hurried down the narrow corridor lit with chrome sconces on the wall. At the other end, Keiko made an abrupt right turn and pushed her way through a closed door with a bar latch. They entered the concrete stairwell and began their descent.

Fluorescent bulbs cast a sterile, eerie glow on the white cinder block walls and gray concrete steps. The Americans chased after their host as she hurried downward, often taking two steps at a time.

When they reached the main floor, she pulled open the door leading into the lobby and then cut to the left. "The back door is this way."

She took off with Tommy right behind her, but Sean paused. A man in a similar outfit to those waiting outside Keiko's door was standing by the main entrance to the building. He was wearing sunglasses despite being indoors, and had his hands in his pockets. His head twitched to the side as he saw the sudden movement at the other end of the room.

"Crap," Sean said to himself. He rushed after the other two even as the man by the door darted toward them.

Keiko and Tommy fled through a short hall that ended in another doorway. She pushed the latch and passed through. Sean caught up in no time, his pace quickened by the new threat on the ground floor.

"You got a car?" Sean asked as he hurried through the open door and shoved it hard to hasten its closure.

"Yes, it's in the garage." She pointed to a covered walkway that led to a three-story garage.

"Go get it. I have to take care of something here."

Tommy frowned. "Take care of something?"

Sean braced his shoulder against the door a second before a heavy thud slammed against it from the other side.

"Yeah," he nodded. "We have company. Would you mind getting the car?"

Tommy and Keiko obeyed, realizing someone had seen them. They took off toward the garage while Sean pushed hard against the metal door. If the guy had a gun, he might try to fire it. That would be a foolish move considering the bullet could possibly ricochet back at him. The problem was that at some point Sean was going to have to let go of the door to go get in the car. When he did, the man on the other side would get through.

He looked down as the guy kept pounding and shoving on the door. A cinder block sat on the ground near the wall. It wasn't ideal, but if he could reach it, maybe he could wedge it against the door in such a way that the man on the inside couldn't get out.

Propping his foot against the bottom edge of the door to keep leverage, he leaned his body over and reached for the block. It was only a few inches away from his hand, but he couldn't get it. Loosening his foot against the door just for a second, he stretched out again to grab the block. The door shuddered and gave way as the guy inside plowed into it with his shoulder and stumbled forward into daylight.

For a moment, Sean was out of view because the door swung around in front of him. He glanced toward the garage and was glad to see Tommy and Keiko were already out of view. But they wouldn't be for long.

The door slowly swung back toward its frame, and Sean stood up. The other man had his back to him, looking around for any trace of the escapees. Sean took advantage and rushed him, driving his shoulder into the guy's back and knocking him to the ground like a linebacker. The man's head smacked against the concrete sidewalk, and Sean felt the body go limp. As he stood up, Sean noticed the man's chest rising and falling slowly. He wasn't dead but definitely unconscious. It was lucky he'd hit his head like that—well, not lucky for the gangster. Right now Sean didn't care about that. He had to get moving before the guy came to and called down reinforcements.

He heard tires screeching, and a second later a little red four-door Toyota appeared. He could see Tommy and Keiko inside and took off toward the vehicle. Sean pounded the ground hard, forcing himself into an all-out sprint until he skidded to a stop, flung open the car door, and dove inside.

Before he even closed the door behind him he shouted, "Go!"

Keiko stomped on the gas pedal, and the little tires squealed again; the sudden momentum slammed the rear door shut as she sped out onto the main street and into the Tokyo traffic.

Once they were out of view and around the next corner, Tommy glared back at him. "Where did that guy come from?"

Sean propped himself up, took his gun out of his pants, put it back in his gear bag, and set it aside. He ran his fingers through his messy blond hair and put his head against the headrest. "He was watching the front door, which is why we were going out the back way to begin with. I guess they decided to have him waiting on the inside instead of watching from out front."

Keiko was still breathing hard from the close call with the gangsters. "Those were the men who killed my uncle?"

The suddenness of the question caught Sean off guard, but he nodded. "No way of knowing for sure, but I'd guess that's them. Whatever it was your uncle hid at that castle must be pretty valuable. If it's a map that leads to the Honjo Masamune, that's something bad people would be willing to kill for."

Tommy nodded. "That sword would go for hundreds of millions on the black market."

Keiko processed the information as she weaved the car through traffic. "So that's what this is about? Money? They killed my uncle for money?" Her voice sounded distant, almost hollow.

"It's sad, but that's the sick world we live in now," Tommy consoled her.

She pinched her lips together and gripped the wheel tightly. Both men could see the anger in her expression, but she didn't cry. She just kept her eyes forward, focused on the road.

"I guess we need to find whatever it is my uncle hid and make sure they don't get what they want."

Tommy grabbed the handle above the door and looked over at her again. "You said it's twenty minutes to the palace?"

She nodded. "Normally. I can get us there in fifteen. I know a shortcut."

6

TOKYO

"What do you mean they got away?"

Hideo stood by the rear door to the building, staring down at the man who sat against a concrete retaining wall while rubbing the right side of his forehead. His subordinate was clearly in pain, wincing each time his fingers touched the huge knot bulging from his temple.

"I saw them come out of the stairwell," the man explained. "They took off in this direction, so I went after them. When I got outside they were gone. Then one of the Americans came out of nowhere and knocked me to the ground from behind. I must have hit my head. I blacked out, and when I regained consciousness, they'd vanished."

Hideo's stern glare softened slightly. Three of his men stood between him and the garage, keeping a lookout for any passersby or anyone of interest. Two others had gone to retrieve their cars from out front.

Hideo put his hand on the man's shoulder. He'd only been with their organization for a few months and was still considered to be a little brother, a shatei. When he spoke, his tone was full of soothing encouragement. "Don't worry about it," he said. "We know where they're going next."

The newcomer looked up, surprised. "We do?"

"Yes," Hideo nodded. "We know everything that happens in this city. Now, are you able to stand?"

The guy nodded and eased himself up onto his feet.

"Good. The cars are coming around to get us and take us to these Americans. No doubt you'll want to repay them for what they did to your head, yes?"

He nodded again and started walking toward the garage.

Hideo corrected his direction, pressing against his shoulder and guiding him off to the side of the building near a dumpster in the shadows of the sunlight. "Stand over here in the shade for a moment, brother. If you hit your head, I'm sure the bright light will only make the pain worse."

"It does. Thank you."

Hideo bent down to the ground and picked up the younger man's sunglasses. He handed them to him courteously. The newcomer gave a curt nod and thanked him.

As he slid the sunglasses onto his nose, Hideo pulled a black pistol out of his jacket. It already had a suppressor attached to the end, something he must have done while the group was coming down from the fifteenth floor.

He raised the weapon and fired a round through the left corner of the newcomer's skull. A pink mist erupted from the other side. As the body wavered, the younger man turned slightly before his knees gave out. The other three gangsters stepped in, catching the body before it hit the ground. One lifted the lid on the dumpster while the other two much stronger men hefted the fresh corpse into the bin and onto a pile of garbage bags. The lid slammed shut as two black Mercedes appeared around the corner and pulled into the loading area.

One of the men opened a rear door for Hideo, and once he was inside, closed it and got in the front with the driver.

Hideo unscrewed the suppressor from his weapon, handed the cylinder to one of his men, and stuffed the gun back into his jacket. "Where are they?" he asked the driver.

"They've gone to the palace."

Hideo nodded. "Get us there. Hurry."

7

TOKYO

As predicted, Keiko's shortcut led them quickly to the palace grounds. The Americans figured that tourism would be somewhat slower during the wintry months. Turns out, people came to see the historic area all year round.

The group left Keiko's car a few blocks from the outer wall that wrapped around the royal premises. A moat-like waterway also circled the property, a lasting reminder of the feudal times in Japan.

Stone bridges, built centuries before, led into key areas of the estate. Sean admired the scene. The pagoda-style structure was an eloquent design, perched flush on one of the interior wall's corners, right on top of the water. And while most of the royal palaces in Japan were much larger, more ornate, the Tokyo palace was simpler, a two-story dwelling that seemed more fit for a prime minister or president than a descendant of an ancient royal line. But Sean appreciated that part of it too. Minimalism had strong roots in Japanese culture, and this particular palace symbolized that, at least from the outside.

They made their way along the sidewalk and after ten minutes found the entrance they were looking for.

"That's the gate," Keiko said, pointing at the huge structure.

The Tayasu Gate was a large wooden entryway, bookended by a

massive stone wall on both sides. The wood was thick, sturdy oak cut long ago from enormous trees. There were two open doorways on either side of the main portal, which was also wide open. A sporadic stream of visitors trickled in and out of the gate, their heads turning from side to side and up and down as they took in the sheer size of the thing.

Tommy stared up at it with wide eyes, overstating the obvious. "It's huge."

Keiko nodded. "It is one of the original gates on the property. The white wall above it is a more recent addition."

Once they were underneath the shadows of the gate, the group stopped and looked up and around. Each had the same question, but Tommy was the one to blurt it out first.

"OK, so we're here on the threshold. The next part says we're supposed to rise to find the way." He turned to Sean. "Any thoughts on that one?"

Sean moved fully underneath the gate's frame. Above, the structure below the ceiling was somewhat hollow with the support beams and rafters in full view.

"Rise to find the way," he said with his hands on his hips.

The other two joined him under the overhang and looked up.

"There are certainly plenty of places to hide something up there," Keiko said.

Tommy's voice filled with sarcasm. "Yeah. Would be nice to have a look around. If only there were a way we could get up there..."

Sean shook his head, doing his best to ignore his friend's I-told-you-so tone.

Tommy opened his rucksack and fished out the tangled mess of rope, spilling a water bottle and compass onto the ground in the process. He didn't care. He held up the rope triumphantly and looked at it as if it were a foreign object.

"Oh, I'm sorry. What's this? It looks like a rope. Is that what it is, Sean? I can't tell. Wait, you know what? I think it is a rope. But we would never need a rope in the city, right? I mean, what possible reason could we have for needing a rope in the city?"

Sean had heard enough and, catching his friend off guard, snatched the rope from him and stepped over to one of the gate's interior walls. His fingers worked fast, undoing the knots in the rope and then bundling one end together to give it some weight.

"You're welcome," Tommy said as he watched, suddenly feeling less proud of himself.

Sean took a middle section of rope and spun the heavy end around five times before letting it fly upward. It sailed over the nearest beam about fifteen feet up and dropped over the other side. Sean's fingers loosened, letting the slack pull out rapidly until the bundle reached shoulder level. He stopped the rope's progress, grabbed the clump of rope, and tied off a slip knot. Then he pulled down on the long end, sending the knot back up to the beam until it tightened snugly against the wood. He gave it a few hard tugs and then turned to Tommy.

"You want to go up, or should I?"

Tommy blushed and cocked his head sideways. "I can't climb that thing. You know I couldn't even do the ropes in gym class when we were in high school."

Sean lowered his eyebrows sarcastically. "Oh, you mean you brought a rope to Tokyo, but you need *me* to climb it?"

"I didn't think we'd have to climb it," Tommy mumbled. He stuffed his hands in his pocket and watched.

Sean grabbed the rope with both hands and pulled himself into a rappelling position with both feet planted against the wall. He leaned back one more time to make sure the knot was secure and then started walking his way up one foot at a time, one hand over the other. It took him less than twenty seconds to reach the beam. Sean pulled his legs up so his torso was parallel with the ground.

Keiko watched in amazement from below. Tommy stood next to her, pretending to be unimpressed.

"He does this sort of thing all the time," he said to her.

Clutching the rope tightly with both hands, Sean raised his legs and wrapped them around the beam, straddling it from underneath. Locking his legs in place, he released the rope with one hand and put one hand around the beam, then the other. He shimmied around the side of the wood and a moment later was on top of it with both legs dangling below.

Tommy shook his head. "Showoff."

Sean ignored him. He was already searching the nooks and crevices of the ceiling area.

On the ground, a middle-aged couple walked by and stared up curiously at the American. Tommy dismayed them by saying, "He's doing maintenance on the support structure."

They frowned at him and kept walking.

He turned to Keiko. "I don't think they understood me."

She stared at him as if his head was on fire.

"OK." He looked back up at his friend, who was standing on the beam, keeping his arms out wide to maintain balance. "See anything up there, buddy? People are starting to notice."

"Yeah," Sean replied. "There's something wedged against one of the front beams that's holding up the wall." He pointed in the direction he was looking. "It looks like a box of some kind."

He placed one foot ahead of the other, carefully negotiating the beam like an amateur gymnast. At one point he wavered a little, nearly losing his footing. Keiko put her hands over her mouth, gasping at the tenuous moment. Falling wouldn't kill Sean unless he landed on his head, but it wouldn't be a great outcome; injuring an ankle, arm, or foot would greatly hinder their progress.

"What happened to your whole fear of heights thing, buddy?" Tommy taunted.

Sean kept his eyes locked on his destination. He was only five feet away from the intersection where another beam joined the one he was on, forming a T.

"That only kicks in when I'm over twenty-five feet high or so. You know that."

Tommy twisted his head and looked at Keiko. "He has selective fear of heights."

She said nothing, still watching breathlessly as Sean traversed the beam and switched over to the shorter one that connected to the front interior wall.

Sean took a final step and crouched down cautiously. Planting his hands on the flat surface just in front of him, he lowered his body down to a sitting position and once more let his legs dangle. Squeezing the beam with his thighs to keep steady, Sean reached over and pried the little box from its hiding place. The bamboo container was only about eight inches long and a few inches wide.

"What is it?" Tommy asked, trying not to draw too much attention from other passersby.

"It's a bamboo box," Sean answered.

He pushed on one end of the top and found that the lid slid into place along a pair of opposing grooves. His index finger pushed it a little farther, revealing a tiny roll of paper inside.

"There's something inside. It's a piece of rolled up paper."

"What does it say?" Tommy pressed.

Sean looked down at him derisively. "I haven't taken it out yet."

"Right."

Sean pushed the lid back into place. "I'm going to drop it down to you."

"Wait. What? I don't want to break it!" Tommy protested.

"There's nothing to break, buddy. It's just wood and a piece of paper."

Tommy looked around. An old woman strolled by, staring at him for a moment before turning her gaze forward to the street.

"How do you know? You said you didn't open it. There could be some kind of acid vial in it or something."

Sean's eyebrows scrunched together. He shook his head slowly. "Acid vial? Really? I'm telling you, it's just paper and bamboo. Here." He leaned over the beam, still gripping it tightly with his thighs.

This position shortened the drop by two feet, and he held the little box by the end to reduce the fall by another few inches, just to ease Tommy's mind.

Tommy still wasn't sure about the idea, but he positioned himself directly under the box and held up both hands.

Sean released the end of the box. Tommy caught it with an exaggerated motion, lowering his palms quickly as if he were catching an egg. Satisfied nothing inside was broken, he straightened his back and examined the object. Up above, Sean was already heading back to the rope, carefully navigating his way through the rafters and across the support beams.

Keiko stepped close and looked at the box. Her shoulder grazed Tommy's, sending a chill down his spine that he was certain she had no idea about.

On the lid, Japanese characters were burned into the surface.

Tommy spoke in a hushed tone. "What does it say?"

She choked back her emotions and translated. "It's a name," she said. "Iemasa Tokugawa."

Sean's feet clopped onto the ground as he let himself drop the remaining six feet. The noise startled their somber moment. "Sorry, buddy, but we're probably going to have to leave the rope. No way I can untie that and get down at the same time."

"Aw man, seriously?"

"I'll buy you a new one." He sidled up next to the others and stared at the box, now more clearly visible in the sunlight. "You just gonna stand there, or you gonna open it?" Sean took a quick look around, surveying the area. He wasn't completely convinced they were alone. He hoped it was paranoia, but the incident at Keiko's building had roused old instincts, instincts that weren't easily shut off.

Tommy nodded and pushed the lid open. The paper inside was wrapped tightly and tied with a single red ribbon. From the looks of it, the cream-colored paper was old. The signs of time and wear were clearly visible in the faded exterior.

"Do you think we should get it to a lab before we open it?" Sean asked. While he had a great deal of knowledge in the field of archaeology and history, Sean always deferred to Tommy's expertise when it came to delicate matters. He was one of the smartest in the business when it came to those things.

"Should be OK," he said, shaking his head. "If Tokugawa put it here, it's only seventy years old. Not likely to fall apart. But I'll be careful. You never know."

He sidestepped over to a park bench close to the wall and eased onto it. Tommy gently pressed a finger against each end of the tiny scroll and lifted it out of the box. He carefully untied the ribbon and set it aside. Sean and Keiko huddled around him, leaning in as he tenderly peeled back the top layer to unwrap the paper. It made a soft crinkling sound that caused Tommy to freeze for a moment, fearful he may have torn it, but upon inspection he realized it was fine. Years of sitting in the bamboo box in the same position had almost petrified the paper.

As he continued the unrolling process, faded black Japanese characters were revealed. When the entire page was visible to the group, Sean stared down at it, his mind working hard to translate images he didn't understand.

Keiko did understand them. "It says, 'The three tests of the holy begin on barren heights. There you will find the way written in stone.'"

She frowned. Frustration filled her voice. "Another riddle."

"Yeah, that happens to us a lot," Tommy said.

"Three tests of the holy?" Sean asked. "Does that mean the person who is searching for the sword must prove they're holy?"

"I hope not," Tommy joked. "Afraid both of us will fall short in that category."

Sean repeated the second phrase. "The way written in stone. I guess that means either we'll find the sword, or we'll find another riddle. If I had to speculate, I'd say it's the latter. If there are three tests, that must mean we will have to find three clues before the location of the sword is revealed. Barren heights suggests that the first one could be hidden on a mountain." He turned to Keiko. "You don't happen to know which mountain that might be, do you?"

She shook her head. "We have many mountains in Japan. It could be any of them."

Tommy interjected. "Just once I wish we could find the treasure on a sandy beach where X marks the spot."

Sean could tell Keiko's mind was turning; did she have an idea about the mountain in question?

Before he could ask her, Tommy spoke up again. "Let's get this back to the hotel and call the kids. Maybe they can offer up some help. They're good with piecing together information like this, and unfortunately, my knowledge about Japanese mountains is somewhat lacking."

He started to get up but froze in place, his eyes fixed on something through the gap between Keiko and Sean.

Sean noticed his concerned look almost instantly. He didn't have to turn around to know that something was wrong. "They're here, aren't they?"

Tommy gave a subtle nod. "Yep."

"How many?"

"Five. And they're right behind you."

8

TOKYO

"Thank you so much for leading us to the cipher," Hideo said. He and his four men stood in a semicircle surrounding Keiko and the two Americans. "I am most grateful."

Sean turned around slowly, keeping his hands out to his side. His rucksack was sitting on the ground at Tommy's feet. He'd absently set it there, next to his friend's bag, not thinking he would need the weapon inside. Now he cursed himself for the mistake. Not that it would matter much. Firing a weapon in broad daylight around a bunch of people would almost do more harm than good. And as the men in the matching outfits came into view, Sean realized that even if he had his gun in hand, he'd be cut down before being able to get off a single shot.

Shaved Head stood between two other men in such a way that anyone who walked by wouldn't be able to see the pistol in his hand.

Being at an extreme disadvantage and with no play to make, Sean resorted to using his other special ability. Sarcasm. "Nice haircut," he said with a smirk.

The gunman's expression didn't change. "Give me the cipher."

Sean acted unconcerned. When he responded, his voice escalated with each word until he was almost shouting. "Or what? You'll shoot us? Here? In front of all these people?" Drawing the attention of anyone within earshot was exactly what he wanted.

Anger flooded Shaved Head's eyes, but he remained calm. The two men at each end of their semicircle pulled knives out of their jackets. The blades were at least seven inches long and glinted in the sunlight.

"That won't be necessary, gentlemen. Not here anyway," Shaved Head said. He held out a hand to the two men. They obeyed and put the blades out of sight. "I would prefer not to have to shoot you, especially here. Like you said: too many people around. So either you give us the cipher and we let you live, or you come for a ride with us, we take it from you, and you die a very painful death. The choice is yours."

Tommy stood slowly while the leader was speaking. He held the paper in a trembling hand. It wasn't fear that made him shake. He'd stared down the barrels of enough guns. It was anger.

He stepped forward. "You think you can solve this riddle? Good luck. We have degrees in this stuff and don't know what it means. It's all gibberish anyway."

The leader lowered his head slightly and glared at Tommy from underneath his eyelids. "I will be the judge of that."

Tommy moved around in front of Keiko, who stood firmly in place, paralyzed with fear. He figured she'd never been held at gunpoint before, and the last thing he wanted was this idiot accidentally putting a bullet in her.

"What do you think, Sean? Should I give it to him?"

"I'd rather you not." Sean kept his eyes locked on the enemy. "Don't get me wrong. I honestly don't think you can figure out what this thing says. It's just that I don't like you very much. I know we haven't been formally introduced, but there's something about you that just screams scumbag."

Shaved Head gritted his teeth. The longer he delayed, the more confident Sean was that the guy had no intention of pulling the trigger. And getting them to go quietly would be an issue too. Sean had already shown them that by raising his voice.

"Looks to me like we have ourselves what we call a stalemate. Know what I mean?"

Off to the right, in the gate entrance, a security guard had taken interest in the rope hanging from the rafters. No one in the standoff saw him inspecting it, and they didn't see when he suddenly realized what was going on between the two groups.

"What is the meaning of this?" he said in sharp Japanese.

The Americans didn't understand the words, but they got the gist.

"These men are causing trouble," Keiko answered, suddenly emboldened. "They're trying to rob us. Call the police."

Shaved Head's eyes blazed, twitching furiously.

Sean took a slow step back toward his rucksack, using the guard's distraction as a chance to grab his things. While he was there, he picked up Tommy's bag as well.

The rent-a-cop was only equipped with a stun gun, but he drew it quickly and pressed a button on his shoulder radio. He said something in a flurry of words, probably calling for backup.

"This is none of your concern," Shaved Head said to the security guard, or at least that's what the Americans figured he was saying.

"Tommy," Sean whispered.

"Yeah?"

"I have the riddle memorized. Toss the paper in the air toward that ditch."

"What?"

"Take the cipher, and throw it up in the air toward the ditch," Sean repeated. "And let their leader see you do it. These guys don't fool around. They're going to kill that guard, and then they'll kill us."

His assessment of the situation had changed. He'd thought it to be a stalemate, but Sean realized that these men operated without fear of authority, which meant they had connections, the kind of connections that could let them get away with almost anything.

Tommy understood immediately. And he didn't disagree. "Hey!" he shouted, waving the paper in the air as he took a wary step back toward the ditch.

A steady stream of water flowed into the moat surrounding the palace grounds. He stopped a foot away from a guardrail and held the little scroll high. "You don't want this to get wet, do you?"

Shaved Head's attention swiftly turned to Tommy, and his face filled with panic. It was the first they'd seen the statue-like expression change. Tommy lowered his hand dramatically and kept it at waist level for a second, letting the tension build. Then he tossed the little scroll straight up as hard as he could. All five gangsters freaked out and broke toward the sailing roll of paper.

"Now!" Sean shouted.

He grabbed Keiko's arm and jerked her to the left as he and Tommy darted toward the street. Behind them, the scroll ceased its upward journey and started falling fast toward the steady liquid stream. They scrambled, bumping into each other clumsily, grasping at air to catch the falling paper. One man tipped it with his fingers, bumping it a little higher before Shaved Head was able to step up onto the rail and lean over, snatching it just seconds before it fell out of reach and into the running water.

One of the men turned and pointed at the three people disappearing around the corner, shouting at the others that they were getting away.

Hideo stopped them. "Wait," he said. "We have what we came for. We have to take this to Taka at once. He will be most pleased."

The men obeyed and straightened their clothes. A few tourists stared at them awkwardly as they passed by. Hideo shoved his weapon back into his jacket and sneered at a young couple who walked by holding hands. They sped up their pace and hurried away through the gate.

Out on the street, Sean pushed Keiko in front of him just in case the gangsters pursued and started firing. It was his instinct to protect others that way. He'd rather take the bullet than someone like her. She was innocent. Him, not so much.

They hurried by a row of cars and crossed the street at the next intersection, running out in front of a line of three cars that had just gotten the green light. The drivers honked angrily, but Keiko and the Americans kept running. The cold air burned their throats and lungs as it passed through in big gasps. Sean could see Tommy's speed was already slowing.

"Don't slow down, buddy," Sean warned and cast a quick glance back.

There was no sign of the gangsters, but that didn't mean they weren't coming. Better to make the gap as big as possible than to make the famous mistake of the hare racing the turtle.

With legs getting heavier with each step, the group finally made it to the car. Before she reached the door, Keiko had already hit the button on her key fob, unlocking the vehicle. The three flung the doors open, jumped in, and ten seconds later the little red car sped away into the midafternoon traffic.

Tommy was in the front seat, gasping for air. Keiko's breathing was also somewhat labored but not nearly as exaggerated. Sean was a little winded, but he was accustomed to running much longer distances than that.

As he started to recover, Tommy swallowed and told Keiko the name of the hotel they'd reserved for the night. She nodded and said it would only take twenty minutes to get there.

Then Tommy turned around and looked at Sean for an explanation. "Any idea how those guys found us there?"

Sean sat up straight and shook his head. "Not sure, unless they heard us talking about it when they were out in the hall." He directed his line of questioning to Keiko. "Does your apartment have thin walls?"

She didn't answer immediately. It was clear she wasn't used to running for her life or having a gun pointed at her.

Tommy put a calming hand on her shoulder as she steered the car through traffic. "It's OK. We're fine. We'll get you to a safe place and let the police know what happened. They'll take care of it."

She shook her head. Her voice trembled. "We can't go to the police. Yakuza owns the police. Not just in Tokyo. All over the country. They've infested the city and country like a virus. There's no stopping them now. And there's nowhere to hide."

Sean turned around and looked out the back window. "They're

not coming after us," he said after staring down the street for several seconds. "If they were, we'd see them by now. They got what they wanted."

Tommy laughed. "Lot of good it'll do them if they can't figure out the riddle."

"Maybe," Sean said. "But I'd feel a lot better if we could put some distance between us and them. Get on the phone with the kids, and see what they can come up with. And Keiko?"

Her eyes looked back at him in the rearview mirror.

"Keep driving. Let's get out of the city for a little while until things die down."

She nodded but had a questioning look in her eyes. "The kids?" she asked.

"They're my assistants," Tommy said. "They're just young, that's all."

Keiko didn't seem reassured, but she kept driving.

As she navigated her car through traffic, Tommy got on his cell phone and dialed the number for his laboratory back in Atlanta. The two they affectionately called *the kids* spent most of their waking hours there. It wasn't just because Tommy paid them extremely well; they enjoyed the work and were always finding new things to test and research. It helped that Tommy provided them with the best toys. Their hyper-quantum computers were able to process queries faster than any other machine on the planet, and there were only a few in existence. For Tara and Alex, it was like being kids in a candy store. So when he called, they almost always answered.

"Hey, Tommy. How's Japan?" Tara asked. He could hear her smacking some gum through the earpiece.

"Hello, Tara. Same old story. Looking for an ancient artifact gone missing, ran into some goons who want to kill us. The usual."

"Yeah, I was more interested in hearing about the food, the weather, that sort of thing. But it's good to hear you're in your comfort zone."

"Old dogs, I guess."

"Indeed. So I'm assuming you're calling because you have a question for me. How about you give us a challenge this time."

Tara and Alex were always up for a good riddle, especially the kind Tommy seemed to frequently run into.

"I'm glad you said that, although you might not be when I give it to you."

"Try us. I'm putting you on speaker so Alex can hear."

"Hey, boss," Alex chimed in.

Tommy greeted him and then got back on task. "Hey, Alex. OK, so as you know, we are looking for the Honjo Masamune. We found a cipher on the grounds of the Imperial Palace, which used to be the Tokugawa family land. They were the original holders of the sword. The last man to have it, Iemasa Tokugawa, hid the cipher there. Although it was more of a riddle than a cipher. We didn't have to decode anything."

"So what's the problem?" Alex asked.

"We aren't really sure what the riddle means. It's a tad on the obscure side, and since we're on the move, we need you to help us figure it out."

"Understood," Tara said. "So what's the riddle?"

"I'm going to hand you over to Sean. He has it memorized."

Tommy handed the phone to Sean and mouthed for him to tell them the riddle. Sean had always had the better memory of the two.

He took the device and put it to his ear. "Hey, Tara, Alex. The riddle says, 'Three tests of the holy begin on barren heights and that there the way will be written in stone.' We figure that the real clue in the riddle has to do with barren heights. So it's probably a mountain or something."

"Hold on a second."

Sean could hear her smacking gum in the background as she tapped away at the keyboard.

Alex spoke into the speaker. "We're cross-referencing any possible matches featuring the keywords three, test, holy, mountains, that sort of thing."

"I'll wait."

Keiko jerked the car to the left suddenly and then back to the right, dodging a bicycle courier who'd merged into the right lane out of the blue. The car came to a stop at another red light. The bicyclist pulled up next to them, staring straight ahead as he waited for the light to turn green.

"This is interesting," Tara said after a short period of silence. "Most of the results have to do with the three mountains of Dewa. That ring any bells for you guys?"

"Three mountains of Dewa?" Sean said out loud.

Keiko looked into the mirror and nodded. "Those are holy mountains in the Shinto religion. Very sacred places. Buddhists still travel to them every year on pilgrimage."

"Sounds like we may have a winner," Sean said to Tara. "Tell me more about these mountains."

The light turned green and Keiko stepped on the gas, throttling ahead of the cyclist.

"Well, let's see. I'm checking out the images of some of them right now. Looks like two of them are in pretty dense forests. The third, Mount Gassan, doesn't appear to have any trees at all. Lots of rocks, grass. If I had to describe it I would say the slopes are barren."

"Sounds like we may have found a match then."

"Could be. There's a Shinto shrine at the top. Maybe you'll find something there." She paused for a moment and then spoke again. "Wait. Hold on a second."

"Problem?"

Tommy turned around, staring at Sean with a questioning glance. He replied with an *I don't know* shrug.

"Yeah," Tara replied. "The mountain is closed during the winters. Apparently, there's a lot of snow up there right now. Makes it nearly impossible to get to."

Sean thought about the issue. "So no roads to the top? No hiking trails?"

"There are trails, but right now this says they're covered in, like, five feet of snow. No way you want to try to get up there until sometime in the summer."

"What if we flew in? There any flat areas a helicopter could land up there?"

Alex and Tara mumbled to each other, talking over a few spots they must have been looking at on the computer monitor.

"Not really flat, per se. But there are some potential places on the ridge where a helicopter might be able to land. Of course, it could be windy up there. Lots of shear. Would make for a rough flight."

Sean considered the options. "OK, Tara. We'll get back to you. Thanks for your help."

"Anytime, boys."

Sean ended the call and handed the device back to Tommy.

"What does she think?" Tommy asked.

"Well, she says that Mount Gassan might be a good place to start. But it's closed to visitors right now because of heavy snowfall."

"Yes," Keiko agreed. "That area gets much snow in the winter. Climbing to the top would be almost impossible."

"Which is why you asked her about a helicopter," Tommy continued.

"Right. She seems to think we may be able to land a chopper up there but it could be sketchy with the wind shear."

Keiko turned right at the next light, onto a less crowded street. She immediately noticed the lack of other cars and pedestrians.

The bicyclist turned with them as well, maintaining a steady speed just behind the car.

Tommy offered his solution. "I'll check around and see if I can find a pilot crazy enough to take us up there. Maybe we'll get lucky."

"Hope so."

Keiko eased the car to a halt at a stop sign and looked both ways. The cyclist suddenly cut around the vehicle, stopping right in front of them. He pulled out a pistol and pointed it straight at the driver. She freaked out for a moment and took her hands off the wheel.

Tommy was about to tell her to punch the gas when a silver sedan screeched to a halt to their left. Another matching vehicle appeared in front of them, blocking the way in both directions. Sean turned around, hoping they could back up, but another sedan also blocked that escape route.

The man on the bicycle lowered his head and shouted. "Get out of the car! *Now!*"

"How did they find us?" Tommy asked, staring at the cyclist. "I thought no one was following us."

"I knew there was a reason they didn't chase us from the palace," Sean muttered. He cursed himself for not keeping a better watch.

The man with the gun shouted again, ordering them out of the car. Sean nodded and put up his hands. Tommy did the same.

The rear doors of the car next to them opened, and men exited quickly, opening the rear door and yanking Sean out. The vehicle in the rear also emptied two men from the back who hurried to the front doors, opened them, and pulled out Tommy and Keiko.

"Hey, take it easy!" Tommy shouted. "We're just American tourists!"

Sean didn't protest. He saw the tattoos peek out from under button-up shirts. These men were Yakuza. And Sean knew he and his companions were probably about to die.

9

TOKYO

It was hard to tell how much time had passed in the artificial darkness. The men that dragged Sean and his companions out of their car had immediately put hoods over their captives' heads to make sure they didn't see where they were being taken. Tommy had protested up until the point he was shoved into one of the three cars. When the door closed, Sean didn't hear his friend's voice anymore. He assumed Keiko was also put in a separate car. Smart, he thought. Together, they could be trouble. Divided, much easier to handle.

The bumpy car ride lasted around ten minutes, as best as Sean could guess. When they got out, the smell of garlic and fried something filled his nostrils. He figured it was noodles, but there was no way of knowing. A door creaked open somewhere. He stepped in a puddle as the men moved him from the car and into a building where the scents were strengthened and mingled with new ones: spilled booze, fish, and some spice he couldn't identify.

The men walked him down a hallway and then forced him to the right. Sean figured the corridor was narrow even though he couldn't see it. And his hands were bound behind his back so reaching out and touching it was impossible. At one point he felt his shoulder brush against it and sensed the man next to him crowding close. Not that it mattered. Busting out of here would be next to impossible, even for someone who specialized in the impossible.

"Where are you morons taking us?"

Sean heard Tommy's voice up ahead. At least they were being led to the same place. "Take it easy, Tommy."

"Sean? Thank goodness. Where's Keiko?"

"I'm here," the feminine voice echoed through the passage.

"Shut up," one of the men ordered. They made a left and then came to a sudden halt.

There was a short sliding sound and then a click. Then the sound came again, and they heard another click. Sean had seen entries like this before; a guy on one side would open a little window to check who was at the door and then unlock it. He figured that was what just happened.

Once more they were on the move, being ushered down another short passage until it ended in a set of stairs that descended into the bowels of whatever building they were in. At the bottom, the man next to Sean yanked him to the left and led him ten more feet until the hand on his shoulder forced him to stop.

A second later, he felt the hand move up to the hood and yank it off. For a moment, his eyes had to adjust to the few points of light in the center of the room: a set of five lightbulbs hanging from the ceiling at varying lengths. A man sat in a chair about fifteen feet away, his face covered in shadow, just out of reach from the glow of the lights. He was wearing a silver suit and black tie, his thin hands folded over his chest.

Sean looked to his right and left: Tommy and Keiko were standing on either side. Whoever had brought them here, they weren't small-time. Ten men lined the walls, five on each side, and every one of them rippled with muscles. They didn't try to hide the guns hanging from their shoulder holsters. One of them had knives tucked into sheaths on his belt. He looked especially sinister. Sean knew to always beware of a guy who brought knives to a gun party. It was usually for a reason, and the reason was almost always brutal.

The man in the shadows interrupted his thoughts. "Welcome to Tokyo, gentlemen."

Sean knew to keep his mouth shut, but Tommy wasn't as adept at dealing with these types.

"Who are you? Why did you bring us here?"

There were three guards standing behind the hostages, one for each of them. The one behind Tommy silenced him with a swift elbow to the kidneys. Tommy grunted and dropped to one knee, clutching his back. The man who struck him immediately helped him back to his feet, an odd courtesy after such a swift and harsh punishment.

Tommy winced and stayed half-hunched even after the guard's *assistance*.

The man in the silver suit continued. "As I was saying, welcome to Tokyo. You should know that I know pretty much everything that happens in my city. Everything worth knowing, anyway."

His English was good, unbroken. He was clearly educated, which was a new kind of danger Sean hadn't encountered before.

"Are we worth knowing about?" Sean asked.

He waited for the guard behind him to strike, but the boss's hand shot up quickly, halting any similar attack.

"You are not tourists," he replied. "I don't mind the tourists. They fill my pockets with money, eat at my restaurants, drink at my bars, and buy my souvenirs. Most of them are of no consequence. You three, on the other hand, are of great consequence."

"And why is that?"

"Because you are looking for something of great value, something priceless, something no one has ever been able to find in seventy years of searching."

Sean was careful to keep his tone polite. "And you want it for yourself."

The man leaned forward, revealing his face. Then he stood up and straightened his jacket. He had gray hair, wrinkles stretching out from the corners of his eyes, and facial skin that sagged slightly. He also had puffy bags under his eyes. Sean guessed him to be in his late sixties, fairly old for a Yakuza boss.

"You make a typical assumption, Mr. Wyatt."

"I guess I shouldn't be surprised you know my name, although I do try to keep that somewhat a secret."

The man smiled. When he did, his cheeks puffed out, making him look like a little boy with gray hair. "Your name was easy enough to come by. Your background remains a mystery. But you can rest easy, Sean. I have no interest in your history. As far as I'm concerned, the past is of no matter. I usually find that when someone's background is as secretive as yours, they either did a lot of bad things for a lot of bad people, or they did a lot of bad things for a government. Either way, you're the right man for the job."

Now Sean was curious. "Job?"

He had a feeling he knew where the conversation was going but waited to hear the old man out.

"Surely you know that I am Yakuza." Sean nodded. "And since you know that, given all the men I have in this room, the cars, and the ease with which I tracked you down and abducted you, it is safe for you to assume I am powerful."

Sean answered casually. "I'd say that's a given. And, no offense, given your age, I'd say you're fairly good at navigating the difficult avenues of the underworld."

The old man nodded. "A skill honed through much difficulty."

"They say to beware of old men in a career where most men die young. You certainly deserve a high level of respect if that is the case."

Sean was going pretty deep with the butt kissing. But Tommy and Keiko didn't interfere. Keiko was too afraid. And Tommy knew his friend could feel out a room better than anyone. He imagined Sean had probably found himself in similar situations to this one more than a handful of times.

"You say all the right things," the old man said with a grin. He bowed low. "An American who has learned respect. Or at least how to present himself as respectful."

"It's not fake if that's what you're saying. Someone who

commands this many men has to have leadership of some kind. Whether it's on the right side of the law or not isn't my call. We're all just soldiers."

The man peered into Sean's soul, searching him for the truth. There were no lies in the American's eyes. And Sean had just offered him a taste of what his past looked like. It was enough for the old man.

"My men call me Aoki," he said after another moment. "You may call me that as well."

The guards in the room eased visibly.

Sean bowed low. "It's an honor to meet you."

Sean knew exactly who the old guy was now, though he couldn't believe he was standing face to face with him and still breathing.

Upon hearing the name, a chill had shot down Sean's spine. He'd heard of Aoki. The old man was at the top of the food chain with the Yakuza. While it was hard to figure out if there was a single kingpin over all the other subgroups in the gang, Aoki certainly could be it. Behind the kind-looking, gentle mask was a cold-blooded killer. Sean had heard some gruesome stories about the kind of justice this guy dealt out. It was the stuff of nightmares.

And he wasn't lying about all the different kinds of businesses he owned. Most of them were acquired for an obscene amount of money. Others, less scrupulously. But the previous owners always sold. They didn't have a choice. They were welcome to move somewhere else and start over if they wanted. Those who tried to defy Aoki met a terrible fate.

"I can see from the look on your face that you have heard of me," the man said with a hint of puzzlement on his face.

"Your reputation isn't an easy one to miss, even in America."

"And yet you stand here, unafraid."

Sean shrugged. "The way I see it, if you were going to kill us, you'd have done it already." He prayed he was right about that part. His instincts told him it was the right assumption, but assuming was never a sure thing. "Which means you either want something from us, or you're up to something else."

Aoki smiled. "Perhaps it is a bit of both. And you are correct," he waved a finger at Sean. "I don't want to kill you. I need you to do something for me." He had cut to the chase, ending the little charade.

"Well, if you want us to bring the Honjo Masamune to you, why didn't you just ask instead of sending those goons after us?"

Aoki folded his hands behind his back and briefly looked down at the floor. When he raised his head, he spoke plainly. "Those men who followed you were not mine."

Tommy was finally able to stand up straight, though his lower back still throbbed from the blow he'd taken. "Oh yeah? Who were they then?"

The old man smirked, turned to his left, and took a few paces before stopping and pivoting back toward the visitors. "They work for a man named Taka. He was one of my prodigies. Unfortunately, Taka found his way up the ladder a little too quickly. The power went to his head, and his ambitions became too lofty."

"So that was the guy with the shaved head?" Tommy asked.

"No. That is a man named Hideo. He is Taka's main enforcer. A ruthless character in his own right. And he will do anything Taka tells him to so long as he gets to ride his boss's coattails to the top."

Sean was starting to see where this was going, though he would never insinuate that Aoki was afraid of this Taka character. "And Taka wants to take you out. That sound about right?"

Aoki nodded. "Very astute, Mr. Wyatt. Yes. It isn't just about that, though. There are any number of men who want to kill me."

"Heavy sits the crown," Tommy added.

"Correct. That is my life, my existence. You get used to it. But Taka is different. He has no sense of honor. All he cares about is power."

The irony wasn't lost on Sean, a crime lord talking about honor. He wondered how much honor there could have been in the innumerable people he'd killed or screwed out of their livelihoods through the decades.

Again, Aoki read his mind. "I may be a criminal, but I have honor, Mr. Wyatt. Taka has none."

Now it was Sean's turn to cut to the chase. As intriguing as this little visit was, it was time to either get executed or get moving. They were losing time with every second of chatter.

"I don't mean to be rude, sir, but why *did* you bring us here?"

Aoki spun around and paced back the way he'd come, stopped, and faced the visitors again. "You were correct in your assumption that I want you to find the Honjo Masamune. But the sword does not belong to me. I am not the rightful owner. It belongs to the Tokugawa family, and only they should possess it. You must make sure that Taka does not find the sword...at all costs. He wishes to use it as a sign of power, a sort of symbol. If he retrieves the sword, many of the Yakuza will follow him. Of course, I will be finished in Tokyo, a small consequence of the outcome."

Sean tilted his head to the side and frowned. "Small consequence?" He didn't like the sound of that.

"Yes," Aoki said. "Taka wishes to bring all Yakuza under his banner. When that happens, he plans to throw the country into anarchy. Of course he doesn't see it this way. He believes, ignorantly, that he can set up his own sort of monarchy."

"That sounds a little insane," Tommy said.

"Indeed it does, Mr. Schultz."

"Wait a minute, how do you..."

"You needn't worry yourself with the inconsequential, Mr. Schultz. How I know your identities and why you are here doesn't matter at this point. What matters is that you do not fail. Taka must be stopped."

Sean spoke again, crossing his arms as he did so. "OK, so if you just want us to find the sword and get it to the rightful owners, why bring us down here and slow us down? We figured out where we were going. This meeting has set us back at least an hour."

Aoki smiled and nodded at one of the guards to his left. The man produced a tablet and flipped the screen around so the visitors could see it. The image on the screen was of a red compact car, or what was left of it, burning out of control. Huge black plumes of smoke poured out of brilliant orange flames.

"My car!" Keiko exclaimed. For a moment, the Americans had

almost forgotten she was in the room, so silent she'd been during the conversation.

"Taka's men put an explosive device under the carriage. It is why they didn't follow you from the palace grounds. For the immediate future, it's safe to assume that they believe you to be dead. We will put in a report with the local authorities that two Americans and a local woman were killed in the blast. That should buy you a little more time."

Tommy wasn't sure he liked the idea. "Thank you?"

"You are welcome." Aoki ignored the sarcastic gratitude. "I am sorry for the loss of your vehicle," he said to Keiko. "We will provide one for you. And I am also going to provide you with one of my guards to help you along the way."

"We work alone, or..." Tommy struggled with the explanation. "Well, the two of us together work alone. I mean, we're helping her, but we work alone."

Sean interrupted his friend's fumbling words. "What he means to say is we appreciate the kind gesture, Aokisan, but we can handle ourselves. And we can probably move faster if we don't have another person with us."

Aoki raised an eyebrow. "It wasn't a question, gentlemen. But if you choose not to accept my offer, that is your decision to make. Just make sure you do not fail. If you do, it will be the last mistake you make."

Bad people had threatened Sean before, so Aoki's threat rolled off his back like it was nothing. Instead of cowering, he wondered if the older man might have a solution to their immediate problem. "I just have one question for you."

"Yes?"

"Do you have access to a helicopter?"

10

TOKYO

Taka hovered over the boardroom table. He stared at the little piece of paper held down at each corner by stones he'd taken from a nearby vase. Taka had been looking at the riddle for over twenty minutes, unable to decipher its meaning. A vein on the side of his head pulsed as his frustration grew. Part of his anger was with his inability to understand the clue. The other half was with Hideo for not getting the solution before killing the Americans and their friend.

Hideo stood at the other end of the table with his hands folded behind his back. He stared at the far wall with a blank expression. As he understood it, once they procured the riddle, the Americans were no longer necessary. Sure, a Japanese citizen would be killed in the process but so what? They killed innocent people all the time. Part of Taka's mantra was that no one on earth is innocent. Everyone is guilty of something, and therefore it is not tragic when people die. They are merely getting what is due to them. Hideo could tell his boss was irritated but said nothing to defend his actions. All he'd done was relay what happened at the palace grounds.

The Americans had thrown a wrench into the plan and delayed

things momentarily. The palace guard had been a problem; though he wouldn't be anymore. After Hideo caught the cipher, the guard continued to nag at them until Hideo instructed one of his men to kill him.

One of the henchmen stepped around behind the guard, pulled out a knife and shoved it through the base of his neck, close to the collarbone. It was a swift death, and about as clean as could be hoped for with a knife. Usually, people who had their throats cut sprayed blood everywhere. Puncturing the neck near the collarbone and severing the artery would allow the blood to leak down into the lungs, and thus keep the killers clean for their walk back to the car.

Standing around in a huddle, they dumped the body into the ditch and watched it tumble into the waterway before heading toward the street. Once they were safely inside their vehicles, Hideo had detonated the bomb.

"The Americans won't be a threat to us anymore," he'd told Taka. "They and the girl are dead."

The latter part of this news disturbed Taka, but he didn't mention it. "You're sure they're dead?"

"The police reports say two Americans and a Japanese woman were killed in the blast."

Taka frowned. Something wasn't right. "They have a report on their identities so soon? That sort of thing usually takes a day or two for them to determine."

Hideo shrugged. "Perhaps their identifications weren't damaged in the fire."

Taka wasn't convinced. "The police cannot be trusted. I know. I pay them. They are bigger criminals than we are." He waved a dismissive hand. "It doesn't matter if they're alive or dead. We have this, and they do not. Now all I need to do is figure out what it means."

"If I may, it seems to me that the riddle is referring to the three mountains of Dewa. My grandparents were devout Buddhists and would go to the mountains on a pilgrimage every two years. It might be a good place to start."

Taka was pleasantly surprised at the epiphany. "Thank you, Hideo. Now that you mention it, I think you're right. Many Buddhists consider those three mountains to be holy." He scratched his chin as he thought about the possibility. "The question is which one?"

"If I may make an observation, Mount Yudono and Mount Haguro are both covered in thick forests. The land is green and full of life, while Mount Gassan is nothing but rocks and grass. Most of the winter it is covered in snow. If the journey to find the sword begins on barren heights, my guess would be somewhere on Gassan we will find the answer to our riddle."

Taka was impressed, but he didn't want his underling to forget his place. "Thank you, Hideo. Get a team together, and prepare to head for Gassan. I am grateful for your help."

Hideo was caught a little off guard. "I'm sorry, sir. Are you certain?"

Taka shrugged. "It's as good a place as any to look. Assemble a team, and check out this Gassan place."

Hideo lingered, still hesitating. "Sir, the mountains in that region will be treacherous. It's likely Gassan will be covered in snow."

"So? Figure it out. That's what I pay you for."

After another moment of uncertainty, Hideo nodded and left the room. Taka remained at the end of the table, staring down at the little piece of paper. He hoped his right-hand man was right. If he wasn't, no matter. Time wasn't an issue. If what Hideo had said was accurate, the Americans were dead along with the Japanese woman. It was a shame she'd died, an unfortunate casualty. Then again, that kind of collateral damage was to be expected from time to time, especially when the stakes were highest.

He stepped over to the window and gazed out at the city: his city. The sun was starting to set in the west. Soon the cold night would take over. Taka turned around and picked up the paper. He'd memorized the clue and no longer needed the physical copy. His hand dipped into the front right pocket of his pants and removed a cigarette lighter. He flipped open the lid and sparked the flame to life and then touched it to the paper.

The little scroll caught fire quickly and was soon engulfed in flame. Taka held on to the top corner until the last moment before dropping the burning page into a nearby waste bin. Now he and Hideo were the only people on the planet with a clue as to the whereabouts of the greatest Samurai sword ever made. At least he hoped that was the case.

11

MOUNT GASSAN, NORTHERN JAPAN

Sean wasn't sure whether the helicopter pilot was crazy or if he just didn't have a choice. The Americans had hoped for a peaceful flight into the mountains of the Yamagata Prefecture (the ancient province of Dewa). For the most part it had been. But when they reached the higher peaks near Mount Gassan, things started to turn ugly.

They'd found a hotel the night before after a five-hour train ride and were able to get some tenuous sleep. Sean didn't get much rest, but Tommy and Keiko slept like the dead. Early Thursday morning, as the sun was rising over the ocean to the east, Sean woke up, took a quick shower, and got dressed. Despite not sleeping well, he still felt refreshed, as if he'd taken a power nap in the middle of the day.

When he was ready to go, Sean woke the others so they could do whatever they needed. Waking early was something Sean hated but at the same time couldn't help. After getting up early for so many years, his body wouldn't allow him sleep in. It was infuriating sometimes because all he really wanted to do, especially when at home, was sleep in. For whatever reason, 7 sharp each morning was the latest he could stay asleep.

Sean always tried to do a little reconnaissance before he went headfirst into any situation. So he pulled up his computer and started investigating Mount Gassan while Tommy was taking a shower. When his friend stepped out of the bathroom, Sean was studying images of the monastery at the top of the mountain.

"What ya doing?" Tommy asked as he dried his hair.

"Trying to get a feel for this place. I'd rather not fly to the top of a freezing cold mountain and spend a ton of time wandering around, searching aimlessly for something."

"Good idea." Tommy pulled up a chair next to Sean's and sat down, still only clothed in a towel wrapped around his waist.

Sean frowned. "Would you mind putting some clothes on first?"

"What?" Tommy asked. "Afraid of the male body?"

Sean snorted and turned back to the computer. "I'm afraid of *your* body." Before his friend could reply, he tapped on the screen. The image was one from the summer, and the entire monastery was visible along with its surroundings. "These memorial stones right here might be what we're looking for."

"You mean like the stone from the riddle?"

Sean nodded. "Would make sense. They're going to be there forever, and death is eternal. Well, depending on your beliefs of course."

Tommy stared at the screen. "Interesting." He slapped Sean on the back. "Good job, buddy. We'll have you back and working for IAA before you know it." He stood up and returned to the bathroom to get dressed, leaving Sean sighing and shaking his head.

Before they'd left Tokyo, Aoki had promised that the group would receive whatever help they needed in their quest for the missing sword. Sean was leery of using mob assistance for anything, but he got the distinct impression it was an offer he couldn't refuse.

Aoki had recommended a guy he'd known for years, or at least claimed to have. He said the man could get them a good pilot, a helicopter, and all the supplies they would need for the journey. Both Sean and Tommy were suspicious, but there was no choice. They accepted the crime lord's offer and took off.

True to his word, Aoki made a phone call to his associate in the coastal city of Sendai. Upon arriving, their contact, a chubby middle-aged man named Yoku, had been extremely accommodating. He provided a pilot and a helicopter to carry the visitors to their destination.

The rolling hills gave way to steeper slopes of dense forests in the mountains. As the helicopter flew over the higher elevations, the snow below them grew deeper and deeper. It was like a winter wonderland with tall coniferous trees decked out in fluffy white powder.

But as the helicopter ascended toward the barren peaks and bowls at the top of some of the ridgelines, the wind picked up and shoved the aircraft back and forth. Keiko hadn't said much during any part of the journey. It was clear that she was not comfortable with the idea of flying in these conditions, but she didn't say much about it, instead staring out the window and occasionally grabbing a hand-hold on the door.

Tommy and Sean had tried to convince her to stay in the hotel in Sendai. No one would be looking for her there. At least that's what they believed. The truth was, there was no way to know for sure. Keiko must have realized they couldn't guarantee her safety in either situation so she insisted on staying with the two Americans.

Yoku had taken care of everything, right down to getting some heavy winter coats for the adventurers. He even got the sizes correct. They shouldn't have been surprised. Someone like Aoki didn't get into the position he was in without paying attention to details.

Sean unzipped his big coat and rechecked the weapon he'd stuffed inside. Fortunately, Aoki's men had brought their gear bags with them when taking the visitors out of their cars. Satisfied with his third inspection of the gun, Sean zipped the coat back up and glanced out the window at the wintry landscape passing by underneath.

Oddly, he wasn't afraid of flying. His fear of heights was relegated to tall buildings, precipices, and other structures. For whatever reason, he actually enjoyed being in an aircraft. It felt like he was in a seat in the air. As the helicopter approached the summit, Sean was glad Aoki's guy in Sendai had seen to one additional detail. It had seemed odd at first, but upon seeing the snow-covered ridges on the mountaintop, Sean knew the man had been correct.

There was no way they were going to be able to land the helicopter up there. The snow would make it nearly impossible. Fortunately, Yoku had another plan. He equipped them with skis, boots, and poles. After they figured out what they needed at the shrine on top of Mount Gassan, they could ski down to a rendezvous point where it was safer for the helicopter to land. Sean had gone over the map with the pilot to make sure he understood the layout and where he needed to go once they left the shrine. For a moment, it reminded him of his days working with the government. Extract zones, rally points, and all that stuff were things he'd left in the past. Except sometimes the past had a funny way of creeping back into his life.

Sean and Tommy both knew how to ski. They'd learned at a young age on the bunny slopes of North Carolina. The snow had been mostly artificial, but it did the job. Luckily, Keiko said she knew how to ski, too.

The pilot's voice crackled through headsets, interrupting everyone's thoughts. "That's where you're going," he pointed at a small structure on the mountain's peak. "We'll be there in sixty seconds." His English—like the fake snow of Sean's childhood—was choppy, but it did the job.

Sean reached down and grabbed his skis from the floor.

"The snow is several feet deep, so when you drop, your landing should be soft. I will be waiting for you at the rendezvous point."

Sean nodded and slung his rucksack over his shoulders. Tommy and Keiko were also preparing to jump out.

In less than a minute, the building on the horizon became clearer, and the group could see the shrine in more detail, though the roofs were almost completely covered in snow.

"Is there anyone in that thing?" Tommy asked, uncertain if the pilot would even know the answer.

The man shook his head. "Only one. There is a priest there at all times. During the winter months, he is there alone for long periods of time."

"Jeez. What does he do to pass the time?"

The pilot turned his head a little to the side, still keeping an eye on the mountain ahead. "Meditate."

He slowed the aircraft's speed until he found a place where the ridge leveled off a little. "This is going to be as good a place as any."

Sean nodded and turned the latch on the side door. He slid it open and looked down. It was only about eight feet down, nothing to worry about. A sudden burst of wind rolled up the slope and tipped the helicopter to the right.

"You should jump now. This wind is getting dangerous." There was definite concern in the pilot's voice as he struggled with the control stick.

Sean looked over at Keiko. "You ready?"

She gave a steady nod, and before he could double check, she jumped out the door and into the deep powder below.

Tommy and Sean looked at her as her legs disappeared into the snow, all the way up to her knees. Then they looked at each other and shrugged.

"I guess she's not scared," Tommy said.

"Why?" Sean smirked and removed his headset. "Are you?"

Before Tommy could answer, Sean tucked his skis under his armpits and leaped into the snow five feet to the right of Keiko.

Tommy shook his head. "Thanks for the lift," he said to the pilot. He jumped out to the left of Keiko, who had already dug her way out and had shoved the end of her skis into the packed snow so that they were sticking upright into the air.

Sean and Tommy did the same and began working their way onto the upper layer of powder. Wearing ski boots wasn't the best way to navigate deep snow. Fortunately, along the ridge, it had packed down enough to allow them to walk along without too much fuss.

Sean pulled his goggles over his eyes, relieving them from the bright sun glaring off the snow and the brutal wind, which caused him to tear up. He stared over at the snow-covered staircase that led up to the shrine. It was only fifty yards away, but with their terrible footing, it may as well have been a thousand. He started plodding along, one foot in front of the other in a deliberate traverse toward the shrine. The wind picked up again and nearly knocked him over sideways, and very well might have if his ankles weren't buried. He turned around and looked back at the other two to make sure they were OK. They were following along behind him, making slow progress, but progress nonetheless.

A discouraging thought ran through Sean's head. What if they couldn't find what they were looking for in all this snow? Conditions were less than ideal, and the closer he got to the path leading to the outer wall, the more that became a real possibility. He reached the bottom of the steps, or what he assumed were steps. The snow covering the way up to the shrine's gateway, or *torii*, had a vague outline that looked like a staircase. Sean took another quick look back to make sure his companions were still close behind and then started up the steps.

By the time he was halfway to the gate, Sean's legs were already burning from the effort of hiking through the drifts. The air was a little thinner, too, due to the fact that the mountain's peak was over six thousand feet. That lack of oxygen made the exertion that much tougher, and Sean found himself breathing heavier than he normally would. He worried Tommy was struggling but kept pushing forward.

After four minutes of trekking up the steps, Sean stopped underneath the torii and looked out over the land. Wind blew dust-like snow across his goggles, making visibility almost zero. It was much harder to see than it had been in the helicopter. Of course, inside the aircraft, they were above all this.

Just beyond the gate, the exterior stone wall jutted out to the left above a strange pile of snow. Judging by the lower level of snow piled up on the near side of the wall, Sean figured it would be a good place to get out of the wind for a minute. He motioned to the others with his mitt-covered hands and then clomped off the path and over to the wall, finding a place where it was stacked up a few feet over his head. Spinning around, Sean pressed his back to the wall and leaned into it, taking a second to rest. Tommy and Keiko did the same, happy to get out of the brutal wind for a moment.

Sean pulled down the top of his coat so the others could hear him more clearly. "I'm starting to think this was a bad idea!" he shouted.

"No kidding!" Tommy yelled back. "How in the world are we going to find anything up here?"

Keiko leaned close and joined the conversation. "How do we know which stone the next clue is written on? There are hundreds of them making up this wall." She pointed to the front entrance. It was locked. "And we can't go inside. If the clue is there, we won't be able to get to it until the summer."

Sean shook his head. "I don't think it's inside the shrine. Let's start on the front side with the memorial stones. That's probably our best bet." He pointed at the torii. "Up there. Let's get through that gate. I think what we're looking for is just beyond it."

His face was stinging from the biting wind, and his nose had flushed red. Sean pulled the coat's face covering back up over his mouth and nose and scurried over to the nearest support beam for the gate.

Tommy and Keiko followed, passing him and going to the beam on the other side.

"What should we do?" Tommy put his hands out wide. "How are we going to find anything out here in this mess?"

"Yeah," Sean answered. "I guess we didn't really think this through all the way." He turned his gaze toward the front of the monastery. "Over there!" he shouted through the howling wind and pointed.

"What are those?" Keiko asked, pointing at three odd humps in the snow.

The anomalies were barely noticeable, situated in front of the left wall and next to the pathway. But the two Americans knew exactly what they were.

Tommy answered. "I think those are the memorial stones we saw in the pictures, but I'm not sure." He turned to Sean. "I guess we dig them out?"

"That's our only option. But not with our hands. Let's go back and get our skis. We can use them to dig. Will make the work faster."

"Good idea. Keiko, I'll get yours."

Sean wanted to throw in a little sarcastic comment about chivalry not being dead, but it was too cold. Instead, he led the way back to where the group had stuck their skis into the ground. He picked his up first and then Keiko's, handing them to Tommy as he clumsily tried to handle his own.

"Here you go, Romeo."

"I was just trying to be polite." His explanation could barely be heard over the howling wind.

Sean didn't feel like talking. He wanted to get to the bottom of this riddle and get down to the tree line, out of this wind, and into the comfort of the helicopter's warm interior.

He headed back to the little nook where the three odd humps in the snow jutted out like white ghosts. Keiko had propped herself against the wall for protection against the elements but joined the two Americans and took her skis from Tommy.

"Thank you," she said.

He was sure she was smiling, but it was hard to tell under the coat's collar and behind the goggles.

Sean unclipped his skis and jammed one into the nearby snow-bank. He started digging with the remaining one, pulling the snow back toward the mountain's slope. "Pile the snow over here," he said, pointing behind him. "At least we can build up a snow wall to give us a little shelter from this brutal wind."

The other two nodded and followed his lead, shoveling the white powder over to the side. Every minute or so, Sean dropped his ski and spent thirty seconds packing their new wall a little higher. In five minutes, they had dug halfway down to the base of the stones and built a wall up to their shoulders. In another five, their heads were below the top of the man-made snowbank, and the wind was signifi-cantly less taxing.

"Good call on this thing," Tommy said, pointing at the wall. "That wind isn't nearly as bad."

"Yeah, well, it won't matter if we don't find what we're looking for."

He stared down at the three stones. One was much taller than the other two and featured Japanese characters in neat rows on the front. The others had the same unique lettering but were smaller, less prominent pieces of rock.

"What does it say?" Tommy asked Keiko.

She crouched down and read the words. Then she shook her head. "It's just names. I believe these were the priests who have served here at the shrine over the years."

Sean bent down and examined each stone's surface. The rock had been worn smooth, probably by human hands. That or they'd been taken from a creek or river. The stones' texture wasn't what interested Sean. He was searching for something out of place, something that didn't quite fit.

He found what he was looking for at the base of the smallest of the three stones. "What's this?" He pointed at a short sequence of letters carved into the rock, almost flush with the ground.

Keiko had to get down on her hands and knees. The engraving was faint, worn down by time. It was different from the rest of the characters cut into the stone, clearly not done by the same person or with the same attention to consistency.

"It's another riddle," she said, getting so close to the stone that her nose almost touched it. She brushed away a little loose debris and then spoke up again. "Pass through the red gate. A dragon watches the way to the holy ground, a toll to be paid for illumination."

"Any idea what that means?" Sean asked her.

She shook her head.

Tommy interrupted. "We can figure that out later. Let's just get back down to the helicopter and out of this cold."

Sean nodded. "Good call."

"I gotta admit," Tommy said, "that's some mighty fine work we just did. And it took us less than an hour."

Sean cringed on the inside. "Don't jinx us. We're not off the mountain yet."

Tommy laughed. "What, you not confident with your skiing abilities?"

Before Sean could shake his head, he heard something strange amid the whistling and howling of the wind. He snapped around and stared back in the direction they'd come. The ridge was still barren, void of any life. The sound went away for a second, and then he heard it again. Clearer, more distinct than before.

It was the distinct sound of a snowmobile motor.

12

MOUNT GASSAN

"Move," Sean ordered. "Get around to the other side of our wall."

"What's the—" Tommy caught himself before he finished. He could hear the whining engine now as well. "Aw, man."

He scrambled out of their makeshift pit and into the deep snow above the wall. He held out a hand for Keiko and helped her climb out. Sean grabbed their skis and poles and handed them over before taking his own.

"Sounds like snowmobiles," he said as he climbed out of the pit. "Get your skis on, and get ready to go."

Keiko hesitated. "Maybe it is just someone delivering supplies to the priest."

Sean stepped close to the other two and peeked over the top of their manmade snowdrift. He shook his head upon seeing the headlights of five snowmobiles coming their way.

"Nope. Those are definitely not people bringing supplies."

"I don't mean to be the bearer of bad news," Tommy said, "but we can't outrun those things. Once they see us, they'll come after us. There's no chance we can get away."

Sean already knew that. He sloughed his rucksack onto the

ground. He unzipped his jacket and pulled out his gun. "You should probably get your gun."

"Right." Tommy obeyed and dug into his gear bag. He withdrew a similar weapon and checked to make sure there was a round in the chamber. "So what's the plan? Gunfight on the mountain? I doubt the Buddhist priest would approve."

The comment caused Sean to snicker briefly. "Yeah, I doubt he would. The good news is we're outnumbered."

"Just like always."

"Yep." Sean turned to Keiko. "Wait until I give you a signal, then you take off down the mountain. We'll catch up to you. Just head for the tree line. If they follow us into the forest, it will be harder for them to navigate through it."

Keiko nodded. There was fear and uncertainty in her eyes, but she placed the skis on a flat section of snow and stepped into them before tightening the straps on her boots. She lay over on her side to stay out of sight but remained in a position that would be easy to stand again and make a quick takeoff.

Sean and Tommy stepped into their skis too, bracing themselves against the snowbank to keep their balance.

The snowmobiles kept coming, passing the point where the Americans and Keiko had dropped out of the helicopter, and only stopping when they reached the base of the path where the slope became much steeper. The five men were all wearing heavy white coats and snow pants. Away from their machines, the outfits were outstanding camouflage against the mountain's white powdery backdrop. One man was busily pointing around at the others, making wild gestures with one hand. All of the men carried submachine guns, slung over one shoulder with a narrow strap. Sean recognized the HK-5s immediately. From this distance, they wouldn't be terribly accurate. But with all five men shooting, one was bound to get lucky.

The one giving out orders had to be Hideo, the one with the shaved head Sean met at the palace. Judging from his height and build—winter coat notwithstanding—he figured his assessment was correct.

They were only sixty feet away at the bottom of the steps, so Sean pulled Tommy down out of sight before the men began their ascent.

"You think it's the same guys from the palace?" Tommy asked.

"No reason to assume otherwise. I guess they were able to figure out the riddle."

"And here I thought we had a monopoly on that sort of thing."

Sean twisted his head. "Guess not, buddy."

"So what's the plan? I know she's going first. Then what?"

"We have the element of surprise. They're armed, but I doubt they're ready for a firefight. When they're halfway up the steps, open fire. They'll scramble for cover first, probably dive into the snow. When they do, put as many rounds as you can into their snowmobiles. Aim for the gas tanks if you can. I doubt they'll blow, but without fuel, they can't follow us very far."

"Right," Tommy nodded.

"Make sure you have an extra magazine ready. Just in case."

Tommy did as instructed, quickly taking a fully loaded magazine out of his gear bag and sliding it into his front jacket pocket. Then he put the bag back over his shoulders and hunkered down, keeping the weapon just in front of his face.

Sean peeked around the edge of the snowbank. The men were making slow progress but were already a third of the way to the Americans' position. Sean held out a mitt behind him, telling the other two to hold. Ten more seconds went by like sap dripping from a maple tree. Satisfied they'd come far enough, Sean turned around and motioned for Keiko to go.

She pushed herself off the ground, pounded her poles into the snow, and shoved forward. Four quick strokes, and she was gone.

Sean watched as the men on the stairs suddenly noticed the skier. They turned and raised their weapons. "Now!" Sean barked.

He and Tommy popped up from behind their wall and opened fire. Their targets were still thirty feet away, hardly the optimal range for accuracy in these conditions, but a few rounds found their mark. The man in front, the one Sean figured was Hideo, took a bullet in the side. He twisted sideways and then dove to his right, sliding clear of the barrage. Another man took a round squarely in the chest. He dropped to the ground on his knees and then fell over on his side. The other three immediately turned their attention to the shooters, pointing their weapons at the snowbank in a panic.

They squeezed their triggers while diving away from the open area, sending a reckless spray of bullets into the snowbank and the rock wall surrounding the shrine. Now the path was clear, giving the two Americans straight shots at the snowmobiles.

"Hit the machines," Sean ordered.

Tommy complied, and the two emptied the rest of their magazines at the parked snowmobiles. Snow splashed around the vehicles as the rounds missed their mark. Two of the machines were hit, though. One was struck near the bottom of the fuel tank and was already leaking precious fuel onto the pure snow. The other took a round in the center and was also losing gas rapidly.

"Better go," Sean said as he pressed the release button on his weapon.

The magazine fell into his free hand, and he pocketed it quickly. In the same motion he grabbed the one he'd put in the same pocket earlier and slid it into place. The weapon clicked, and he tugged back on the slide to chamber another round. Tommy copied his friend's moves, although a tad slower. When he was ready, Sean gave him a nod toward the slopes. Keiko was already a few hundred yards away and speeding toward the base of the mountain. A gust of wind picked up, and she disappeared in the blowing debris.

Sean whirled around and fired another two shots at the gangsters' positions. "Go," he said to Tommy who was standing ready by the edge of the hill.

"Haven't done one this steep in a long time," he said, hesitating.

"Now you're scared?"

"I'm not scared I'm just—"

Sean shoved his friend in the back, sending him over the edge and speeding down into the deep powder. Taking one last shot at the men on the near bank, Sean spun around and pushed hard with his poles, diving ahead into the driven snow dust.

He didn't look back, instead making sure he kept Tommy ahead of him. His friend weighed at least fifteen pounds more, a fact that actually helped Tommy during this particular getaway.

Gravity pulled Tommy down the slopes as he cut left and right, stabilizing his speed so that he could maintain control. Sean slalomed as well, maximizing pace to put as much distance between him and the gangsters as possible. Going downhill into the wind made seeing more than twenty feet ahead almost impossible. Tommy flashed in and out of Sean's field of vision, dipping into the rolling gusts. Even if the men on the snowmobiles followed them, the Americans and their companion would be difficult to see until they got near the tree line.

Or so Sean thought.

The slope suddenly evened out, and his momentum nearly toppled him forward onto his face. He corrected and maintained, plunging his poles into the snow to keep up his speed. The plateau ended abruptly and dropped off in a steep decline. Sean sailed over the edge, flying fifteen feet through the air until he felt the back of his skis touch down. He cut hard to the left to steady his speed and pushed on ahead, making sharper turns to keep control on the steep embankment.

Down at the lower elevation, the wind had diminished from the fierce gusts up on the bowl. He slowed his pace to take a quick look back at the white dust storm above, then stared downward. A thousand feet away, he could see the thick evergreen trees rising up from snow. Tommy was barreling ahead at breakneck speed. Sean was relieved to see that Keiko had made it to the forest. She slowed her pace by making a V out of her skis and then disappeared into the skinny stands of tree trunks, weaving in and out of view.

The faint, intermittent whine of the snowmobile engines grew louder. The men were coming. No way Sean was going to make the trees in time. He straightened his skis, bent both knees, and tucked down into a racing position. His coat and snow pants were hardly conducive to high-speed aerodynamics, but that couldn't be helped. Ahead of him, Tommy glanced back and saw Sean's posture. Realizing there must be danger approaching, he mimicked the position and tightened his body into a compact ball.

The Americans picked up speed as they raced through the powder, charging for the perceived safety of the trees. Sean risked another short look back and saw the first of the headlights appear, then the second and third. He hit a hump in the slope and flew through the air, soaring twenty feet before hitting the ground in a splash of snow. He managed to keep his balance in spite of the jarring landing and pushed forward.

A familiar chain of pops echoed from behind. Sean didn't need to look back to know the men on the snowmobiles were firing their weapons. At the speed they were forced to maintain and given the uneven surface, accuracy would be minimal.

Only a few hundred feet to go.

A bullet ripped through his jacket's left sleeve, narrowly missing Sean's arm. He looked back again to find the snowmobiles gaining quickly. The two in front carried one man each. The third one held two, which meant it could only go so fast. The fifth gangster must have been left on the summit. Sean figured he was either dead or would be soon.

The first two machines would be on him within ten seconds, and he could do nothing to prevent it; however, he could buy some time for Tommy and Keiko.

Sean cut hard to the right, veering toward a section of forest that stretched in a bend toward the mountain's peak. Traversing the slope would slow him down, but it would also give him more options. Streaking straight ahead granted speed, but that didn't matter against the horsepower of the snowmobiles.

The driver in front turned right and kept after Sean, followed closely by the second guy. The machine with the two riders went straight ahead, chasing after Tommy.

More shots rattled off, causing plumes of white powder to explode around Sean's skis. He noted another sudden drop-off coming up and crouched down again to gain more speed. He ducked back and forth to make himself as difficult a target as possible, but the men were only thirty feet behind him now and closing fast.

Just as Sean reached the lip of the drop, he twisted his skis sideways, digging the edges into the snow. He went over the sudden drop amid a wave of snow. The fall was only five or six feet, the result of a random rock formation jutting out of the ground. He landed on his feet facing the direction he'd come. Sean stayed low, knowing what would come next.

The sound of two motors roared closer. Sean crouched as much as he could without slipping. A second later, the two machines revved high and soared over Sean's head. The tracks on the snowmobile to the left narrowly missed his beanie and splashed fresh snow onto his shoulders and face. He shook it off and watched the machines land hard on the steep downslope thirty feet beyond his hiding spot.

One of the drivers hadn't seen the drop in time and when he became airborne, was lifted from his seat as the heavier machine fell to earth. Upon landing, he was slammed back into the saddle and rocked free of his grip on the handlebars. He rolled to a stop in the soft powder, his snowmobile coasting down the hill and veering off to the left.

Without a moment to spare, Sean kicked out and took off downhill after them. The man who'd fallen off his ride recovered quickly, scrambling to his feet. Snow poured off him, and he swiped at his goggles to regain his vision. He was disoriented but soon located his snowmobile as it drifted along the side of the slope—until gravity started to pull it down toward the forest a few hundred feet away.

Sean zipped through the powder toward the fallen attacker, grabbing his pistol from inside his jacket as he picked up speed. The man started trudging through the snow in a vain attempt to catch up to his machine while the other rider—realizing what happened to his partner—changed course and turned back to come up the hill. Too late, the man on foot sensed Sean approaching and spun around, fumbling with his weapon. By the time he got a grip on the gun, Sean had raised his pistol and fired from twenty feet away. Sean had spent years perfecting his technique in situations that were less than ideal, so with his muscles loosened and acting as shock absorbers for the movement of his legs, he fired five times. Three of the rounds found their mark.

The attacker's torso twisted to one side and then the other as each bullet hit: upper right chest, left shoulder, and then his stomach. He lurched forward for a second before falling on his back into the snow. Sean immediately saw the remaining rider coming at him, the machine nearing its limit as the engine groaned loudly, pushing the skis and tracks up the steep hill.

He saw the rider heft his weapon over the windshield and prop it on the top edge, steadying it to fire. Sean beat him to it. His finger pulled on the trigger three times in rapid succession. Two rounds missed completely. The third struck the side of the machine as the rider jerked the handlebars to the right. It was a panicked, ill-conceived decision. He attempted to bring his weapon around to fire, but now his broad side was exposed. Sean dug his skis into the snow and turned left, heading right at the snowmobile. He lined up the sights on his weapon and unleashed another volley.

This time, the bullets didn't miss. One found the outer part of the rider's knee; the other two burrowed into his torso. The impact knocked the rider backward, flipping him head over heels into the snow. Sean waited for a moment to make sure the guy wasn't going to get up. The rider didn't move. His machine, on the other hand, coasted another fifteen feet up the hill before losing its momentum and stalling.

Sean heard gunfire coming from the direction Tommy had been heading. He looked back at the snowmobile and shrugged. *May as well. That rider won't be needing it anymore.*

13

MOUNT GASSAN

Sean pressed the throttle all the way to the grip on the right handlebar. The tracks spat snow fifteen feet behind him as he sped toward the other snowmobile and its two riders. Based on the size of the two dead men he'd left on the slope a few moments before, he assumed one of the men on the last machine was Hideo. Tommy was almost to the tree line, but the men were firing relentlessly, causing him to swerve back and forth. The technique made him harder to hit, but it also slowed him down.

With Sean having far less weight on board, the gap between the two machines closed quickly. He crossed the slope at breakneck speed, heading down to intercept the other snowmobile before they could get within point-blank range of Tommy. Sean wondered how far Keiko had traveled into the forest. He hoped she'd pushed on to the rendezvous point. The distance kept shrinking between him and the last snowmobile. Only a few hundred feet. His eyes flashed over to the forest on his right, and he realized he wasn't going to make it.

Thankfully, Tommy had disappeared into the thick trees, slaloming his way through the conifers as he kept pressing ahead. The other driver pursued, undeterred by the forest, keeping his thumb on the gas.

Sean's eyes narrowed. *This is going to be close.*

He shifted the handlebars to the right and aimed the nose of his snowmobile at the right side of the other machine. Sean ducked down behind the windscreen, eyes fixed on his target. *Fifty feet. Thirty.* They were almost into the trees when Sean bailed from his saddle. He jumped hard to the side, landing in a soft blanket of snow. The powder stopped his roll quickly. The now-riderless snowmobile sped at the other machine, closing the final ten feet in less than a second. The rider on the back twitched his head to the right and saw the approaching vehicle, but it was too late.

Sean's snowmobile smashed into the other, spinning it in a 360-degree turn. The passenger on the back flew through the air and fell unconscious to the ground after violently striking his head on an outlying spruce tree. The driver's right leg was bent at an awkward angle and crushed from the knee down. He screamed in agony, grabbing at the wounded appendage as he hunched over the side of the snowmobile.

Sean scrambled to his feet and waded through the snow toward the wreckage; surprisingly, the motor was still running. The driver, realizing the threat, tried to ignore the pain coming from his leg and reached out in an attempt to grab the weapon he'd dropped. Sean raised his pistol and pointed it at the man's head.

"Don't!" he shouted.

The driver's eyes stared through his orange-tinted goggles at the approaching American. They flashed back to the gun on the ground, only ten inches away from his fingertips.

"I said don't," Sean barked.

The rider lunged for the weapon. Sean moved his aim slightly down and to the left, following the target and aiming for his shoulder. He took another step and squeezed the trigger, but as he did his footing slipped under the narrow ski boot, and the barrel shifted ever so slightly back to the right. The weapon popped loudly, sending the bullet through the top of the driver's skull. His body fell to the ground at an ugly angle, pressing the top left side of his head into the snow, staining it red from the spurting hole in his head.

Sean sighed and lowered his weapon. He hadn't intended to kill the man. He wanted him alive for questioning. Sean turned his attention to the unconscious passenger lying by the narrow spruce tree. The guy wasn't moving, and it was hard to tell if he was still breathing. Sean didn't have time to stick around and check the guy's vitals. He needed to get to the rendezvous point.

"Hey!" Tommy's voice reverberated through the trees.

Sean turned and searched the scattered rows of trunks and branches until he found the source. Tommy was standing sideways with ski poles in hand, looking back up the slope. Sean gave a flick of his head. He'd left his skis by the body of the other rider a few hundred feet away. He could trek through the snow and retrieve them, or he could just hop on the still-running snowmobile.

The latter option was far more appealing.

He steered the beaten up machine through the trees until he reached his friend. Keiko came into view as she waited another hundred feet farther down.

Tommy raised his goggles and examined the snowmobile. "Nice ride."

"You like it? Figured I'd borrow it from those gangsters for the rest of the day."

Tommy looked up the hill at the dead man in the snow, his shoulder and head buried in the powder. "Yeah, I don't think he'll mind. How you think they found us here?"

Sean shrugged. "They had the riddle. If someone was able to figure out the phrases...I mean, it wasn't that hard to figure out. The kids did it in less than five minutes."

"True," Tommy nodded. "Looks like these guys won't be bothering us anymore."

Sean twisted around and stared at the unconscious man. "I hope not. Better get moving. Our pilot will be waiting for us, and I want to get out of this cold."

Tommy gave a nod and turned to head down the slope. Before he pushed off, Sean stopped him. "What's she doing down there?" He pointed at Keiko, who was still standing in the snow, watching them.

"Dunno," Tommy shrugged. "We told her to push on to the rendezvous point. I guess she stopped to see if the guys were still following us. That's what I did. When I didn't hear their engines anymore, I turned to see what was going on. That's when I saw your little maneuver."

"You like that?" Sean passed a sly grin.

Tommy rolled his eyes. "What happened? Out of bullets? Don't you normally just shoot everyone?"

"I think I still have one more if you'd like to see it."

Tommy chuckled, shook his head, and shoved off. He picked up speed, cruising down the slope at a comfortable pace, slaloming through the conifers. Sean glanced back one more time at the unconscious man on the snow. He'd not moved since his head hit the tree next to him. At best, he'd have a concussion. At worst, he'd have suffered blunt force trauma, and if he wasn't dead yet, he would be soon.

Sean wasn't about to wait around and find out. He pressed on the throttle, and the snowmobile plowed ahead.

He caught up with the two skiers and followed them down the rest of the mountain until they reached a clearing in the forest. As planned, the helicopter was waiting for them—something Sean wasn't entirely convinced would happen. After all, the pilot had been supplied by a gangster. But it was there, and as soon as the pilot saw them coming, he fired up the engines. The long, flexible propellers started spinning around slowly at first but began to pick up pace rapidly. The pilot kept the helicopter's engine at an idle as the group approached.

The wind seemed almost nonexistent at the lower elevation, and the temperature was significantly warmer. Sean recalled something he'd learned in high school about temperature and elevation. The teacher told him that the temperature changed by about three degrees Fahrenheit for every thousand feet of elevation. While it was still cold down at the rendezvous point, it was easily six or seven degrees warmer than up at the shrine.

The pilot opened the door on the side of the helicopter as the two

Americans and their companion arrived. Tommy and Keiko stepped out of their skis. Sean dismounted from the snowmobile. He noticed the pilot staring through his aviator sunglasses.

"You're probably wondering where I got this." Sean pointed at the vehicle with a jerk of his thumb.

Tommy helped Keiko into the cabin of the helicopter, loaded his bag onto the floor, and then climbed aboard.

The pilot continued to stare as if he were trying to solve a puzzle. He noticed the shattered faring on the right side. It was stained with a few smears of blood. "I'm not sure I want to know."

Sean puckered his lips and nodded. "Yeah, I'd say that's best."

14

SENDAI, JAPAN

The group huddled around a table in the elegant hotel lobby, eyeing the piece of paper Sean had used to write down the riddle from the stone on Mount Gassan. A fire burned in the gas fireplace nearby. It was positioned in the center of the room and radiated heat through an opening on both sides. The warmth of the fireplace soothed them to their bones.

On the other side of the room, a bartender stood behind a black granite counter, pouring sake for three businessmen. From the sounds of their laughter and loud banter, it wasn't their first round of drinks.

The lobby had a modern feel to it with gray walls, swooping silver sconces, a brushed metal chandelier that hung from the ceiling near the entryway, and lights dangling in various places from exposed wires.

Sean read the lines out loud for the others to hear. "Pass through the red gate. A dragon protects the way to the holy ground, a toll to be paid for illumination." He looked up from the table at Keiko, a questioning stare filled his eyes. "Any ideas on this one?"

She shook her head. "I apologize. I'm afraid I don't have any for you."

Tommy scratched his head just above his right ear. His eyes glazed over as he stared at the paper. "A red gate. It must mean another torii."

"Yeah," Sean agreed. "But if I had to guess, I'd say there are any number of red toriis in this country."

"He's right," Keiko nodded. "Many of them were painted red, though I'm not sure why."

"OK," Tommy said, "but we don't have to worry about all the shrines in Japan. We already know that the riddle has to be referring to one of the other two holy mountains of Dewa. Right?"

Sean and Keiko both nodded.

"Right," Tommy continued. "So all we have to do is figure out which of the remaining two contains the next clue."

"So what does the next part mean?" Keiko asked. "Are we looking for some kind of lizard?"

"Could be," Sean said. "If they keep Komodo dragons there in a pen or something, maybe that's what we're looking for."

Tommy frowned. He wasn't sold on the lizard thing. He opened up his bag and pulled out a tablet. After fiddling with the settings and connecting to the hotel's Wi-Fi, he tapped on the screen's keyboard, entering some keywords he thought might be useful.

The second search result looked interesting, and he tapped the link. A fresh web page popped up, and Tommy scrolled through a number of images of toriis, mountains, and shrines. He shook his head and went back to the search results.

"Hunting for dragons?" Sean asked, half joking.

Tommy rolled his eyes. "Actually, yes." He pressed the link on the fourth result and was taken to another web page. "I'm trying to see if there is another possibility for the riddle. Obviously we don't believe in dragons."

"Obviously."

"But dragons are fairly prominent in Asian cultures. What if we're looking for a painting of a dragon, or one of those paper dragons from a parade?"

"Or a statue," Keiko offered.

Sean and Tommy turned their heads and looked at her.

"Right," Tommy said. "And wouldn't you know it," he pointed at the screen, "this place has several dragon statues."

The other two scooted their chairs closer to Tommy's and looked at the screen. There was an image of a massive red torii set against a backdrop of lush green forests atop picturesque hillsides. In the foreground of the image sat two metal dragons, bodies bent in the shape of the letter S, with sharp ears and whiskers pointing toward the sky. Their mouths were open wide, pouring water into a basin.

"That's a fountain, Tommy."

"I know, but it could be something."

Keiko interrupted the other two. "What's this down here?"

Tommy scrolled down the screen a little farther. Another kind of dragon, fatter and with curls around its head, sat on a pedestal. It featured large round eyes, and its mouth was open, displaying a fearsome-looking tongue. Its ears were pricked back as if ready to attack.

"Look at the caption," Sean said.

Tommy read it out loud. "This dragon marks the beginning of the path to the holy grounds of the mountain. Sadly, we couldn't take pictures beyond this point because it is forbidden. All I can say is that this area is one of the most beautiful I've ever visited. It's a shame I can't share the imagery."

Thick forests and rolling hills filled the image's background. Another picture to the right displayed a narrow path that wound its way around the hill, ascending to the holy area on the mountain.

"You think that might be the place?" Tommy asked. He looked over at Sean with a hopeful gleam in his eye.

"Makes as much sense as any. And like you said, we know it's either this mountain or the other one. Check Mount Haguro and see if you can find anything about dragons."

Tommy went back to the search engine. His fingers pecked away quickly at the screen's keyboard. "I can type so much faster with a laptop," he complained.

"Yeah but those are bulkier, and you wanted to pack light."

Tommy snorted. "As I recall, that was your suggestion."

"Would you just hurry and enter the keywords."

Tommy tapped the return button, and the screen flickered again. It opened to a fresh set of search results, and he scanned the descriptions until he found one that he thought might be most useful. A new page appeared, and the three huddled around the tablet, analyzing the images that were arranged in neat rows and columns.

After three or four minutes of scrolling, the combination they were looking for hadn't appeared. Several of the links led to images of a five-story pagoda, a famous landmark on Mount Haguro, but nothing about dragons or the red gate showed up.

"Looks like Yudono is our next stop," Sean commented.

Tommy chuckled to himself. "You don't know."

Keiko and Sean looked at him as if his face was covered in moths.

"Seriously?" Sean said.

Tommy threw his hands out to the side. "What? It's funny. Yudono... you don't know."

"It's really not funny."

"Fine, but OK, it appears that's where we should head to next. And looks like we won't have to deal with the wind and super frigid temps we saw up on Gassan." The thought caused him to shiver.

"Right. But it's still going to be cold." He turned and faced Keiko. "And I want you to stay here in the hotel."

She shook her head defiantly. "No. You need my help. Neither of you can read Japanese."

The two Americans glanced at each other.

She pressed on. "If you find something that is in Japanese—and you will—you won't be able to understand it. Face it: you need my help."

From the moment they'd met Keiko, she seemed quiet, afraid, and beleaguered. All were understandable considering the recent events surrounding her uncle's death. Now, seemingly out of nowhere, she had found a touch of courage.

Tommy was intrigued.

"What do you think, buddy?" he asked Sean.

Sean wasn't so sure. But he couldn't very well tie her up in a hotel room and leave her there. One way or the other, she wasn't going to stick around. He could see the determination in her eyes.

"It's going to be dangerous. You saw what happened on the mountain. There could be more men with guns. Bullets flying everywhere. I can't guarantee your safety."

"I know all that." She glanced down at the thin carpet and then back at Sean. "But I have to see it through. My uncle, he wanted me to be a part of this."

"He would have also wanted you to stay alive," Tommy interjected.

She nodded. "True. But I don't think he ever wanted me to live scared. He sent me that message for a reason. It is my burden to make sure the Honjo Masamune is found. If I can help, then I will. I must."

Tommy wished he could lean over and kiss her, but he repressed the ridiculous notion. Instead, he made the call for both him and his friend. "OK. You can come with us. But stay close. If anything goes haywire, I would rather one of us take a bullet than you."

Her head bobbed up and down again, acknowledging his wishes.

A waiter in a black vest and white shirt strolled up to the table. He was carrying a red teapot and a round tray with three matching red teacups. He set the tray on the side of the table and then placed the cups before pouring the tea for the visitors.

When he was done, he politely asked if they needed anything else. Keiko thanked him and sent him on his way.

He smiled, brushed his cropped hair to the side, and walked hurriedly back toward the kitchen.

Tommy reached over and grabbed his teacup. He took a long sip of the steaming liquid. After he swallowed it, he smiled and set the cup back down. "Now that is how green tea is supposed to be made."

Sean took a shorter sip of his while looking out one of the big windows at the far end of the room. A thin flow of pedestrians trickled by, probably on their way to eat somewhere or on their way home from work. It was the darker part of dusk, just before night took over completely. There would be no more searching done today.

He had the hopeful thought that maybe, just maybe, they could get a good night's rest without anything crazy happening.

His mind drifted to sleepless nights abroad in various countries and cities. They seemed to occur more often than not. Just one more reason he'd left the agency, and working for his friend at the IAA. Yet here he was again, dodging bullets and looking over his shoulder. Sean had recently concluded that it was never going to end. And that was why he'd left the IAA. The more he thought about things in that light, with his newfound freedom, the more at ease he felt. That didn't change the fact that he was extremely tired right now.

"So tell us about yourself," he said, trying to change the subject. He raised his cup again, took a big gulp of the soothing hot liquid and then stood up. "What's your story?"

Keiko was caught a little off guard, but she smiled politely. "My story?"

"Yeah," Tommy jumped in. "I'm curious too." He passed her a corny grin that Sean desperately tried to ignore.

"Well," she began, "I'm afraid there isn't much to tell."

"Oh come on," Tommy urged. "Here you are, on an adventure with two strange Americans. You're obviously not afraid of much. I'd say you handled yourself pretty well on the mountain and at the palace grounds. So what gives?"

Keiko shrugged and looked out the window for a second. "It isn't that I'm not afraid. But I haven't always lived in a nice area. When I was younger, I spent a lot of time in some of the rougher areas of Tokyo, places that were run by Yakuza." Her voice faded, becoming distant as she continued. "Gunshots were something we got used to. I remember once, when I was a child, a bullet shattering the window of my parents' kitchen. I was terrified. So were they. Those things were why they left. Why they didn't take me with them, I'm not sure. Maybe they couldn't afford it. But they thought I would be safer with my uncle. That turned out to be an incorrect assumption."

Tommy appeared genuinely sympathetic. "I'm so sorry. You want to talk about it?"

"Don't be sorry. It made me who I am. I don't mind talking about it now. It was a long time ago. They went to America to get away from the violence here. I haven't heard from them since. They thought if they left me here with my uncle I would be safe. I miss them but I am stronger for the experience. My uncle taught me martial arts, and how to use weapons. I know how to handle myself." She paused for a moment as if trying to conjure the right words. "I just didn't think I would be thrown into a situation where I'd need to. I have a career now and a home in a decent neighborhood. But when these things started happening again..."

"It brought it all back," Sean finished her sentence for her.

Sean's eyes narrowed for a second as they caught sight of something curious outside: a figure in the shadows across the street. A man in a charcoal-gray winter coat and a black skullcap. Was he waiting on someone? A taxi perhaps? Or was his reason for being there more sinister? Sean diverted his attention back to the conversation before the other two noticed his distraction.

"Yes," she nodded. "But I will be fine." Her voice filled with resolve. "You needn't worry about me. I can take care of myself."

She put out her hand and took hold of the cup directly in front of her. Even as she brought it to her mouth, Sean could see her hand trembling. Either she was putting on a fairly good act, or she was just nervous from talking about her past. He wasn't certain.

"I believe you," Tommy said, overplaying the sympathy. "I'm sure you can handle yourself just fine."

His cheesy grin was more than Sean could stand. "OK, Romeo. I'm going to look into getting us some more supplies for the trip back into the mountains. Do yourselves a favor, and get some rest. Could be a long day."

Before Tommy could respond, Sean stepped away from the table and sauntered away. He swung around the bar and disappeared around the corner, heading toward the elevators.

What Tommy and Keiko didn't see was that he passed the elevator doors and continued down the corridor toward an alternative exit. He'd not let on to the others about what he saw out on the street through the window during their chat.

15

SENDAI

"What do you mean they got away?"

Taka's voice raged through the earpiece.

"Tell me you were able to get the location of the sword, or at least a clue."

Hideo heard a fist pound on a table. He imagined his boss pacing around in his office or the boardroom with an angry scowl on his face. It was a look Hideo actively tried to avoid. Not because he was afraid but because Hideo wasn't stupid. He knew exactly how to climb the ladder in the Yakuza world, and it wasn't always best to be the top dog.

At any given moment, Hideo had command over dozens of men, all willing and anxious to do his bidding, even if the bidding was coming from someone else, like Taka. That didn't matter. Hideo still reaped the benefits. He was feared, respected, wealthy, and able to do pretty much whatever he wanted, all as a result of his loyalty to Taka. Now, however, the boss was unhappy. So was Hideo.

He'd allowed the Americans to escape with the only clue to their next step in the hunt for the Masamune. Letting them get away from the palace grounds wasn't such a big deal since he'd been able to procure the clue left behind by Tokugawa. Now, however, that event acted as a catalyst for his employer's anger.

Hideo hung his head, ashamed at his failure and certain of his fate. "No, we did not retrieve the next piece. My men are dead. I alone escaped, albeit with significant injury."

He reached back and touched the place on his head where it had struck the tree. It was unclear how long he'd been unconscious. The only positive out of the entire incident was that the back of his skull had been pressed against the snow, which had likely kept the swelling down until he regained consciousness. Groggy, sore, disoriented, and beaten, Hideo had stumbled through the heavy snow to a small town at the base of the mountain where he now sat in a cafe, sipping some hot tea as he delivered the bad news to Taka.

Hideo waited for another outburst from his boss, but it never came. The silence was almost a more disconcerting reaction.

"All your men are dead?" Taka asked after taking a minute to let the information settle in.

"Yes. These Americans were heavily armed." That part was an exaggeration, but Taka didn't need to know that. "We were unprepared."

The truth was, Hideo never expected the reaction he received from the Americans, especially the skinny, taller one. He'd proved to be a worthy adversary in the field of combat.

"You had them outnumbered, though, yes?"

"We did. And I take full responsibility for this failure."

"I don't have to tell you the price of failure in my family."

Hideo stared down at the pale green tea in the white cup sitting in front of him. "I am aware."

"Good," Taka said curtly. "Then do not fail me again. I consider you a brother, unlike some of these others who work for us. It would pain me dearly to lose you."

Hideo's face hardened. He was the one who usually dealt out the punishment for Taka. His cruel and often unorthodox measures had helped create the almost mythical terror so many felt when mentioning Hideo's name. The threat was not unexpected, but the offer of mercy was.

"Thank you, sir."

Taka ignored the gratitude and got back to business. "Fortunately, I always have a backup plan, my old friend."

"Backup plan?"

"Yes. You see, I have someone else following these Americans. So I will know their every movement."

His eyebrows stitched together. Hideo wasn't pleased to hear that his boss potentially doubted his abilities. At the same time, Taka hadn't been wrong to do so. "Who is this person?"

"You needn't worry about inconsequential things such as that, my friend. Just know that we are tracking the Americans at this very moment. They have holed up in a hotel in Sendai. I imagine they will wait until tomorrow to make their next move."

The last sentence was said with an apparent degree of certainty.

Taka continued. "I will contact you in the morning to let you know where they are headed. Find a place to stay for the night. You will also get reinforcements. We have a presence in one of the cities on the western coast. Just remember how forgiving I have been for this. It is a treatment few ever receive."

Hideo nodded. "Thank you, sir."

The truth was, he could get away if he wanted to. It was a big world. Taka's reach was extensive in most of the major cities in Japan, maybe a few others on an international level, but disappearing wouldn't be that difficult. He could find a place to hide out in another country. Maybe he would always be looking over his shoulder, jumping at shadows in the night, but it beat the alternative. At least he would be alive.

Hideo shook his head. He stared down at the tea. His fingers surrounded the little cup, cradling it gently. That wasn't the way he did things. It wasn't like him to run from a fight or from a threat. He always took his medicine. And living a life of fear and paranoia was no life at all. He'd rather stare down the barrel of a gun or at the edge of a blade before trying to exist like that.

Taka interrupted his thoughts. "Get some rest. Your new men will arrive in the morning. Make sure you don't fail like this again."

"Yes, sir. I won't."

The call ended, and Hideo put the device back in his pocket. His right hand involuntarily reached back and rubbed the base of his skull. It still throbbed like a jackhammer going in slow motion. He fished a packet of ibuprofen out of his coat pocket, tore it open, and dumped the two pills into his palm. He'd already taken four. Two more wouldn't hurt. Hopefully they would take the pain away until he could get something a little more powerful, which would likely not be any time soon. He popped the pills into his mouth and picked up a nearly empty glass of water next to his cup of tea, tipped the clear liquid into his mouth, and swallowed. He shook his head back and forth for a second to make sure the gel caps made it down his throat.

The manager of the establishment was standing over near the bar, staring at him with an odd gaze. It came across as a look of disgust, but maybe Hideo was just imagining it. Funny how some people could pick out Yakuza even when their tattoos weren't showing. He returned the look with a threatening one of his own. The manager immediately turned away and pretended to be busy doing something else.

Hideo's appearance was rough, and he knew it. He probably smelled too, though that was more difficult to determine. A hot shower would feel good right now, as would a warm bed. A soft body next to him would be the icing on the cake, but he doubted that would be something he could get out here in the boondocks. He'd have to wait until he got back to Tokyo.

He took a final sip of the tea and set the cup down hard on the table. The noise startled the patrons in the booth near him, but he didn't care. He passed them a sneering glance, dropped a wad of yen on the table, and made his way to the door. Getting a new weapon would be a priority. He figured the men Taka was sending would take care of that for him. Usually they carried more than one.

As Hideo stepped out into the cold evening, he pulled his coat around his torso and turned left, heading toward the hotel and disappearing into the crowd.

16

SENDAI

Sean stepped out of the hotel and onto the sidewalk. The cold night air washed over him in an instant. He zipped up his coat before losing any more body warmth. He was at the side of the hotel and wouldn't be visible through the main doors or the lobby windows. Something troubled him about the man he'd seen on the other side of the street.

During the conversation with Keiko and Tommy, Sean had let his eyes drift back to the window several times to make sure he wasn't just being paranoid. The man in the gray coat remained there, leaning against the wall of a restaurant. More than a few taxis had passed by, so he wasn't waiting on one of those. And if the guy was waiting on a ride from a friend, he could have just as easily waited inside the restaurant or even the hotel lobby. Standing outside in the cold made no sense. Unless he was supposed to be watching someone.

Sean rushed across the nearly empty side street, between a few parked cars on the other side, and crouched behind the last one nearest the intersection where the alley met the main road.

He leaned forward, peered beyond the front bumper of a green Honda sedan, and searched for the man in front of the restaurant.

The guy was still there, although now he was holding a phone to his ear. From Sean's vantage point, he could see the device's touch screen wasn't illuminated, which meant the guy was faking the phone call in an attempt to look natural. Sean sighed and shook his head. *Amateurs.*

Sean kept an eye on him and stood slowly from his hiding place behind the car's hood. He crept to the corner and then turned right, blending in with the few stragglers brave enough to venture out in the frigid temperatures. He turned his head and glanced over his shoulder. The guy was still standing there, pretending to talk on the phone. Sean had to give it to him: he was keeping up the act, even nodding and laughing a little to give the impression he was having an actual conversation.

At the next block, Sean detoured to the left and hurried through the crosswalk to the other side. He turned left again, making his way back toward where gray coat was now acting as if he was sending a text message to someone. *At least he's mixing up his routine a little.*

Sean pulled the hood over his head and tucked his chin under the top front of his coat to conceal as much of his face as possible. It was a natural move considering the wintry weather, and would raise little suspicion from the observer. He was only fifty feet away now, and the gap was closing as Sean quickened his pace. Looking like someone in a hurry to get out of the cold would further serve his intention to sneak up on the unaware target. He stuffed his hands into his pockets as he approached and kept his eyes mostly locked on the sidewalk directly ahead, only looking up under the brim of the hood every four or five seconds to make sure gray coat hadn't become suspicious.

One more quick look told Sean he was only twenty feet away. He probably would have been able to walk right up to the man, subdue him, and pull him into an adjacent alley without the guy ever knowing what happened. Unfortunately, a random gust of wind changed all that. It blew through the street corridor like a banshee, whipping flags, banners, ribbons, and awnings into a momentary frenzy. With his hands inside his coat pockets, Sean couldn't move them fast enough to keep the wind from blowing his hood back, revealing his face.

Instinctively, he reached up with both hands to grab the hood, but the sudden movement only served to draw more attention from his target.

Gray Coat's head snapped to the left as he realized what was happening. His eyes widened upon seeing his mark so close. The next thing he did came as somewhat of a surprise to Sean.

He expected the man to attack him, but instead the guy spun to the right and took off at a dead sprint. Sean sighed. *Really?* He was in no mood for a cold evening run right now.

In an instant, he was at full speed, charging to the corner where Gray Coat had been standing, now thirty feet behind the fleeing man. Sean watched him duck around the edge of the building, disappearing from view. He'd already noted that the street was a somewhat busy tributary compared to the one he was on. That didn't mean the guy wasn't waiting just around the corner, ready to drop him as soon as he appeared. Taking a wide turn, Sean rounded the sidewalk corner with enough room to keep him safe if Gray Coat was waiting to trip him, or worse. What Sean found was the running man had opened up a bigger gap between them than expected.

Sean sighed again and pumped his legs harder. The shorter Japanese man made up for his lack of a long stride with a much quicker one. His feet were a blur as they lifted and dropped on the balls of his feet, pounding the pavement with each step. He cut left and crossed the street in front of a slew of cars, narrowly missing one. The irritated driver honked the horn. Sean could see the furious look on the driver's face in the sterile glow of a streetlight. That didn't stop Sean from veering across the street in pursuit, further angering the driver and those behind him.

Leaving the honking horns and squealing tires behind, Sean charged ahead, closing the gap between him and the fleeing man. They ran into a much darker side street, surrounded on both sides by modern apartment buildings. The alley was lit only by a few pale night lights, fixed to the walls about twenty feet apart. Between the reach of the whitish glow, the runners were cast into shadow for a moment, and then back into light.

Ahead, the side street opened to another avenue, less crowded than the last. Gray coat was only twenty feet away now, and Sean could tell that the man's pace was slowing. He could feel his own legs getting heavy, but Sean had learned a long time ago that to win a race, the human mind could push the body to do things it didn't think possible. He forced his muscles to pump even harder as the runner wasted a precious second, turning his head to see if the pursuer was still there. The move cost him since he had to slow down to look back. Sean picked up several more feet because of it.

Gray Coat took off again, his energy renewed by a sense of fear. He cut across the less crowded street again with Sean close behind. The runner was only ten feet away. One slip, and Sean would have him.

The man's stride elongated, a sign that his muscles were giving out. Sean was close enough to hear him gasping as the two dashed into the next side street, one that was much darker. The brick buildings appeared to be older, warehouses most likely. Then Sean saw the end of the line fifty feet away. The street ended in a brick wall where the buildings on either side connected.

The runner jogged to a stop as he realized his fatal mistake. There was no escape. He spun around, gasping for air, and faced his pursuer.

Sean was out of breath too. In spite of his consistent cardiovascular training, a four-minute sprint was something that would wear out even the best athletes. After ten seconds of nearly heaving, he managed to recover enough to ask, "Who are you?"

Gray coat didn't answer. He had a look of terrified panic in his wide eyes. His head turned back and forth as he examined the walls, hoping there was some way of escape that he'd missed.

"We don't have to do this the hard way," Sean said. His breath came easier with each passing moment, though his legs felt like they were filled with sand. "Just tell me who you are or what you want and I'll let you go."

The guy shook his head, still panting like a dog on a hot summer day.

Sean shook his head slowly and sighed. "Do I really have to beat it out of you? I'd rather you just tell me what's going on and we leave here as friends. No reason to get the crap kicked out of you." He paused his thoughts and took a few cautious steps forward. "Do you even understand what I'm saying?"

The man's eyes narrowed, and he lowered his head. "I understand."

"OK, good, because for a second there I was thinking maybe you didn't speak English." He took another step forward.

Gray coat's demeanor changed. His posture transformed from one seeking escape to a more defensive stance.

Oh, come on, Sean thought. *I'm not in the mood to fight right now.*

"We don't have to do this," Sean said. He put both hands out, palms facing the guy. "I'm tired. I had a long day. I'm still significantly jet lagged. You are obviously interested in whatever it is my friends and I are doing. Why don't you just tell me why?"

The man shook his head slowly and unzipped the heavy coat. Underneath was a white tank top. Under that were tattoos covering most of the man's torso and arms. He was Yakuza.

Based on the way he'd tried to run from the scene, Sean figured him to be a little brother. While he didn't know much about the Yakuza, Sean's rough understanding of the culture led him to believe that the people who occupied higher levels of standing were more likely to engage in confrontation, sometimes blatantly in public. For this guy it seemed like a last resort, and showing off his tattoos was likely a last ditch attempt to scare Sean away.

"Impressive ink," he said, pointing vaguely at the tattoos. "How long did it take to get all that done? Did you do it in one sitting or was it over the course of several sessions."

The man yelled something unintelligible and lunged forward. He led with his left foot, trying to land a kick to Sean's chest. The American was ready for it, despite his casual stance, and instantly stepped aside. The gangster landed with his upper body exposed for a second, a mistake Sean took advantage of. He faked a jab at the man's face, causing his opponent to reach up for the block. A split second later, Sean's right hand struck the gangster in the abdomen, instantly bruising the muscles within. As the man doubled over, Sean swung his left fist around at the exposed jaw. The gangster's hands had dropped down to protect his belly, which was a critical mistake. Sean's knuckles found the right cheek and snapped to a stop about three inches behind the target. The gangster's head rocked sideways, and he fell away to the side before Sean could grab him.

For a moment, Sean thought the blow might have been enough to knock the man unconscious, but he wasn't surprised to see him roll over on the asphalt and push himself back onto his feet. It was never that easy. Especially with men who were driven by fear.

The gangster steadied his stance and then launched another assault. The attack was much faster than the first, possibly from desperation or possibly due to the knowledge that his opponent wasn't a total idiot when it came to hand-to-hand combat.

His fists fired out, and he took three quick steps forward. The punches came in a flurry, one right after the other. Sean had already switched his feet sideways to make for a smaller target. He deflected the first punch, then the second, and then the third, ducked the fourth, and then countered with a hard right. This time, the gangster was ready and parried Sean's punch, countering with another jab that landed on the cheek.

The blow stung at first and then instantly turned to a deep, throbbing pain. There was no time to recover as the gangster switched from a boxing pose to something Sean recognized from his martial arts training. The gangster kicked hard, over and over again, faster than almost anything Sean had ever encountered. He leaned to the left, blocking the strikes with his forearm, which sent a new pain through the appendage with each strike. On the fourth kick, the gangster faked it, dropped the foot to the ground, and then jumped, bringing his right foot around in a wide arc. It was a good move, and one that caught Sean completely off guard. The top of the foot bone smashed into Sean's left cheek and sent him tumbling to the pavement.

Sean's elbows hit first. His hands caught his momentum just before his chin hit the ground. The dark alley spun a little, and his vision blurred. What at first appeared to be an easy scrap had just turned into a fight for survival. Sean's fingers clawed at the asphalt, and his toes dug in as he scrambled forward toward the brick wall, now desperate to get back to his feet. He heard quick footsteps behind him and turned even as he kept moving away from the attack.

The man's foot flashed out again, snapping like an angry cobra at Sean's face. The American was ready, though. Sean fought off the daze and once again took command of his muscles. His hand moved fast, snatching the gangster's foot out of the air before he could retract it. In one fluid, sudden movement, Sean twisted his torso, pulled the man's ankle hard, wrapped his left arm over the shin, and tucked it under his armpit. Then he tugged and pivoted, yanking the man off his standing foot. The move was so fast that there was no way for the gangster to catch his balance. Instead, his ground foot lifted, and his back smacked against the pavement. His head snapped backward and hit the ground in a short, sudden thud. Disoriented, he struggled, rolling his head back and forth to shake off the concussion.

Before he could regain his bearings, Sean dropped to his knees, straddling the man's torso. He held his hand menacingly above the guy's neck with fingers open like a claw.

"If you try to get up, I will rip your throat out and leave you here to die. Do you understand?"

The man's eyes blinked rapidly and flitted around, but he nodded vaguely.

"Good. Who are you, and who do you work for?"

"You don't understand. I'm dead anyway."

It wasn't the first time Sean had heard that from someone he'd beaten down. Although each time he had hoped it was the last.

"What do you mean you're dead anyway? Who are you so afraid of?"

He shook his head, refusing to say anything else.

Sean considered his options. He took a quick look back to make sure no one was around and then grabbed the man's right hand and started bending the index finger at an awkward angle. The guy screamed in pain and only stopped when Sean relieved the pressure.

"Funny things, fingers. They're so small. but when one is about to break it is excruciating. Plus, without them, life gets a lot more complicated. He bent the finger again, almost to the point of snapping the bone.

It was accompanied by another painful howl until Sean released it.

"I can break all your fingers, dislocate other joints, and come up with some pretty sick stuff that I don't think you'd like me to do. And honestly, I'd rather not have to. Been out of that line of work for a long time now. I just want you to tell me who you're working for and why you're following me."

"Aoki," he blurted out. "I work for Aoki. He sent me to make sure you were doing your job, looking for the Masamune."

That was easy.

"That's why you're not armed? You were just sent here to watch us?"

He shook his head. "Not just you. Anyone else who might be following you."

The last sentence sent a chill through Sean's spine. "And did you see anyone?"

He waited a second for the answer, letting the man collect his thoughts. "No," he said finally. "I haven't seen anything suspicious."

Sean's eyes turned to slits. He wasn't completely sold on the story yet. "If you were just sent here to watch, why did you run from me? And why did you fight me just now?"

"If Aoki finds out I failed, he will have me killed." He drew in a short gasp of air. "Like I said, I'm probably already dead. Once I report what happened, he'll have me executed. Failure isn't tolerated."

Sean understood, but if this guy was telling the truth, it might be beneficial to have an extra pair of eyes watching their backs. "Then don't tell him."

The gangster's eyebrows knit together, confused by the comment. "I have to report everything to him."

Sean shook his head. "Not everything. You tell Aoki that the Americans are making good progress. Nothing else. He doesn't have to know that I know you're watching me."

The man relaxed visibly.

"I won't tell if you don't," Sean added. "Just keep an eye out. We encountered some of Taka's men earlier. Most of them are dead. But one still might be out there. If you see us heading into a trap or trouble coming, you let me know."

The guy shook his head. "How do you want me to do that?"

Sean shrugged. "I don't know. You'll figure something out." He stood up, looming over the man on the ground for a few more seconds. "I need to get back to the hotel. Thanks for the exercise."

He stalked away, leaving the gangster lying on the pavement. Sean didn't look back. The man wasn't armed, not from what he could tell. And the fact that Sean had shown him a little mercy might go a long way. He just hoped he hadn't made a mistake in letting the guy live. If he had, it wouldn't be long before the error was realized.

He turned the corner out of the alley and picked up his pace. This whole thing was getting more complicated by the minute.

17

MOUNT YUDONO

Sean and the others elected to drive to Mount Yudono the following morning, which took considerably longer than the helicopter ride they'd had the previous day. Fortunately, the weather had taken a turn for the better, producing conditions that kept the roads clear of snow and ice at the lower elevations. The drive was a long one, something the Americans planned for, which is why they woke up early and left the hotel while it was still dark outside.

The sun crept upward in the eastern sky behind them, reflected as a bright fiery orange in the rearview mirror and slowly changing to whitish yellow as it crept higher. Only traces of a few wispy clouds were visible as they stretched across a clear blue backdrop. The rolling foothills grew larger as the travelers continued westward, eventually leading to the tall, snow-covered peaks they'd seen the day before.

Sean couldn't help but feel as if he was in western North Carolina, on the border of Tennessee. The area was so much like the Smokey Mountains; aside from the people, road signs, and most of the buildings, it felt almost like home, only colder and with more snow.

Most of the group was too tired to say much during the first hour of the journey. Instead, they sat in silence, staring out at the picturesque forests, villages, and mountains as they passed by. It wasn't until they began their ascent toward the Yudonosan Shrine visitor area that Tommy finally spoke up from the driver's seat.

"Maybe it's too late to ask this since we're almost there, but you haven't noticed anyone following us up to this point, have you?" He glanced back in the mirror at Sean who was staring out the window. Keiko raised a concerned eyebrow in the front passenger seat.

Sean shook his head. "I've been keeping an eye on it."

Tommy switched his stare back to the road for a moment and then flicked another look at Sean. "That's sort of an answer to my question."

"No," Sean turned his gaze to meet the eyes of the driver. "I haven't seen anyone following us up to this point. And I've been watching for that since we left Sendai."

Keiko relaxed a little.

Tommy nodded. "OK, no need to get testy. Everybody needs a little reminder now and then. It's not like the old days where we were out here doing stuff like this all the time."

No. It just feels like that, Sean thought. Truth was, he'd been finding himself in sticky situations with ridiculous regularity. He'd recently decided to stop running from it and even offered to help out with any special situations in which Tommy, or Axis, might need assistance. A leopard couldn't change its spots. Sean had tried to for a few years, running from what he truly was. He couldn't run from it anymore.

He watched the dense forest pass by. It was mostly occupied by coniferous varieties: spruce, hemlock, and fir. In the colder, wetter climates, these trees were able to thrive, producing a breathtaking landscape of greens and browns the entire year.

Tommy turned the car onto a side road and accelerated. He steered it around the winding curves, wary of the narrow strip of road and the tight turns. Whenever he encountered such slim stretches of asphalt, he wondered how many crashes there'd been there in the past. Given their destination, he doubted many people were in much of a hurry most of the time. And on this day, they saw no other traffic.

The rise in elevation from the base of the mountain to the shrine came with an increase in the amount of snow on the ground until it was completely coated in a white blanket of fresh, sparkling powder. Fortunately, the area hadn't received any new precipitation overnight, and the roads remained clear for the most part.

They reached the parking area at the base of a small hill where Tommy found an empty spot near a set of broad steps. He turned off the engine and stepped out, taking a look around the nearly empty lot. The two passengers did the same.

Sean stared up the big staircase toward a giant red torii. The gate seemed to loom over everything, even the shrine behind it to the left. Positioned in front of the torii, next to the steps, was a small fountain and basin. It was the one they'd seen during their online investigation of the site. The two dragons Sean and Tommy had noticed in the pictures were sitting opposite each other with mouths open wide. No water spewed forth, though. The monks must have turned off the pumps for the winter.

"I guess we go this way," he said, pointing up the stairs.

Tommy nodded. "Very astute."

Sean shook his head and ducked into the car to retrieve his gear bag. Tommy opened the back door on his side and did the same, slinging it over his shoulder. They closed the doors, and Tommy locked the vehicle with the key fob, hearing the locks click as they moved up the steps. Once through the red gate, they proceeded beyond the shrine to a trailhead a hundred feet to the rear.

There were no signs of life other than a few birds chirping in the trees and an occasional burst of wind that shook the branches. Only two other cars were in the parking lot. Sean assumed they were either tourists or people on a pilgrimage. The latter would explain why no one was in sight.

"Kind of creepy," Tommy whispered. "Where is everybody? Shouldn't there be monks roaming around or something?"

"It's cold out here," Sean said. "They're probably inside where it's warm."

"Right." Tommy nodded. "That's true." He hushed his mouth, flushing a little either from the chilly air or embarrassment or both.

Keiko pointed ahead at a sign next to the trailhead. "It says the holy mountain is this way. That is where we will find the dragon from the pictures."

"This way it is," Sean said cheerfully. "Care to lead the way, buddy?" He motioned to Tommy.

"Sure, why not?"

He took off at a moderate pace, one that Sean was certain his friend couldn't maintain for long. That was part of the reason he'd asked Tommy to take the lead. Letting his somewhat out of shape friend set their tempo would make sure he didn't fall behind. There was another reason that Sean put his friend in front, though, one that he thought it better not to mention.

Over the years, Sean had developed a keen sense of perceiving subtle movements. Whether at a distance or close by, it was nearly impossible for someone to sneak up on him or surprise him. The skill was one born of necessity during his years with Axis. It had also served him well with IAA when working with Tommy on special operations. And it was something that wasn't easily turned off. As Keiko walked by, following Tommy onto the path, Sean gave a quick look back at the parking area, the shrine, and the surrounding area. The birds were still chirping in the trees sixty feet away. That was a good sign. He'd learned a long time ago that when the animals were spooked, something was up. Satisfied with his rapid surveillance of the locale, he turned and fell in behind the others.

The trail narrowed and wrapped its way up and around the mountain. The path was surrounded on both sides with tall, skinny tree trunks that stretched high into the air, shading the already cold forest floor.

For the most part, their hike was uneventful and, fortunately for Tommy, didn't last long. Somehow, even though the temperature was only a few degrees above freezing, he was managing to perspire. To be fair, the beanie cap he wore on his head didn't help.

The group reached an area that opened up in front of a stepped path with a metal railing. Sean took a water bottle out of his bag and drew in a huge drink. He looked out across one of the vistas and let out a sigh. "Pretty country right here, buddy," he said.

Tommy answered in between gasps. "Yeah. It's..it sure is." He looked back down the trail and then looked uphill. It seemed like a green and brown tunnel to him, narrowing further as he stared at it. "I have to say, this trail is a little steeper than it looked from down at the bottom."

Sean started to respond with a comment about his friend still needing to get in shape, but a quick warning glance from Tommy kept him mum on the subject.

"Just once," Tommy went on, "I would like to investigate something on the Great Plains or maybe a prairie." He took a water bottle out of his bag and guzzled half of it in mere seconds. After another few gasps of air, he spoke again. "You know, somewhere flat. Everywhere we go...mountains...hills...more mountains. And of course, more steps." He glared at the continuing uphill climb.

"And don't forget all those stairs at the monastery in Bhutan that followed an hour-long hike up the mountain."

The comment nearly made Tommy pop. He leaned over as if about to vomit, but kept his composure. He slowed his breathing and shook his head, holding out a warning hand. "Please, don't bring that part up again. What a nightmare that was."

"I have to say, after our last adventure, I'd think you'd have learned." Sean crossed his arms and stared at his friend with a chastising gaze.

"I know. I know. I need to get in better shape. But who has time these days? What with everything that's going on." He stood back up straight and seemed to have regained his energy. "Come on, let's keep moving. We haven't got all day up here, and it's cold." He shoved the bottle back into his bag and walked over to the start of the stepped path.

Sean chuckled to himself. He bit his lower lip to keep from saying anything else. He could tell Keiko didn't know what to think about the interaction between the two Americans. Then again, she'd pretty much been all business since the get go. Her silence was odd but still understandable, just a young girl thrown into a crazy mess with a bunch of evil people and two Americans she didn't know. Sean decided not to pry too much, especially since he imagined Tommy had the night before.

Next to the path, the dragon statue they'd seen online sat facing out at them as if issuing a silent warning with its open jaws, flashing tongue, and fearsome wide eyes. A sign was close by, advising visitors that no photography was allowed beyond this point and that the ground they were about to tread was holy.

Mountain worship was one of the older folk religions of Japan. Yudono, along with the other two mountains of Dewa, were three of the main locations for such practices. Many people made pilgrimages to all three mountains every year, but the holy ground at Yudono was, to many, above all others.

The three visitors huddled around the dragon. It appeared to be carved from granite. Sean examined it closely, searching the surface for clues.

"See anything?" Tommy asked. He began his search at the base of the dragon's pedestal, hoping the clue would be etched into the stone as it had been on Mount Gassan.

It only took him a minute to realize this part of the puzzle wasn't going to be so easy.

Keiko looked as well, checking over every single inch of the statue. She pointed at a block of wood that seemed oddly placed. "What's this?"

"I was wondering the same thing," Sean said. The piece of wood was wedged between the dragon's front legs. The creature's left paw rested on a ball covered in engraved stars.

Tommy stood up straight and looked at the block. He pressed on one end of the wood and it came out with surprising ease. After pushing the wooden piece out the rest of the way, he lifted it up and gave it a thorough look over.

"Anything?" Sean asked. His curiosity was growing.

"No. It's just a piece of wood." Tommy slid the object back where he found it and looked around in exasperation. He stared out at the snow-covered mountains and the valley between. "I should have known it wouldn't be as easy as the last place." He sighed, and a small cloud of fog escaped from his mouth, dissipating into the frigid air.

Sean grinned. "Oh come on, buddy. You know that most things in life worth having don't come easy."

He ran his hand along the smooth stone of the dragon's back. "It does make me wonder, though." Sean sidled around to the statue's left side and pressed his face in close to get a view of where the dragon was facing. "The clue we found on Gassan said the dragon watches the way, a toll to be paid."

"So?"

"So maybe the dragon isn't what we're looking for. And maybe this path of steps here isn't the way we're supposed to go." Sean pointed over to an area at the base of the hill forty feet away. Sticking out of the powdery white surface was a rectangular stone box. Just beyond it, a faint indention snaked its way up the mountain through the trees, disappearing just over the ridge. It was almost unnoticeable, like a path worn down by small woodland animals. But now that he stared at it, Sean was convinced it was what they were looking for.

Tommy and Keiko followed the direction his finger was pointing.

"It's an offering box," Keiko said, realizing what it was. "People put money in it and hope to gain favor from the mountain god."

"The toll that must be paid," Tommy whispered.

A light gust of wind rolled through the area, whistling in the visitors' ears in spite of their caps and hoods. Snow dust picked up and flew against their sunglasses, momentarily settling on the lenses. Sean always wore protection against the bright rays of the sun. He found it even more imperative when surrounded by snow due to the incredible reflective glare.

Sean mindlessly started trudging through the snow across the open space toward the offering box. The loosely packed powder crunched under each footstep. Two red poles hung on either side of the container, though he wasn't sure what importance they could have. Tommy and Keiko followed close behind until they reached the other side. They surrounded the box and bent over, investigating the little slit in the top where money could be deposited. Sean spied the hole and then looked up at the nearby trees. Ribbons of various colors hung loosely from some of the branches, leftover from prayers that had been tied to the trees by pilgrims on their way to the holy hilltop.

Sean reached into his pocket and pulled out the trusty money clip he always carried.

"What are you doing?" Tommy asked.

"Making a donation," Sean replied. He loosened the clip, took out a bill, folded it, and slipped it through the slot in the top of the box.

"I'm pretty sure we didn't actually have to do that."

Sean shrugged. "You never know."

He slapped his friend on the back and started up the narrow path with Keiko right behind him.

Tommy groaned. "Not another hill." Before Sean could retort, Tommy took a deep breath and hurried after the other two.

18

MOUNT YUDONO

The climb up the mountainside was steep. While there was no danger of falling, the path to the top yawed at around a 30-degree angle, which caused the travelers' legs to burn almost immediately. The hike was a workout, but Sean was grateful. Exerting a little extra energy helped fight the biting cold that had started to creep back into his bones as they were trying to figure out the meaning of the dragon in the riddle.

Sean could hear Tommy grumbling behind him, though the grueling exercise was keeping him from saying too much. Instead, he was using most of his concentration on breathing and taking the next step upward.

At the beginning of the trail, the snow only came halfway up their shins, but as the three continued their ascent the powder deepened, nearly reaching their knees.

"Is...is it me?" Tommy gasped. "Or is this snow getting deeper?"

Sean nodded. Even he was starting to get a little winded from the workout. Luckily, they were nearly to the top of the rise and could see a clearing just beyond the thick patchwork of skeletal trees.

"Just more drifts up here. Don't happen to have any snowshoes in that bag, do you?"

Tommy let out a short laugh and returned to his heavy breathing. "No."

The slope started to level off dramatically, and Sean stopped for a second to take a look back. Keiko had stayed right behind him the entire way, though she, too, was panting for air. Tommy was a good twenty feet back now. Sean had passed him not long after their hike began, but he was surprised to see Tommy keeping up for the most part.

Down below, the flat area where the dragon stood was gone, hidden from view by thousands of trees and a rolling hillside. Because of the seemingly endless forest, getting a clear view of the surrounding area was nearly impossible. Only a few peeks through the trees allowed the visitors to catch a glimpse of the nearby valleys and other mountains.

Sean was disappointed, but he turned around and pressed on. He wasn't here for sightseeing. They were on a mission, and the sooner they could figure out this part of the riddle, the better. The warmth of the hotel room and a nice hot meal was already beckoning to him. And it wasn't even noon yet.

After trudging another fifty feet, the ground flattened out completely, and the terrain opened into the clearing they'd seen a few minutes before. Sean stopped at the edge and waited for Tommy to catch up again. His friend slogged his way through the final few steps and found a nearby tree trunk to lean against as he caught his breath. For a second, Sean wondered if he was going to vomit.

"You OK?"

Tommy doubled over and put his hands on his knees, sucking air into his lungs as if he'd just sprinted two hundred yards.

He held up a hand, demanding a pause, but nodded.

"Take your time," Sean said with a grin and a shake of the head.

Tommy spit into the snow, but he stood back up straight and swallowed. "Sometimes I wonder why you and I are friends. You know that?"

Sean's grin broadened. "Because you love me?"

Between breaths Tommy said, "Yeah. But I'm not sure why. And right now it kinda feels more like hate."

Keiko watched the interaction between the two, unsure if they were joking or serious.

"Oh, stop being so dramatic. Now come on, looks like there's something over here in the snow."

Sean pointed to an object that jutted out of the clearing's white floor. Parts of it stuck out of the snow, revealing gray stone beneath. From their initial inspection, it was impossible to tell what it was. Finally starting to catch his breath, Tommy took the lead as they waded through the snow and into the center of the clearing to the strange mound.

When they were only a foot away, the three spread out and surrounded it. The snow piled on top stood about four feet high, and the drifts around it were nearly that wide.

"Fascinating" Keiko said.

"Looks like some kind of altar," Tommy answered, beating Sean to it.

"Only one way to find out," Sean said.

He stepped forward and began brushing the snow off the top. Tommy did the same with the sides, and less than a minute later the loose powder was mostly gone; all that remained was a stone plinth with an intricately carved matching stone lantern on its top. A creamy white candle inside was half-burned away, the wick a dark black from its previous use.

"Well, I guess that explains that part of the riddle," Sean said.

"Looks like someone has been here before." Tommy leaned in for a closer inspection. "Not recently, though. This thing hasn't been lit for a long time."

Sean turned to Keiko. "Any reason why this would be way out here in the middle of nowhere?"

She shook her head. "This must be a very sacred place. I would guess that only the monks are permitted here to pray and meditate. Perhaps they use it at night."

Her explanation made as much sense as any other he could think of. But that still didn't give any insight as to the why the trail of clues had led to this point.

Tommy tried to tilt the stone lantern up from its resting place, but it didn't budge. "This thing is all one piece," he said.

Sean tilted his head to the side and nodded. "Gotta admit, that's some Old World craftsmanship right there. The attention to detail is impressive."

The altar on which the lantern sat was plain, nothing more than a rectangular granite box. The lantern itself, however, was incredibly ornate. The frame had been painstakingly carved to display a cherry tree on one side, a bird on another, and a lotus flower on the third. The side Sean was facing was more open, simply framed with two straight pieces of stone braced in the center by a single cross section.

Tommy stepped back from the altar and tried to get a better look from a few feet away. "Whoever made this didn't intend it to be moved," he commented.

"Maybe we are in the wrong place." Keiko spun around in a circle. She stared out into the woods, but there were no other paths leading away.

"I doubt it," Sean said. "The last clue was pretty clear, especially given that we found this thing." He ran the passage through his head again, keeping it to himself for his own private reflection. After a moment, he spoke again. "It mentioned illumination. Maybe if we light this candle, something will reveal itself?"

Tommy shrugged and nodded. "Could be." Then he frowned. "You got any matches?"

Sean chuckled and shook his head back and forth. "You have rope but nothing to start a fire?"

"I didn't plan on a camping trip," Tommy defended.

Sean decided not to press his friend further; instead, he opened up his bag and pulled out a butane torch lighter. "It's OK. I got it," he said, holding the little device close to the wick.

It only took a few seconds for the candle to flicker to life. Sean pulled away from it, but as soon as he did, a breeze rustled through the trees and blew out the flame.

Tommy sighed. "I guess we should huddle around it." He looked at Keiko awkwardly.

She apparently didn't notice the semi-uncomfortable expression on his face and pressed closer to the little altar.

"Open up your coats, and hold each side out wide to help block the wind," Sean directed. He unzipped his own coat in preparation, and the others copied him, huddling around the lantern and opening their outer shell.

"Jeez, it's cold," Tommy said, feeling a burst of frigid air hit his core.

Sean nodded. "Yeah I know. Hopefully this won't take too long." He ignited the torch again and shoved it inside the lantern, touching the blue flame to the smoldering wick. It sparked to life again, the pale yellowish glow lost in the glare of daylight.

The three huddled around the flickering candle. Another short burst of wind shot through the meadow. The Americans thought for sure the flame would extinguish again, but this time it held on and continued to burn. They watched the lantern closely, every heartbeat bringing a new wave of tension as they waited to find out what the tiny source of heat would reveal.

"It's possible that we're wasting our time," Tommy said after nearly a minute of waiting produced no results. "Maybe this isn't where we'll find the clue. It's possible we were supposed to be on the other trail. Right?"

Sean stared at the surface of the lantern. He refused to give up so easily. If the clue had been written down in invisible ink, the writer wouldn't have put it on the lantern's top. He would have written it on the underside to be protected from the elements. On the surface, rain would have eventually washed it away. Underneath, it could remain dry for much longer.

He bent down and tilted his head to get a better look up inside the stone object. After a second, he smiled and glanced at Tommy. "Take a gander, buddy."

Tommy's face curled in a frown as he knelt down opposite of his friend. "Gander?" he teased. "We in the 1950s now?"

"Just look."

Tommy cocked his head to the side and gazed up into the lantern's ceiling. "Huh. I guess this was the right place."

On the underside of the lantern's roof, a single Japanese character scribbled in black stood out against the gray backdrop of stone. For a moment, the two Americans didn't say anything.

Keiko, realizing they were too entranced to tell her what they saw, got down on the ground next to Tommy and stared up at the marking. "It says Gojuto."

Tommy snapped out of his mesmerized state and looked over at her. "Gojuto?"

Her head bobbed, confirming the answer. "Yes. Definitely."

"What's that?" Sean asked, getting up off his knees and dusting the loose snow from his pants.

She stood as well and shrugged. "I apologize, but I'm not sure."

Tommy joined them in standing. "Gojuto is a five-story pagoda on Mount Haguro." He smiled awkwardly as he answered. "It's considered a national treasure here in Japan."

At this point, Sean could tell he was trying to impress Keiko. And the goofy look on Tommy's face was getting worse by the minute.

Sean rolled his eyes and reached into his jacket pocket. He pulled out his phone and checked for a signal, not surprised to discover there wasn't one. He stuffed it back in the jacket and turned back to the others.

Keiko explained why she hadn't heard of the apparently famous pagoda. "Growing up in the city, I never had much chance to hear about these things. It's fascinating to learn about this history all around me." Her face sank a little. "I can see why my uncle spent so much time researching."

"It's a funny thing, history," Tommy said. He gazed into her eyes like a desperate, confused puppy. "On the surface a lot of people think it's boring, but once you really start to dig into it, it becomes much more exciting."

Sean was about to cut off the exchange when he noticed something on the edge of the woods where the path met the clearing. It was subtle. But his well-trained eyes caught it.

"I don't mean to interrupt your little discussion," Sean said, "but I think it's time we leave."

"What, you getting cold now?" Tommy joked.

Sean didn't laugh. Instead, he responded with a cold stare that his friend had seen too many times before.

"It's not the cold, buddy. We were followed."

19

MOUNT YUDONO

"Followed?" Tommy's eyes scanned the forest but saw nothing. He also knew better than to ask Sean if he was sure. "What do we do? We're sitting ducks out here." He tried not to look panicked.

When Sean answered, he barely moved his lips and spoke in a hushed tone. "I'm assuming they haven't attacked yet because it may look like we haven't found anything."

"But the..." Keiko started to say and then stopped herself short as she realized what Sean was saying.

"Right. So if they think we are still looking, we may be able to buy a little time." Sean pointed off to the far side of the woods, opposite of where they'd entered the meadow. He nodded as if he were showing the other two something important. "Nod with me. Pretend like I'm telling you that should be the next place we investigate."

The other two joined the ruse. Tommy took the cue and pointed a finger off to the right. He spoke a little louder, making more of a show of the situation. "What about over there? I noticed something that direction."

Sean nodded in fake agreement. He shoved a hand into his pocket and pulled out a receipt he'd mistakenly kept from a previous meal.

Now the piece of paper proved more useful than he'd ever imagined. To the hidden observers, they could easily believe it was a clue to the Masamune riddle. From their vantage point, they wouldn't know the difference.

Tommy displayed a ridiculous grin, hoping whoever was watching the charade would assume that everything was OK. "So what's the plan?"

"Unless I'm mistaken, if we go off in the direction you were just pointing, we should eventually merge with the other trail we saw down below."

"OK. But what about them?" Tommy flicked his eyes toward the woods.

"They'll try to keep their distance. Again, if they thought we'd found something, they'd have already come at us. If they think there's a chance we will find what they want, they'll let us—and then try to take it."

"Right. So we make for the edge of the clearing, and while they're hanging back, we make a run for it."

Sean gave a solitary nod. "Exactly."

"The snow," Keiko said, "it's so deep. We won't be able to move very fast."

"We're going to take it slow until we get to the woods," Sean explained. "If we take off running now, they'll know we've seen them and are trying to get away."

Tommy's eyes narrowed. "One of them just peeked around a tree. I don't think he knows I saw. But we should get a move on."

Sean nodded. "You two go in front. I'll watch the rear. Remember, when you get to the first few trees and start your descent, take off."

Tommy didn't need to be told twice. Instinctively, he grabbed Keiko's gloved hand and started toward the woods. Sean waded through the snow behind them, keeping a careful watch on the trees to his right and left with his peripheral vision. Halfway across the clearing, he felt exposed, like a deer who'd wandered right in front of a hunter's tree stand. He could feel the eyes on them as they kept pressing to the edge of the clearing. The eerie sense of having weapons aimed at his back was something he'd never gotten used to. Facing a gun was different. At least there was the possibility of fighting it off, or at the very worst, knowing what was coming. His abdomen tensed as he tried to fight off the stress during the tenuous traverse.

Only twenty or so feet away from the woods, the nerves continued to escalate. They were so close. Tommy didn't turn around, but Sean knew what his friend was thinking. He was predictable if nothing else. Tommy was thinking, *We're going to make it; we're almost there.*

Sean knew better than to think such things. There was still the rest of this little mountain to descend, and even then, once they started running and the men following them realized it, a hail of bullets would be zipping their way.

They were almost there, to the relative safety of the trees. At least the trunks would make it more difficult to get a clean shot.

"Once we're there," Sean reminded, "go as fast you can. Use the trees for cover. Weave in and out of them. It'll make you a much more difficult target."

Tommy nodded but kept his eyes forward. Keiko was much less subtle. Sean noticed her head moving a little, left to right. She was clearly scared, out of her element in a scenario like this. He felt a little guilty for allowing her to come along, but they needed her. And he knew she wanted to see an end to what her uncle had started.

The three reached the first tree, and after a few more steps the ground began a gentle slope downward. Just ahead, it steepened, heading down toward the main trail and the valley beyond.

"Wait for it," Sean whispered. He wanted to make sure they were just out of view before making any sudden movements.

Tommy kept his pace steady. "On your call, buddy."

Sean stole a quick glance out of the corner of his eye. He noticed a flicker of movement about fifty yards away behind the trees. He turned his head around and watched the stone lantern disappear behind the hill's crest.

"Go," he hissed.

Tommy broke out in a clumsy run, like a Clydesdale clomping

through a wintry beer commercial. Poor Keiko nearly fell face-first into a drift as he tugged on her arm, dragging her down the hill after him. Sean followed in their wake. His going was made easier by the path his friend was plowing in front.

Pulling his rucksack around close to his side, Sean opened it carefully and put a hand on his pistol. His thin gloves did little to keep the cold away from his fingers, but the trade-off was that he could handle his weapon much more easily. He didn't pull it out of the bag. To do so would send the wrong signal. Maybe the men behind them just thought they were in a hurry to get back down the hill and not running from anyone. If he removed his gun, they'd know the group had been startled.

A familiar pop cut through the forest. Ten feet away, a piece of bark shattered on a tree trunk. Sean saw Tommy hesitate for a second but urged him forward. Near the top of the hill, Sean could see the men in white coats moving toward them with guns outstretched. Another muzzle flashed just as Sean disappeared behind a huge fir and then reappeared on the other side.

"Sean?" Tommy said.

He didn't need to say anything else. Sean knew what his friend was trying to convey. "I know. I see 'em."

Too late for cat and mouse now, he thought.

Sean jerked the gun out of his bag and chambered a round even as virgin powder splashed around him. There were two ways to play it. He could take up a position and try to hold off the shooters, which would result in him either being captured or shot. The upside to that strategy was that Tommy would be OK. He and Keiko would probably make it back to the car safely. The other option was to keep moving and shoot while he ran. The shots would be wildly inaccurate, and he'd be lucky to hit trees or snow. However, that strategy could buy him and his friend enough time to get back to the car and get away. Maybe.

Of course, there was a third option. Sean could go on the offensive, charge up the hill, and hope that the men would be frightened enough to take cover, thus opening up a gap for him and his friends to escape. It was a fanciful idea, but it wouldn't work, a realization that was proven as Sean got a look at the number of men chasing after him. There were at least a dozen guys in white coats and matching ski pants, making them nearly invisible. Had they been lying still on the ground, he could have tripped over one before noticing them.

Another round whizzed by his head and cracked off a branch just behind him. Instinctively, he ducked down and scurried over to the nearest large tree trunk. He pressed hard against the bark, keeping his body compact so as not to provide an easy target for the rushing attackers.

Sean peeked around the tree and noticed a fatal flaw in the men's attack. They were all charging down the hill, plunging clumsily through the snow with no regard for a tactical approach. This left every one of them out in the open, and while they weren't easy targets due to the columns of trees, they could most certainly be easily scared.

One of the men saw Sean hiding behind the tree and slowed his approach to squeeze off a shot. That particular guy was carrying a pistol, but some of the others had submachine guns slung over their shoulders and carried at their hips. Not the most accurate at this distance. If he had a rifle, maybe an AR-15, Sean could take every one of them out in less than twenty seconds.

He'd have to make do and settle for scaring most of them.

He took one more look down the hill and saw Tommy pulling Keiko along. They were making good headway. *Time to give them a little more room.*

Sean spun around the tree and fired at the nearest gunman. The shot caught the man by surprise, as did the bullet that ripped into his abdomen. Sean instantly found the next target to the left and pulled the trigger. The first round splashed in the snow, but he fired again. The second ripped through the man's thigh and dropped him to the ground, screaming. By the time Sean targeted the third gunman, he and the other attackers had scrambled to take cover wherever they could. No longer brazen with the element of surprise, their approach slowed and then halted.

One man attempted to hide behind a tree half his size. Sean instantly planted a bullet through his shoulder and one into his right chest cavity. The man fell facedown in the snow, writhing in pain. Sean didn't wait to see him stop moving. He moved his sights to the next assailant, a shooter behind a tree with a submachine gun dangling out beyond the circumference of the trunk. Sean saw his shoe sticking out in the snow and fired. He missed, but it was enough to scare the man into an uphill retreat.

Ten feet to the left, another popped out from his cover and opened fire. His submachine gun peppered the snow and trees surrounding Sean, but the American was safe behind the thick wood. Emboldened by their comrade's courage, another weapon opened fire, and then another. The hailstorm of hot metal sprayed all around Sean's temporary haven. The tree behind his back took the brunt of the onslaught. He could hear the bullets thud into wood over and over again. Snow exploded all around his feet and beyond. Branches snapped off on trees a few feet away, clipped by the streaking rounds. For ten long seconds that seemed more like minutes, Sean pressed hard against the tree trunk and waited out the barrage.

Then suddenly, it all stopped. He could hear one of the men barking orders. It wasn't anything Sean could decipher, but based on the reckless use of ammunition, he guessed the shooters were reloading and moving forward.

He pivoted around the front of the tree and stepped forward, finding a gangster removing a magazine from his submachine gun. The man looked up through a pair of darkly shaded ski goggles and started to turn around. His retreat was too slow. Sean fired twice. The first shot winged the guy in the shoulder, ripping through the jacket on its way to the earth beyond; the second round sank deep into his back and dropped him prostrate into the snow. Immediately, Sean twisted left and found another target: a man with a pistol. The guy had just pulled the slide back and was readying himself to fire when one of Sean's bullets tore through the base of his neck.

All of a sudden, the odds that had so heavily favored the attackers were cut in half. Sean pressed forward to another wide tree trunk and fired the remaining rounds in his magazine at the last six men. Fortunately, they panicked and retreated up the hill, taking cover where they could. Sean knew it wouldn't take long for them to regroup and come up with a strategy to flank him.

He turned and ran after Tommy and Keiko, flying down the hill. The other two were out of sight. The slope ahead steepened, hiding the running visitors from view up above. As soon as Sean reached the next ridge, he could see his friend through the trees, arriving at the path below.

With no time to lose, Sean pressed on. He nearly tripped on a rock hidden in the snow, a mistake that would have sent him tumbling down like a human snowball. But he managed to keep his balance, hands waving wildly in the air as he ran forward with huge, clumsy strides. Every second, he expected the men behind him to start shooting again, but the shots never came. Had he scared them that badly? He risked a glance back just to make sure they weren't catching up. The only thing he saw was snow and trees.

His head turned just in time to see a skinny spruce trunk just in front of him. He planted his right foot and jumped around it, narrowly avoiding what would have been an aggravating and painful mishap. Near the bottom of the hill, Sean whipped around a tree and out onto the path. He gave another look up the mountain but saw none of the six men coming his way. His eyebrows furrowed. *They should be coming over that last ridge any second,* he thought. But there was no sign of the attackers.

Sean pushed ahead, bounding down the path as fast as the slippery conditions would allow. He ran his left hand along the metal railing in the middle of the trail to keep himself steady, all the while clutching his weapon with the right. The gap between him and Tommy had closed considerably due mostly to the fact that Sean could move much faster alone. But he also figured Tommy was probably struggling to keep going.

By the time Sean reached the trailhead near the monastery, he was only sixty yards behind the other two. He watched as his friend and Keiko made it to the car and flung open the doors. Something wasn't right, though. Sean slowed his pace and paused, catching his breath as he surveyed the scene. The black sedans that were next to their car hadn't been there before. Neither had the SUVs parked beside them. Through the tinted windows, Sean made a horrific realization. The cars weren't empty. He saw the silhouettes of the vehicles' occupants before they opened their doors. Tommy and Keiko had been in such a hurry to get the car started that they didn't realize the danger lurking three feet away until it was too late.

The men in the white coats and black sunglasses were on their prey before Tommy could even make a move for the gun in his bag. Two men wrapped their arms around his neck and torso, pulling him back to the sedan with a gun pressed against his head. Another two did the same with Keiko and dragged her to the rear door of a different vehicle.

Sean ejected the magazine from his weapon, found a full one in his bag, and slid it into the gun's base. He crouched low, sliding the first round into the chamber as he moved toward the giant red column of the torii they'd passed through earlier. He crept to the fence and spied on the situation. Tommy was stuffed into the back seat of the car, though he kicked and squirmed all the way. Keiko put up less of a fight, either because she was smart or because she was afraid. Maybe both.

A plan formulated in Sean's head. Maybe the men in the lot didn't know he was still at large. A wild idea passed through his imagination. He could sneak down the side of the hill, take out the gangsters one at a time, and free his friends.

It would never work. Even if he could eliminate some of the targets, it would put Tommy and Keiko too close to the line of fire. And who knew what those guys would do if desperate enough. They might get the idea to hold hostages.

There was the other problem, too. Where were the men from the top of the mountain? *They should be returning any moment.*

The second Sean felt the hard muzzle press against the back of his head, he knew exactly what had happened. He didn't have to turn around to realize Hideo was standing behind him.

"You didn't think it would be that easy, did you?"

Sean kept facing forward. "Honestly? I kinda hoped it would be, but I had a bad feeling. I guess I'm an old dog at this sort of thing."

As he finished his sentence, the remaining six men from the mountaintop appeared at the base of the hidden trail. A few of them stumbled through the snow until they reached flat ground.

Sean noticed the men's arrival out of the corner of his eye. "Looks like you lost some guys up there. If you go back up, you might find one or two of them still alive. Pretty sure I only hit one in the leg."

The pressure on his head relieved momentarily. But Sean never saw Hideo raise his weapon and swing it at the base of his neck. All he felt was a hard thud.

20

SENDAI

Between blacking out completely and regaining his faculties, Sean either had no recollection of what happened or only fragmented bits and pieces.

At one point he heard some men talking in Japanese. Everything was mostly dark, and he drifted back into unconsciousness.

When he finally did come around, he was sitting in an old metal chair—at least that's what it felt like. His wrists were tied behind it, and it felt like his ankles were also bound. His chin was resting on his chest as his eyes creaked open like a heavy door on rusty hinges. At first, everything in the room was a hazy yellowish light. A voice—one he didn't recognize—started to say something in Japanese. From the sound of it, he was alerting someone else that their captive was waking up.

The room was cool and dry. Outside of the aching pain at the base of his neck and the blurry lights, that was the first thing Sean noticed. His training had taught him to immediately observe his surroundings, no matter what the circumstances. Even in a state of semi-consciousness, Sean assessed the situation in seconds.

A dusty smell filled his nostrils, mixed with the scent of steel. The man's voice echoed slightly, bouncing off walls separated by a good amount of space. If he had to guess without really looking, Sean would say he was in a warehouse of some kind. Maybe an old foundry.

As a small herd of footsteps approached, his vision cleared, and his theory was proved correct. *Abandoned warehouse. How original.*

"You have proved to be quite the irritation."

Sean recognized the voice. And his eyesight had cleared up enough to confirm his suspicions. He raised his head and saw Hideo stop eight feet away with two other men next to him. There was a fourth guy standing off to Sean's right. Again, Sean was constantly assessing the situation.

"Where'd you take the others?" Sean asked. His voice came out as a raspy grumble.

"I'm back here, buddy."

Tommy's voice was a welcome sound, but it was bittersweet. It meant they were both in the same trouble.

"Where's Keiko?" Sean asked.

"We'll get to the girl in a moment. I have to say, your friend here is quite stubborn. He wouldn't tell us anything."

"And you think you're going to get more out of me?" Sean snickered. "You might want to reassess that idea."

"Oh, I have no doubts concerning your abilities to resist various means of persuasion. It would be a waste of time to try to get you to tell us what we want to know by torturing you or your friend."

"Good to know we're on the same page."

Tommy interrupted through clenched teeth. "If you do anything to her..."

It was followed by a punch to the lower back, and his sentence ended with a gasp.

Sean sighed. Tommy had developed quite a knack for getting hit in the kidneys in situations like this.

"You know," Sean spoke up again, "it might be helpful if you told us exactly what it is you'd like us to tell you. Maybe we could start with that."

"The location of the Masamune. Where is it? My men said you

had a piece of paper with you on the top of Mount Yudonosan. I want that paper."

Sean laughed full on out loud, which caused the pain in the back of his head to pulse a little harder. He winced and slowed his laughter.

"You think that's funny?" Hideo asked.

Sean nodded, still grimacing. "Yeah. It really is."

Hideo nodded at the man standing to Sean's side. He stepped over and smacked the prisoner across the cheek with the back of his hand. A fresh stinging pain surged through his face, momentarily replacing the headache.

"Is that funny?" the bald man asked.

Sean snorted in spite of the pain. "That piece of paper your men saw was just a receipt from the hotel. We used it as a ruse to throw them off long enough to escape."

Hideo tilted his head back. His eyes narrowed as he assessed Sean's explanation. "You're lying."

A wicked little grin crept onto one side of Sean's face. "You're welcome to look for yourself, although I dropped that paper in the snow on the mountain. So it might be a little difficult to find it."

Hideo wasn't sure how to react. So instead, he pushed on with the questioning. "If what you say is true, then what did you find on the top of the mountain?"

"We didn't *find* anything," Tommy answered amid coughs.

"There was a stone lantern," Hideo went on, ignoring the other prisoner. "They said you huddled around it but couldn't see what you were doing." The man stepped closer and bent down on one knee, resting his elbow atop his thigh. "Just tell me what you found and where the sword is, and I'll let you both go."

Sean had heard that sort of offer before. He took careful note of the phrasing. "You'll let us go, like you let Keiko's uncle go? Off the side of a building?"

Hideo sighed. "My employer has no quarrel with you. Give him what he wants, and you are free to go. He doesn't see any need for this to get messier than it already is. Sure, you killed some of his men. But he is willing to let that pass if you just tell us where we can find the sword."

"I'll be honest," Sean said with a smirk. "Whatever we found up there is still right where it was before. You and your boys here are welcome to go back up and have a look for yourselves."

Hideo stood and put his hands behind his back. "I had a feeling you would say that. In the interest of saving time, I think we'll just take a shortcut."

He said something in Japanese toward a dark corner of the room. A man appeared out of the shadows, dragging Keiko by the arm. He shoved her forward, and Hideo caught her. Her hair was frazzled, her lip bleeding, and one cheek swollen. They'd worked her over, but apparently she hadn't given Hideo and his men the information they wanted.

"You gutless...leave her alone!" Tommy shouted. His reaction earned him a swift punch to the gut, doubling him over once more.

"As you can see," Hideo said, caressing her bruised face with the back of his fingertips, "she is a strong girl. We encouraged her to tell us where the sword is, but she wouldn't budge."

Hideo forced Keiko to her knees and withdrew a pistol from inside his jacket. He pointed the weapon at the side of her head and waited. Tears streamed down her cheeks, but she said nothing outside of a few whimpers and sniffles.

"So we are going to do things a little differently," Hideo said. "Tell me where the sword is and what you found on the mountain, and she lives. It's that simple."

"Mount Haguro," Tommy blurted out.

Sean's head dipped. *That didn't take long.*

"What about it?" Hideo didn't waver.

Tommy spewed information like a fire hydrant in July. "There's a pagoda there. It's called Gojuto. It's a sacred place to Buddhism and a national treasure to Japan."

Hideo raised an eyebrow. "How do you know so much about this place?"

"It's what I do." Tommy shrugged. "I'm a student of history."

Sean could tell the guy was trying to determine whether or not Tommy was full of it. He stared for a long moment before putting the gun back in his jacket.

"Very well. We will go to Mount Hagurosan. And you are coming with us. If you're lying to me, I will make sure you regret it. I'll start by killing the girl. And then the two of you."

Sean was familiar with the practices of the Yakuza. He'd heard horror stories that made even his blood curdle, and he'd seen some terrible things. The gang had pushed the limits of the demented human imagination and had put into practice some of the most gruesome execution methods since the Middle Ages.

"He's not lying," Sean affirmed. "The clue we found inside the lantern was written in invisible ink, on the object's ceiling. Heat from the candle made it visible. That's where we found the name of the pagoda. The rest was deduced by my friend there." He flicked his head backward in Tommy's direction.

"We will see." Hideo turned to one of his men and barked out orders in Japanese. The man spun around and hurried out of the room through a rusty metal door. Hideo turned his attention to the remaining guards. "Take them to one of the rooms, and keep a watchful eye. These two are clever. We can't have them escaping."

He looked down at Sean. "In the morning we leave for Hagurosan. If you have anything else you feel like I should know, I suggest you tell me before then. Otherwise it will be too late."

Hideo jerked Keiko off the floor, turned, and stalked out of the room, dragging her behind as he went. The Americans were alone with the guards.

Tommy started to protest but sensed another blow to his back coming if he said too much.

"I don't suppose you're going to feed us?" Sean asked as the head man and Keiko disappeared through the door. One of the henchmen stepped close to him and stared down angrily. "Just thought I'd ask."

21

SENDAI

"What are we going to do?" Tommy asked. He'd been pacing around their little cell for the last ten minutes. "And what do you think they're doing with her right now?" The second question caused him visible pain, his face awash with worry.

"Best not to think about that last one, buddy," Sean said. He was sitting on the cold concrete floor, leaning against the wall with his elbows propped up on his knees.

Their room was little more than a big closet, illuminated with long fluorescent bulbs. One flickered weakly, signaling it was nearing the end of its life. With cinder block walls, a hard floor, and two cots they were supposed to call beds, it promised to be a very long night. Sean doubted either of them would get any sleep. He was grateful they'd at least received some form of bedding. He'd expected to have to sleep on the floor.

Tommy didn't feel like trying to see the glass half-full. "Not think about it? What's that supposed to mean? We have no idea what they're doing to her right now. They could be torturing her...or worse!" He threw his hands out, exasperated.

Sean looked up at his friend. "You'll drive yourself crazy thinking about that stuff. Like I said, best not to."

"Easy for you to say."

Sean bit his tongue. "I know it's hard. And clearly you like her. But wondering what's happening to her right now isn't going to help us get out of this situation." He could tell Tommy was about to say something, but Sean cut him off, holding up a hand as he spoke. "Instead of focusing our energy on that, how about we hone it in on something that *will* help us get out of here."

Tommy's eyebrows lowered slightly. "What are you talking about? There's no way out of here." He spun around in a circle with his hands out wide. "We're stuck in here."

The black, windowless door was locked, and there were no windows. Sean figured the room was formerly used for storage, but it could have been an office for someone unimportant to the factory, a floor manager perhaps. A phone jack and a few wall outlets suggested the latter.

Sean's eyes shot up to the ceiling, but his body didn't move. Tommy followed his eyes until he too was gazing at the tiles above them.

Still, he didn't understand. "What about it?"

Sean sighed. "There should be a space just above those tiles. Usually there's enough area to move around. If I can get up there, I can crawl out beyond the wall of this room, take out the guard outside, and unlock the door."

It was starting to make a little more sense, but Tommy still had doubts. "Guard or guards? What if there are two of them?"

"Wouldn't be the first time I've been outnumbered."

Tommy shrugged. "Good point." He paused for a second. "But then what? We escape whatever this place is and run? We can't leave her here, Sean. They're going to kill her."

"I know that. And I'd never suggest we leave Keiko. We'll have to search the building until we find her. Once we do, we get her out, leave the building, and get out of Japan."

Tommy's face scrunched in a frown. "Leave Japan?"

Sean nodded. "Too risky to stay here right now and keep up the search. If we don't leave, she'll be in danger. And so will we. We regroup and go back to the States. We can always come back here later and resume our search."

Tommy shook his head. "By then they could already have the sword. I mean, they know where to look next. If they go there and find it, then we fail."

"Yeah, I thought about that too. I guess you have to ask yourself if it's worth risking your life."

His friend drew in a deep breath. "Sean, this is what we do. Sometimes we find ourselves in bad situations, life threatening, even."

"Sometimes?" Sean chuckled.

"OK, more often than not. But this sword is a piece of Japanese history, and it needs to be shared with the world. If Taka gets it, everyone will bow to him. Who knows what he'll do? And in the long term, Keiko will be in greater danger if we just run away and do nothing."

Sean listened to his friend. He was right, of course. And Sean was never one to run from a fight. "OK, buddy. We'll keep looking for the sword. But first things first. We have to get out of this cell."

"Right." Tommy's face turned crestfallen once more. "Exactly how do you intend to get up into that ceiling?"

The two men looked up again, assessing the situation. It was about ten feet high and reaching it without a ladder would take some ingenuity.

Sean lowered his gaze to his friend. A mischievous expression crossed his face. Tommy shook his head slowly. "No. No way. There's no way, Sean. You can't lift me up there."

A snort escaped Sean's nose, and he shook his head. "Obviously. I wasn't thinking about lifting you. You're going to lift me. The sooner we get out of here, the sooner we can get your crush to safety."

He started for the rear wall, ignoring the barbs shooting from Tommy's eyes.

"She's not a crush."

Sean stopped at the back corner and turned around. "Really? I've seen the way you look at her with those puppy dog eyes. And what about the cheesy lines you've been using?"

Tommy stepped over to where his friend was standing and frowned. "They aren't cheesy."

Sean patted him on the shoulder. "It's OK, buddy. She's cute. I can see why you like her. Just be careful."

Tommy was taken aback by the last comment. "What's that supposed to mean?"

"It means I don't want you to get hurt. She seems to like you, so I'm sure it's fine. But you know how they can be sometimes."

"They?"

"Women. They're roses, buddy. Beautiful, soft, delicate, and they smell good."

"But they also have thorns. Yeah, I've heard the metaphor before."

"Don't worry about it. I'm just talking out of my rear. Here, put your hands together, and give me a boost."

Tommy did as he was told but kept up the conversation, unwilling to let it go so easily. "She seems like a nice girl."

"They all do, my friend." Sean raised his leg and placed his foot in the cup Tommy had formed with his hands. "Lean against the wall to give yourself a little more support."

Tommy shuffled his feet back a little until his back was touching the wall. Then he pressed against it. Sean put his hands on Tommy's shoulders and stepped up. He raised his other leg quickly and put his foot on the nearest shoulder. Tommy wavered for a moment, and his legs began to shake under the additional burden, but he held firm. Sean stood up, tilting forward slightly toward the wall to keep his balance. He was higher than he'd anticipated and had to bend slightly to keep his head from hitting the tiles. He pushed his hands up into the panel directly above and pressed on it. The lightweight material lifted easily out of its housing, and Sean moved it to the right, letting it come to a rest on the framework. The dim lights below did little to illuminate the area above, so he had to resort to feeling around until his fingers came to a metal edge. He tugged on it a couple of times to test its strength and then put both hands on it. He bent his knees to see if the rail would support his weight. It did so without making a sound.

Meanwhile, Tommy was getting impatient. "Would you mind hurrying a little up there? You're killing my shoulders."

Sean ignored him. It wasn't exactly the kind of thing he could rush. He tightly gripped the metal rail with both hands and pulled. Most of his early life, Sean had been unable to do a pull-up. The kids in his elementary school made fun of him for it. Middle school too. When he got to high school, Sean made it his mission to learn how to do a pull-up and develop the strength necessary for it. The process was long and slow, only yielding hints of progress along the way. Eventually, though, he completed his first one. After that, he never looked back. Every week since, he'd spent at least three days a week working on the muscles that performed that exercise. Now he was able to do ten in a single set.

Right now, that hard work was paying off in a way he could have never imagined. He used his feet to walk up the wall and make the work easier for his upper body, but that had more to do with the uncertainty regarding the strength of the railing above his head.

Tommy let out a sigh as his friend's weight was taken off his shoulders. He turned and looked up, watching Sean pull himself into the dark cavity. Only a residue of the flickering light below illuminated his friend's pants.

"See anything?" Tommy whispered.

Sean lowered his head back to the lip of the opening and nodded. He put a finger to his lips, signaling his friend to keep quiet. Then he pulled himself back out of the light and disappeared toward the left corner.

Maneuvering through the darkness was difficult, but Sean's eyes adjusted quickly. The little amount of light coming through the opening gave him a good starting point. Old wires and pipes stretched out along the rafters in several directions. Sean wondered how safe the wires were, considering how long ago they'd been put in place. No time to worry about that. He had to keep moving. At the corner, he found a steel beam that ran out to the front of their cell. He tightened his body to balance on the narrow surface and got up into a bear crawl position. His back scraped against the ceiling above him, causing a cloud of dust to sprinkle down to the tiles below. He froze in place, hoping whoever was outside the room didn't hear the debris falling to the floor. Sean reassured himself no one had heard a thing. He always found that things seemed louder than they really were when a person was attempting to be quiet.

He crept along the beam carefully, putting one foot in front of the other, and doing the same with his hands. The muscles in his shoulders and chest worked hard to keep him steady as he made his way to the front. The longer Sean stayed above the ceiling, the more his eyes acclimated. Soon he realized that little strips of light were seeping through cracks in the panels below, giving just enough light to aid with seeing his way around. Finally, after what seemed like several minutes, he reached the intersection where the room's front wall jutted off to the left.

Sean knew whoever was keeping watch on their cell would be just below, on the other side of the wall. But he had no idea exactly where. This posed a huge problem, one he hadn't even taken the chance to consider. If he dropped down behind one, that wouldn't be a problem. In fact, that would be ideal. But if he were to land directly in front of—or worse, between—a few of Hideo's men, that could be problematic. The other issue was removing one of the tiles without alerting anyone below to his presence. It wouldn't take the most observant person in the world to see a ceiling tile being removed, especially if it made too much noise.

As luck would have it, Sean was given a glimmer of hope. A man said something directly below him. Two seconds later, another man responded. Based on the sound of the second guy's voice, Sean could tell he was several feet away to the left, in the direction of the door. It would make sense that the guards Hideo put in place would be on either side of the entrance to the cell. Sean leaned forward, using the beam over the front wall as a brace and peered down through a little hole in the ceiling tile below. The lights in the hallway were brighter than those in the cell, and Sean could clearly see the shoulder of the guard beneath him.

A plan rapidly formed in his mind, and he shifted his weight, planting one foot on the beam next to his hand. The position was awkward, propped up in a sort of plank position with his legs spread out in a wide V. One thing Sean had learned over the years is not to second-guess things. Letting doubt into one's mind was the first step toward inaction. There was no better time than now to pounce on the guards below. Was the plan perfect? Absolutely not, but the perfect opportunity was something he knew would never come.

He took a deep breath and pushed off, tucking his hands and feet in so he could drop through the framework. The feeble panel gave way easily under his weight, and Sean crashed through in a cloud of dust and debris into the corridor. He shielded his eyes with his forearms but kept them open to make sure he could see what he was going to hit. His aim had been fortuitous. The first thing to strike the guard below was his right knee, digging deep into the base of the guy's neck. Sean's weight took care of the rest, driving him hard to the floor and smacking his face against the concrete, knocking him unconscious.

The second guard was stunned, left staring wide eyed at the scene. As soon as he landed on the ground, Sean rolled to the right and bounced up. He lunged forward at the shocked gangster and jumped through the air with his foot extended.

His intentions were good. The shock and awe of what had just happened had rendered the guard almost paralyzed. But his recovery was much quicker than Sean could have anticipated. The guard twisted his torso to the side and punched hard with his palm, drilling it deep into Sean's abdomen. His momentum made the blow hurt worse than if he'd been standing still, and Sean was knocked back to the floor a few feet away.

The guard went for the pistol in his jacket, eager to finish this fight without throwing another punch.

Sean winced at the pain coming from his midsection, but he pushed himself off the ground and launched at the guard again. He snapped his left foot up as the gangster whipped out his weapon. The top of Sean's foot struck the man's hand and sent the gun spinning through the air. Before it landed on the floor, Sean jabbed his left fist into the guard's jaw. He jabbed two more times, the second hitting the target hard before the gangster recovered and blocked the third.

The guy tried to counter with a left of his own, but Sean parried it to the side with his right and followed through with a hard blow to the other cheek, directly under the man's eye.

The guard staggered backward in a clumsy retreat, but Sean didn't let him escape. He took two fast steps forward and continued the assault—throwing jabs and hooks amid a flurry of weak blocking attempts—until it was all the guard could do to keep standing. Sean's muscles kept pumping through the fatigue until, finally, he twisted and threw an uppercut that landed squarely under the guard's chin. His head rocked back, and he fell to the ground in a heap.

Sean stood over him for a second, making sure he was down for the count. The guy's chest rose and fell slowly, but his eyes remained shut, his head unmoving. A quick look back over his shoulder told Sean that the first guard was still out too—unsurprising considering how hard his skull had struck the concrete.

There was no time to lose. Someone would be checking on these two before long, especially if they failed to check in. And there was still the matter of locating Keiko before trying to get out of this place —wherever this place was.

Sean spotted the pistol on the floor—a Beretta 9mm—and stepped over to pick it up. Not his weapon of choice, but under the circumstances, any gun was better than no gun at all. Next he reached for the doorknob and opened the door. Tommy was standing in the door frame with his chin between his index finger and thumb in a contemplative expression.

"What took you so long?"

Sean twisted his head to the side. "Take this." He handed the pistol to his friend.

Next, he moved over to the other guard and sifted through his jacket until he found a similar weapon, tucked away in a holster. Sean pulled it out and checked to make sure the magazine was full and a round chambered. Tommy did the same as he stepped through the door. When he saw the damage his friend had done, he pursed his lips together and nodded.

"Impressive." He looked at the guy covered in dust and debris. "So you just dropped out of the ceiling on this one?"

"Something like that," Sean said.

"I guess the other one over there must have seemed like he'd seen a ghost." Tommy pointed at the guard lying on his back several feet away.

"Yeah, but he recovered faster than I would have liked." He was reminded of the jab he'd taken to the gut with a renewed soreness radiating from his stomach.

"So what next? I mean, the plan has worked so far. But we have no idea where they took her."

Sean took a deep breath. "I guess we go through that door over there and see what's on the other side."

Tommy raised an eyebrow and then broke out into a broad smile. "As good a plan as any."

22

SENDAI

Sean eased the door open as carefully as possible. In spite of his caution, the door's hinges squeaked loudly, causing both Americans to wince. Once it was open wide enough for the two of them to pass through, Sean stopped and held his weapon at the ready.

"Someone had to have heard that," Tommy whispered.

"We'll know soon enough."

Sean dipped his head around the door frame and peeked to the left and then the right. "It's an empty hallway." He stepped into the next area and kept his gun pointed down the length of the corridor.

Tommy followed and took the other side, aiming in the opposite direction. "So which way do we go?"

Sean peered down the hall. More of the same bare, skinny fluorescent bulbs lined the ceiling. The walls were made from corrugated metal, probably aluminum. The gray paint was flaking off in hundreds of places, another signal to the age of the facility. There were no signs of life in either direction.

"This way," Sean said.

Tommy frowned and spun around, lowering his weapon. "How do you know?"

"I don't. But what I do know is we aren't going to get anywhere by standing here like a couple of idiots pointing guns at an empty space."

"Good point." Tommy thought for a second. "But what if it's this other way?"

"Do you want to go that way? Because personally I don't have a preference. You asked me which way to go; I said this way. You want to go that direction, we will."

"OK, take it easy. I was just asking. We'll go your way. Jeez. Get all sensitive on me."

Sean shook his head and started down the hall at a trot with his friend in tow. "Not sensitive. I just know we need to keep moving. If we stand still, eventually they'll find us."

Arriving at the end of the hall, they found a set of metal grated stairs ascending to the next floor. It was the only way in or out of the corridor from their position. Sean aimed his weapon at the door atop the staircase and then crossed one foot over the other, climbing with ninja-like stealth. At the top, he looked through the narrow window into the next room. Satisfied it was clear, he turned the latch and opened the door.

A gust of cool air burst over his body, accompanied by the scent of rusting metal, grease, and dust. Sean squinted his eyes for a moment and then went through. On the other side, he found machinery that looked like it hadn't been used in decades. He wasn't sure what much of it was for. There were conveyor belts, hydraulic arms, giant wheels, and a number of forklifts that looked like they were left over from World War II.

"What is this place?" Tommy wondered out loud.

Sean shook his head and spoke quietly. "An old steel foundry, I guess." He scanned the area and noticed something strange on the far side of the giant expanse. A weak light radiated from a window in the corner. There was a door close by, guarded by two men dressed similarly to the ones Sean took out just moments before.

"See them?" he asked.

Tommy searched the vast space and then nodded when he

located the guards. "Yeah I got 'em. You think that's where they're holding her?"

Sean shrugged. "Looks like some kind of an office. Probably belonged to the manager of this place. Can't believe they still have electricity here."

"What's the plan?"

"Well, right here we are in plain sight, so I suggest we either get down to floor level or we take this catwalk around. Personally, I don't feel like being a sitting duck up here on this thing."

"Me either. And it doesn't exactly feel secure, does it?"

"No." Sean shook his head and hurried down a set of stairs, taking the initiative. Once he was on firm ground again, he crouched low and made his way over to one of the big machines.

Tommy copied Sean's movement and stopped next to him, taking cover behind the monstrous contraption.

"Now what? Flank them?"

"We *could* do that."

"But?"

"But then we're relying on a brute force attack."

"OK, professor. What do we do instead?"

Sean curled his lips. His voice was full of mischief. "Diversion."

He looked down at a lever attached to the big machine. It appeared to be in a locked position.

Tommy looked at the lever for a moment and then back at his friend. "Do you know what that does?"

Sean shook his head. "No. But I'm willing to bet it's going to release something."

Tommy was dubious. "This thing isn't connected to power. It probably hasn't even run in fifty years."

Sean turned around and grabbed the handle. He squeezed the release trigger and held on to the bar. "Then step back."

Tommy moved a few feet away, keeping an eye on the perimeter in case one of the guards had seen or heard them.

Sean leaned back, pulling hard on the old bar. At first it didn't budge, even with every ounce of leverage he could muster. But after a few hard jerks, the thing came loose and lurched a foot in a counter-clockwise direction. Suddenly, something snapped on the big machine. The next second, one of the big wheels started spinning slowly, moving the conveyor belt a few feet before stopping.

"That's it? That's your plan? I told you it didn't have any power running to it."

"Come on," Sean pulled at his friend's shirt, leading him around behind the far end of the machine.

They sprinted on the balls of their feet to keep quiet, but the sound of squeaking metal parts and loud banging echoed through the area. Once at the other end, Sean stopped at the far corner and peeked around the base of a huge reservoir. The guards at the door had left their post to go investigate the ruckus. They were almost to the other end of the contraption and moving fast.

Sean motioned to Tommy with his hand and crept along the side of the behemoth. The guards were out of sight, but they wouldn't be gone long. It would be to the Americans' advantage to have no weapons fired since doing so would pretty much let anyone else in the building know what was going on. They were nearly halfway to the corner door, and still no sign of the guards' return. Sean kept his eyes forward but risked a glance through a gap in the wheels and bars to see the other side. As he suspected, the guards were befuddled. Both men were looking around the room, checking the catwalk and the floor to make sure they weren't crazy. One of them was saying something to the other in a tone that conveyed confusion in any language.

The Americans took this as their cue to make for the door. Sean cut left and ran hard to the wall. His head was on a swivel, scanning every possible inch of the room to make sure they weren't seen. A sudden shout from the other side of the contraption told the two friends that was exactly what just happened. One of the guards tried to fire a bullet through a gap in the machine, but it missed the running targets, thumping into the concrete base of the wall just beyond. When he reached the door, Sean slid like a base-ball player, turned in mid-slide, and aimed his weapon at the machine's nearest corner—where he knew the guards would appear.

"Get inside!" he ordered Tommy. "I'll hold them off."

Tommy didn't want to leave his friend out there alone with two armed gangsters bearing down on him, but he knew Sean wasn't an ordinary guy. One of him against two untrained gang members was definitely a mismatch—in Sean's favor. Tommy grabbed the handle and flung the door open. He stuck his weapon out in front in case there was anyone waiting inside. What he found was surprising. The short, dark corridor was empty. The only light came from a small office door to the right—the one the two friends had pinned as Keiko's probable location. Tommy ran into the hallway and disappeared into the office.

Sean was out in the open, exposed like a pimple on prom night. His only advantage was that he could see the men coming through the spaces in the big machine, which would allow him to get off the first shots. Still, better to have some cover than none at all. He scrambled to his feet and ducked into the corridor, tucking into the corner of the doorway to get out of sight.

He heard Tommy talking to someone in the other room. From the sound of it, it had to be Keiko. He was asking if she was all right. Then Sean could hear him struggling with something. She must have been tied up. Another sound interrupted the others. Footsteps, running fast toward their position. Sean didn't want to give away where he was, so he didn't issue a warning to his friend in the office, assuming Tommy was still occupied with whatever had him flustered. The footsteps drew closer, clicking louder and louder on the concrete. He knew they were nearly to the door. He grinned wickedly, recalling the story about Bunker Hill and how the revolutionary soldiers were told not to fire until they saw the whites of the Redcoats' eyes.

He spun around the corner and fired. The two guards ran head-first into a hailstorm of bullets. Acquiring the targets came easily given their close proximity, and Sean alternated between them, giving each a healthy dose of deadly hot metal. Sean didn't count how many times he squeezed the trigger. From that range, he couldn't miss. The rounds tore through the men, ripping through flesh, vital organs, and limbs until Sean's weapon clicked.

Tommy hurried out of the office with his pistol held at the ready, but when he saw the two bodies lying in a pile on the floor, he relaxed visibly. A grayish white haze of smoke hung in the air, laced with an acrid scent.

He turned to Sean with a questioning glance. "Did you just empty your magazine on those two?"

Sean nodded. "Better safe than sorry."

"Yeah, but you're usually all about precision. And now you're out of ammunition."

"I don't think so." Sean walked over to the two guards and tipped one over onto his back. His shirt and jacket were stained red, but the gun in his hand was untouched. "I'll just take his since he won't be needing it anymore." He noticed the bags slung over his friend's shoulders. "They stowed our stuff in there?"

Tommy nodded. "Looks that way. I didn't bother checking the contents."

"We'll do it when we get out of here."

A voice shouted from the other end of the room, startling the three companions. Sean looked in the direction the voice had come and saw four more men pouring out of a doorway in the far corner.

"Time to go."

Tommy glanced at a gray double door at the opposite end of the building. "Should we go out the front door?"

Sean's eyes narrowed. "I'd say they would be expecting that, but then again, it's doubtful they'd expect us to escape. Might be heavily guarded."

Tommy stepped over and pried the pistol from the limp hand of the other dead guard. "Then I guess we can't be too careful." He handed the weapon to Keiko, who took it warily. "Know how to use this?"

She shrugged. "Point and shoot, yes?"

"She's a natural," Sean said. "Head for the door. I'll cover you."

Tommy nodded and ran ahead with Keiko right behind. Sean

followed and looked back at the gangsters running at them from across the huge room. They were a good 150 to 200 feet away, too far to be very accurate—even for Sean Wyatt. That didn't mean he wasn't going to at least try to slow them down. Halfway to the door he turned and fired twice. The rounds sparked on the floor around the feet of the man in front and ricocheted harmlessly by. The close call scared the gangsters enough, though, and sent them diving for cover along the sides of the machine in the center of the room. Sean ran harder, twisting to look back every few strides. Gunfire erupted from behind as the gangsters answered Sean's volley.

The rounds bounced off the floor and crashed into the wall around the door. One whizzed by Sean's head, crackling the air in a haunting zip as it flew by. Even though accuracy wouldn't be good at that range, volume could sometimes make up for it. With four guns blazing, the odds of one of the shooters getting lucky were heavily increased.

Tommy reached the door amid the blizzard of deadly metal and flung it open. He shoved Keiko outside and then turned to cover Sean's escape. He squeezed the trigger rapidly at the four targets crouching against the steel contraption. They ducked back to safety, clearly not aware that hitting anything on purpose from that far away would be next to impossible. Miraculously, one of Tommy's rounds *did* catch a guard's thigh. The man grasped his leg in agony and dropped to his knees, reeling.

"I got one," Tommy gasped as Sean turned and glanced back.

"Great! Now keep moving!"

Sean pushed his still-surprised friend out the door and slammed it shut behind.

Outside, they found themselves in a place that looked almost like a junkyard. Old fencing wrapped around the perimeter, topped with three layers of barbed wire. Two ancient, rusted-out trucks sat off to the right amid several other heavy machines that were long out of use. The pavement was crumbling, and it was clear the place hadn't been used for its original purpose for many years.

The chill of the night air seeped into their bones rapidly. Their coats had been removed somewhere along the way, and now they were exposed to the elements, a fact that elevated the necessity to escape and find somewhere warm.

"Those men won't stay back for long," Tommy said, jerking a thumb at the door.

Sean turned his head back and forth until he saw something that would do the trick. A long metal pole was lying on the ground close to a decrepit forklift. He grabbed it and shoved it through the handles on the double doors, effectively sealing it off for the time being.

"That ought to hold them for a few minutes. Come on."

They took off with Sean in the lead and ran to the right. Based on the layout of the buildings and the pavement, he deduced that the entrance would be somewhere in that direction.

Suddenly, a man in a black coat appeared around the corner. He looked almost as shocked to see the three escapees as they were to see him. He started to raise the submachine gun slung over his shoulder, but to everyone's surprise, Keiko pointed her gun and shot first.

She only fired one round, but it struck the guard in the chest and sent him stumbling backward into the shadows. When his back hit the wall, he slowly lowered to the ground and toppled onto his side.

Sean and Tommy both looked at her with amazement.

"Point and shoot, huh?" Sean asked.

She shrugged. "I dated a guy from Texas once."

Sean turned his gaze to Tommy and gave a nod. "OK then."

They pushed forward, weaving their way through the piles of scrap metal, past an old crane, rusty trucks, and by another building that appeared to have served as an office in its former life. Now the windows were dark, and no signs of life stirred in the night.

Sean held out a hand to slow the others as they approached the building's front corner. He peeked around the edge and surveyed the area. The pavement sloped down around a hundred feet until it reached the gate, which was closed ahead of them and chained shut. Sean wondered how the guards were supposed to get out.

Tommy echoed that sentiment. "Now what? The gate is closed. Find another exit?"

Muffled gunfire sounded from the building they'd barred shut.

"Sounds like those guys are trying to shoot their way out."

Sean nodded. "Yeah. Won't be long."

Across the thoroughfare he saw a white delivery van. It was the only vehicle in the area that didn't look like it would crumble at the touch of a finger.

"That van. We can use it to ram through the gate."

Tommy frowned. "No way the keys are in it."

"Don't worry about that. Come on."

Sean waved his hand and took off across the space. Keiko glanced questioningly at Tommy, who shrugged and motioned for her to go ahead. She ran after Sean while Tommy took one last look back to make sure no one had a clear shot at them. Satisfied for the moment, he sprinted ahead.

Sean skidded to a stop at the van and checked the door handle. Surprisingly, it was unlocked and opened easily. He climbed inside as Keiko hurried to the other side with Tommy right behind her. A quick check in the cup holders, ashtray, and visor revealed there were no keys to be found. Tommy slid open the back door and started to get in when Sean looked at him and shook his head. "She's going to need to drive."

Tommy's face curled in confusion. "What? Why?"

"No keys. We're going to have to push it." He turned to Keiko. "Just keep it in neutral, and try not to move the wheel too much or else it will lock. We have enough space to veer it on course, and with the downhill slope it should gain enough momentum to break through."

"Should gain enough momentum?" Tommy questioned. "And what if it doesn't?"

"I'll buy you a Coke."

"Not exactly the kind of wager I want you to lose. Can't you just hotwire it?"

Sean shrugged. "Maybe. If I had five minutes."

"Fine," Tommy resigned. He slid the back door shut and ran around to the back.

Sean gave a nod to Keiko. "Remember, only slight movements of the wheel, OK?"

She nodded and slid into the driver's seat.

"Once I'm on the ground, push in the clutch, and shift it into neutral." He was grateful the van was a stick shift, otherwise this idea might prove to be much less viable.

He hopped down, and Keiko shifted the van into neutral and twisted the wheel ever so slightly to the right. Sean rushed around to the back and joined Tommy, who was already leaning into the rear with his shoulder. Without Sean's help, they had already begun rolling. Sean smirked and pushed hard, pumping his legs as hard as he could.

"Forget what I ever said to you about losing weight, pal. It's coming in handy right now."

Tommy grunted, and the van picked up speed, rolling out onto the main driveway. "Shut up," he said through clenched teeth.

Their feet moved faster and faster as the vehicle gained velocity. Keiko carefully kept the wheel as straight as possible, only adjusting as necessary to keep the thing on course as it cruised toward the gate. Halfway down the asphalt, Tommy could no longer keep up with the van's pace, and shortly after, Sean let go as well, jogging after the vehicle as it sped toward the chained fencing.

Tommy bent over with his hands on his knees, watching as the van plowed into the gate and ripped the feeble enclosure from its hinges. Keiko pumped the brakes to slow the van so it wouldn't roll out into the busy street fifty feet away. She realized that the brakes would only work once or twice and immediately shifted the wheel to the right, guiding the van toward the curb and a grassy strip of lawn beyond it. The vehicle jostled over the curb and slowed to a stop several feet into the grass, coming up just short of a cherry tree.

The two Americans fought through the heaviness in their legs and ran the rest of the way down the hill, over the mangled gate, and over to the van. The door swung open, and Keiko hopped out with a goofy smile on her face.

"That was fun," she said.

The two friends looked at each other and then back at her.

"You all right?" Tommy asked.

She nodded energetically. "Yes. Looks like there are a lot of cars driving by. If we hurry, maybe we can find a taxi."

Sean looked back up the hill and saw the four gangsters appear at the crest. "Good idea. Because our friends are back."

The three sprinted out to the sidewalk as the men on the hilltop opened fire again. Their shots missed wildly from the great distance, and only seconds later the companions disappeared around a building to the left of the foundry's entrance.

23

SENDAI

S ean handed a hotel card key to Keiko. "You'll be in the room next to us," he said. Then he palmed one over to Tommy. "This is ours." He shoved a matching one in his back pocket.

The Americans knew it wouldn't be safe to stay at the hotel where they'd previously been. If Taka and Hideo's men knew they were there, it would be the first place they'd check. The three companions only returned to get their necessities before hurrying away in a cab to another hotel on the other side of town.

The lobby of their new temporary residence was a huge open space. A bronze-colored cylinder hung from the center of the room, casting a sort of odd spotlight on the floor below and the ceiling above. Four men sat at the bar, laughing and clinking glasses together. From the sound of their voices, at least two of them were American. A third was clearly English. The fourth had a German tinge to his accent.

Sean surveyed the room, less out of habit now and more out of a growing sense of concern that anyone could be working for Taka. It was strange how easily they'd been tracked down. He'd been careful, always keeping a watchful eye behind them to make sure no one was following. He doubted the gang leader would have the ability to trace calls or track down the hotel transactions. But anything was possible. More and more it seemed like hackers were causing trouble. It wasn't unreasonable to think that Taka might have a few people in his employ who specialized in such a thing, which was exactly why Sean paid for the rooms in this hotel with cash.

"I suggest we get cleaned up and get some rest. It's been a long day. We can figure out what our next play is tomorrow morning."

He didn't tell the other two, but the base of his skull hadn't stopped throbbing from the blow he took earlier. It was going to take more than a couple ibuprofen pills to get rid of the pain, something he planned to address at the pharmacy across the street once everyone was asleep. Plus it would give him a chance to sweep the area.

All three of them were exhausted. Keiko's eyes were droopy with little circles under them, and Tommy stood there with his shoulders hunched over like he might collapse right there and sleep on the floor. Neither of them put up a protest to Sean's suggestion and turned toward the hallway off to the right where the elevators were located.

Four minutes later, they were on the sixth floor and standing in front of their rooms. Sean sensed something awkward about to come out of Tommy's mouth, but he didn't give him a hard time, instead opening the door and walking inside to leave his friend and Keiko alone for a moment.

Of course, that didn't mean he wasn't going to listen. Sean pressed his ear close to the door as it eased shut.

Outside, Tommy struggled to figure out what to say. He wanted something smooth to come out of his mouth, but all he could come up with was, "Have a good night. Let us know if you need anything."

She nodded and smiled, slid the card into the lock, and disappeared inside her room. Tommy stood there for a few seconds, awkwardly watching the door close behind her. When it clicked, he turned and slowly lowered his head to the door of his room and tapped his forehead against it repeatedly. Suddenly it swung open, nearly causing him to fall inside. Sean was standing there grinning broadly.

"You OK?" he asked in an attempt to be sympathetic.

Tommy stumbled inside, and Sean let the door close behind him. "I just wish I could be smooth like you, ya know? But I never say the right thing."

"I know, buddy. And believe me, like I said before, I'm not always *that* cool."

"At least you are sometimes."

Sean shrugged. "Don't sweat it. Besides, I think she likes you." He walked over to one of the double beds, sat down, and started to go through his gear bag. There hadn't been a moment to check the contents until now, figuring that if a pistol fell out it could cause a little too much of a stir.

Tommy spun around and stared down at his friend. "Really? You think so?"

"Sure," Sean said as he sifted through the bag. He found his Springfield, his cell phone, and all the other gear he'd brought to Japan. His eyebrows knit together. "That's strange."

"What? That she likes me? Why is that strange?"

Sean shook his head. "No. Not that. All my stuff is still in the bag."

"That's a good thing, right? What's the problem?" Tommy lifted his bag off the floor and set it on the end of the nearest bed. He found all of his things inside and looked over them carefully.

"I guess. But it doesn't make sense. You'd think they'd have someone trying to access our phones at the very least."

"Maybe they don't have any tech-savvy people in the Yakuza."

Sean looked dubious. "Doubtful. This is a well-run criminal organization." He reflected back on his thoughts about hackers before. "And why didn't they take our guns? When Hideo knocked me out, I had my pistol in my hand. That means he took the gun and stuffed it in my bag. Why wouldn't he just throw it away or give it to one of his men? Heck, he could have kept it. It's a good piece."

Tommy nodded wearily. "Yeah, but what's your point? Just be glad we have our stuff back. Especially our phones." He took his, found a charging cord in his other bag, and plugged it into the wall.

"Doesn't make sense, that's all. Pair that with the ease of our escape earlier, and you've got something fishy."

Tommy looked at Sean as if he was losing his mind. "Ease of our escape? We were nearly killed."

Sean checked his spare magazine, making sure it was as he'd left it. Again, something that didn't add up. "Out of all those guys shooting at us as we left that factory, not one of them could hit us?"

"Maybe they're just really bad shots."

"Tommy, we dodged, like, I don't know how many dozens of bullets. At least one of them should have been able to get lucky and graze us." He shook his head. "I don't like it."

Tommy plopped down on the bed and put his hands out. "So you'd prefer we were back in that holding cell in the factory? Buddy, we got out. Maybe we were lucky. I don't know. But it sure beats being held captive by a bunch of psychopaths."

Sean still wasn't convinced. He stuffed the magazine back in his bag and rechecked the phone to make sure it had enough battery life for a quick trip around the block.

"No. I wouldn't prefer to be back in there. But something's fishy. I don't know what it is. I'm trying to run through it in my head."

"OK, fine," Tommy said. "Let's go with your theory that they let us go. However silly that sounds, let's for a second say you're right. Why would they do that? They already know the location to check next. If we get away, we can beat them to it. Why would they run that risk?"

"Maybe they think you lied."

"Possibly. But that sure seems like a lot of trouble to go through to validate the story."

Sean snorted. "By the way, good job on holding out on that information."

Tommy stood up and scowled. "They were gonna kill her. What else was I supposed to do?"

Sean smiled and shook his head dismissively. "Nothing, man. You did what you had to do."

"Exactly. And now all I want to do is make sure that Keiko is safe. I don't even care about finding this sword anymore. We just need to get her out of here and protected."

It was a big statement, but Sean understood. He'd have thought the same if it were Adriana involved. Although *she* was different. Adriana knew how to handle herself, better than most people he'd come across. And in his previous line of work, he'd come across some of the world's best.

He stood up and sauntered toward the door.

"Where you going? I thought you said we should get cleaned up and go to sleep."

Sean gave a nod. "We should. But my head is killing me. I'm just going to run out and get something for the pain. I'll be back in a few. Go ahead and use the shower. I won't be long."

Tommy frowned, perturbed at the way the conversation had gone. He threw up a hand and turned back to his things. "OK. Whatever."

Once the door closed outside the room, Sean paused to reflect for a moment. He knew he was right whether Tommy could see it or not. His friend's doubts were certainly valid, but that didn't change Sean's speculation. *Why would they let us go?* The question rattled around in his mind as he walked down the hall, got on the elevator, and then exited on the main floor. As he stepped out into the cold night once more, the question still kept nagging at him.

If they know our next step is to go to Mount Haguro, what possible reason could they have? Come on, Sean. It's right in front of you. Maybe they need us to solve the next clue. But how do we know there is a next clue?

He shook his head as he entered the twenty-four-hour pharmacy. It couldn't be as simple as that. Could it? He didn't know anymore, and the longer he thought about it, the more his head hurt. It didn't take long to find the ibuprofen, and he'd twisted the bottle open before he left the store. After he took a few pills, Sean eyed the street in both directions. They would need new coats in the morning. All he had on at the moment were a pair of regular khakis and a long-sleeve shirt. The winter outerwear was what the Yakuza decided to keep. He wanted to do a quick sweep of the area, but in the cold and with no coat that would get old real fast. It was doubtful he would see anything suspicious anyway. If he and the others had been followed, Taka's men would lie low.

Sean trudged back into the hotel. When he arrived back in the room, Tommy was gone. Either he'd gone for a walk, or maybe he'd gotten brave and went to Keiko's door to see if they could talk. If he was a betting man, he'd put his money on the former.

Since his friend was nowhere to be found, Sean decided to take a shower and go to bed. Tommy could take care of himself.

The hot water soothed his aching muscles, and he spent a good amount of time letting it soak over the sore spot at the base of his neck. When he exited the bathroom, Tommy was still absent. While it was certainly out of character, Sean again reassured himself that his friend was a big boy and would be just fine. Tommy wasn't useless. He could handle himself in a fight. More of a brawler, he'd punched his way out of plenty of tough spots.

The throbbing at the base of Sean's skull started to dissipate as the ibuprofen kicked in. He turned up the fan on the room's A/C unit, switched off the lights, and crawled into bed. In less than five minutes he drifted to sleep, questions in his head melting away into bizarre dreams about dragons, swords, and gangsters.

24

SENDAI

When Sean woke up the next morning, Tommy was already dressed and sitting on the edge of the bed, tying his shoelaces. Sean rubbed his eyes and stretched out his arms. He knew better than to ask where his friend had been the night before. It was none of his business. If Tommy needed some alone time to think things out, no big deal. If he went to try to talk to Keiko, also cool. It didn't concern Sean. And keeping out of other people's business was one of things he prided himself on.

"Sleep OK?" Tommy asked, cutting into his thoughts.

Sean yawned and nodded. "Yeah. What time is it?" He answered his own question by looking over at the clock on the nightstand. "I guess it's time to get going."

"Yeah. We're going to need to get some outer gear: coats, snow pants, that kinda stuff again. I guess those were the only things the Yakuza wanted us to not have."

Sean kept his laughter to himself since he'd thought the exact same thing the night before. "I guess so."

"After we get geared up, we'll head for the mountain. It's early yet, so we should be able to beat all the morning traffic here in the city. Shouldn't take us too long to get there if the roads have been cleared.

I don't think any new snow has come through in the last seven hours."

Sean was impressed with his friend's energetic start to the morning. "Sounds good. I guess we should wake Keiko."

"She's not here."

The comment took Sean by surprise. "What do you mean she's not here? Where is she?" The fact that Tommy didn't sound concerned meant he knew what was going on.

"I took her somewhere safe last night. I know we might need someone who speaks Japanese, but whatever we find on that mountain, we can take a picture or bring it back and have someone translate it for us. I don't like putting her at risk, and I won't allow it to happen anymore."

Sean raised his eyebrows and sat up. "OK, buddy. That's fine. I agree. I don't want her to be at risk." He scratched his head. "Just curious, though. How'd you get her to *agree* to that?"

Tommy's eyes narrowed. "You think you're the only one who can be persuasive when they want to be?"

Sean smiled and twisted his head to the side. "I guess not." He climbed out of bed and slipped into some pants he'd laid out the night before. "This is good, by the way. We can move a lot faster just the two of us."

"I agree. And if someone *does* sneak up on us, I'm a lot more comfortable with it being just you and me."

Sean pulled on a T-shirt. "So you gave my theory some more thought?"

Tommy stood up and looked at his friend. "If there's one thing I've learned in the years of our friendship it's that you're rarely wrong about stuff like this. You may be wrong in other things, but when it comes to sensing trouble, you're like a...well, I don't have a comparison, but you get what I'm saying."

"Thank you. Like I said, I don't know if I'm right or not, but getting Keiko out of harm's way is definitely a good thing."

"Yeah." Tommy grabbed his room key and hoisted his gear bag over one shoulder. "Let's get something to eat and head out. If you're wrong and those men are heading to the mountain too, we don't want to get there second."

Ninety minutes later, the two Americans had new coats, snow pants, sunglasses, and beanies. They'd also procured a car from a rental place recommended to them by the hotel concierge. It wasn't much—a four-door compact—but it was a newer model and had some nice features, the best of which was the GPS screen built into the dash. Getting the rental car reminded Tommy that Keiko's car was now gone, something he fully intended to remedy once this was all over.

Once more, Sean and Tommy found themselves driving through the rolling evergreen mountains of northern Japan. For a while, the only sound in the car was that of the tires rumbling against the road underneath, interrupted intermittently by the clicking of the car's blinker as Tommy switched lanes to pass the occasional slower vehicle.

"Do you get scared?" Tommy asked.

His voice was a sudden change in the mesmerizing quiet of the engine's hum and the road's vibrations.

"You mean other than with heights?"

Tommy laughed, and Sean's lips parted in a smile. "Yeah, I mean like when we're getting shot at. Most people would be terrified. You never seem to be."

Sean rubbed his face in silent contemplation for a few seconds before responding. "Yeah, sure. Sometimes. Usually, I don't have time to think about stuff like that, though. Once I sense trouble, I go into survival mode. Some people switch into the flight option and run away. I switch into fight mode and try to take out the trouble. Everyone's different. You get scared?"

Tommy guffawed. "Absolutely. But I'm not gonna be a sissy and run either. Can't imagine how much crap you'd give me if I did."

Sean nodded. "That's true. I definitely would give you some grief over that." He paused and stared out the window. The evergreens and their brown trunks whizzed by in a blur. "I mean, sometimes, running is the best option."

"A tactical retreat."

"Yes. I like that," Sean gave an exaggerated nod. "A tactical retreat." He kept looking out the window as he continued. "I wouldn't be human if I weren't a little scared, Tommy. I know that you think I did all this training and it makes me more like a robot, but it doesn't work like that. You still think, still feel, still remember everything."

The car's interior returned to relative silence for the remainder of the drive. When they arrived, it was no surprise the parking area was completely vacant. A thick blanket of snow covered the ground surrounding the lot. Winter certainly wasn't the busy time of the year for people to make their pilgrimage to the sacred site. The soupy gray sky above trickled intermittent snowflakes to the ground, but nothing that would cause the visitors to worry. Every weather report they'd checked both before leaving and during their journey said that the region would only get a few flurries.

"Looks like another beautiful day here in sunny Japan," Tommy joked as he got out of the car and looked around.

Sean took in the surroundings too. The serene setting was both beautiful and desolate. With no one else around, an eerie feeling pervaded the area.

Tommy slammed his door shut. "Looks like if Taka's men are coming this way, we beat them to it."

"Which poses another problem," Sean added.

Tommy finished his thought. "Yeah. We go up there. and they arrive before we get back, we're stuck."

"Did you notice that access road on the way in?"

"Yeah. About a quarter mile back that way." Tommy pointed toward the driveway leading into the parking lot. "Think we should ditch it there?"

"Might be our best bet. There's a lot of other tracks there so if the Yakuza pass by, they might think nothing of it."

Tommy sighed at the thought of taking the car back to the side road and then walking back. Sean must have read his mind and offered a solution.

"I'll take the car back and hide it. Why don't you check out the area, scout up ahead a little. I'll be back in under ten minutes."

His friend's face visibly brightened. "OK, thanks. Will do."

Sean hopped into the driver's seat, started the car, and eased it across the snow-covered lot. It was a little less than a quarter of a mile when he saw the access road appear on the left. The single-bar gate was open with a lock and chain dangling from one end. He veered the car onto the little road and continued another hundred feet until the path curved to the left again behind a small hillside. Sean looked back through the window to make sure the car couldn't be seen from the main entrance and, satisfied it was sufficiently hidden, shut down the motor. He reached into his gear bag and pulled out the pistol and two spare magazines, stuffing the latter in opposing coat pockets.

He got out of the car and trudged through the snow back toward the gate, sniffling against the cold as he moved. To make moving easier, he walked in the path his and other tires had created, but the packed snow still crunched a little under his boots. When he reached the gate, he swung it closed and ran one part of the lock hook through the gate loop—giving the casual observer the appearance that it was locked. Satisfied with his dummy lock, Sean started toward the main entrance road when he froze in place. A familiar sound cut through the otherwise perfectly silent forest. It wasn't animal noises, it wasn't tree branches shaking from the extra burden of snow; it was the sound of vehicles coming in his direction. The noise was faint at first but grew louder by the second. And Sean was out in the open.

He turned and ran for a dip between two small rises in the land to his right. There was no time to worry about leaving fresh tracks in the snow. He'd just have to hope the passersby wouldn't notice them. His boots plowed through the powder as fast as he could drive them, while the sound of the vehicles drew ever closer. He forced himself to raise his knees high with each step to increase his speed. The sound of the cars was close now, maybe a hundred yards away. Just before they appeared around the turn near the access road, Sean dove into the snowdrift between the two little humps and disappeared from view. He didn't see the four SUVs drive by two seconds later, but he could hear their tires crunching snow along with the sound of the engines as they eased their way down the road.

Sean's heart pounded in his chest. He gasped for breath as he lay in the snow. A clump of snowflakes melted on his nose. The cold stinging sensation reminded him of when he was a child having snowball fights at school with Tommy.

Tommy, who was now surrounded by the Yakuza.

25

MOUNT HAGURO

Sean moved through the snowdrifts and trees as fast as he could without making much noise. His heart hadn't slowed down since he got up. In fact, it was beating at near capacity. He climbed over a short rise and plunged ahead, the heavy blanket of powder coming up to his knees in places.

Even though it was only a short distance back to the parking area, the going was much slower than it would have been had Sean been able to walk back on the road. He could have even jogged. But off the beaten path, he struggled to maintain a snail's pace. After five minutes of leg-burning hiking, he finally made it to the edge of the clearing. He dropped down belly first into the snow again to keep out of sight and crawled over to a nearby fir tree for cover. The skinny trunk barely provided enough width to keep him out of sight. but it would do for now. Sean peeked around the edge of the bark to see what was going on.

He expected to find Tommy being apprehended by the Yakuza, but his friend was nowhere to be found. *He must be up on the trail,* Sean thought. That would make sense since he suggested scouting ahead. A faint hope sprang up in Sean that his friend had heard the cars coming and gotten out of sight.

Sean watched from his hiding spot as the gangsters filed out of their cars. Most of them were of similar height, build, and with the shaved heads that many Yakuza sported, though upon stepping into the cold, they all put beanies on to keep warm. Sean could see that most of them were carrying Heckler & Koch MP5K submachine guns. A few had pistols. Hideo stepped out of one of the SUVs and looked around. He was wearing sunglasses, but Sean recognized him immediately. The group leader surveyed the area, trying to assess the situation, probably making sure he wasn't walking into a trap.

One more figure got out of the SUV on the nearest end. Sean didn't recognize the person, but they were slightly shorter than the rest, covered from head to toe in snow gear. They'd already put a hat on and had pulled the hood of their coat up over the beanie atop their head. From the facial structure and shape, Sean believed the person was a woman, but he couldn't tell who it was because she was also wearing sunglasses.

Hideo said something to her, and she turned to face him. A second later, she pointed at the wide staircase at the trailhead and said something back to him in Japanese. Hideo nodded and started barking out orders to the rest of the men. The woman looked around one more time, scanning the edge of the woods in a full circle. Sean retreated to the cover of the tree trunk and waited a few seconds until he believed she'd ended her search. He poked his head out again and watched her and the others begin their ascent up the steps toward the pagoda.

Sean cursed himself. If Tommy were up there on the trail, he'd be a sitting duck. Another problem came to mind too. Hideo and his men were going to beat them to the pagoda. If they reached the location first, nothing could keep them from getting whatever secret was kept in the ancient reliquary.

It wasn't until the last man disappeared over the ridge that Sean burst out of his hiding place and took off at a sprint across the parking lot. He reached the first SUV and checked inside, making sure no one had lingered behind. A quick check of the other three vehicles revealed they were empty, too. *So we're dealing with sixteen people,* he thought, recalling how many had exited the SUVs and gone up the trail. He'd been outnumbered before, but this was getting out of hand. He needed a way to thin out the herd, but for the moment his primary concern was making sure his friend was safe. Sean didn't have a clue how to do that yet. Right now the only option was to follow the group up the trail and figure out the rest once they reached the pagoda.

He ran on the balls of his feet to keep as quiet as possible, though it was an exercise in futility considering the heavy boots on his feet and the snow on the ground. Still, it was better than clomping along like a Clydesdale. Sean hurriedly climbed the wide, shallow steps, keeping close to the edge in case one of the last people in the group happened to be watching the rear. The evergreen trees that dominated the forest ran along the edge of the path, so if he had to, he could duck behind one for cover.

As he neared the top of the ridge, Sean slowed his pace and crouched low to keep out of sight. Up ahead, he saw the last man in the line disappear around a bend in the trail, reappearing intermittently among the trees before he was gone completely. The group certainly wasn't taking their time. Sean picked up the pace and jogged ahead, careful to make sure he didn't draw any attention.

He slowed to a stop at the curve and took up a position behind a nearby tree. Pressing his shoulder into it and keeping his weapon near the front of his face, Sean took a peek around the trunk. The gangsters dipped in and out of view amid the hundreds of trees. They were a good two hundred feet ahead of him, which was fine. Sean was about to leave his hiding spot when he heard the snow crunch behind him. He spun around, leading with the barrel of his gun, but his wrist was snatched and held by a firm hand. Sean's go-to move for this sort of scenario was to yank back on his arm, thereby pulling the assailant at him. Using the attacker's momentum against him, Sean would drive his opposing elbow up and into the person's throat. It was an effective move and had crippled many would-be assassins, crushing their larynx and literally leaving them breathless. But as he began to instinctively jerk his arm back, he halted the counterattack midway.

"Easy," Tommy whispered. "It's me."

Sean froze for a second, then relief filled his chest. "You shouldn't go sneaking up on people like that. Could get you killed."

Tommy snorted. "Sorry. I figured shouting at you from the trees, 'Hey, Sean! Over here!' would be less than subtle."

"True."

"What do we do now? They're going to beat us to the pagoda."

"We need to press ahead and keep them within sight. Have to see what they do next. When we get there, we can assess the situation and come up with a plan of attack."

"Attack?" Tommy looked uncertain. "You did see how many of them there were, right?"

"Yeah. But we have the element of surprise," Sean said. He winked and took off up the trail.

Tommy shook his head, bewildered, but chased after his friend. They trotted along the winding trail and slowed down when they reached another long set of stairs.

"What's with Buddhists and all these stairs?" Tommy asked, panting for breath.

"Maybe it has to do with ascending to a higher state of being," Sean said. His breathing was barely faster than normal.

"Right."

Sean started up the steps, and Tommy tagged along, pairing up with him on the other side.

"I was worried they had you pinned in," Sean whispered as they reached the halfway point of the climb.

Tommy shook his head one time. "No. I heard them coming from a mile away. First sound of a car, I took off into the woods and hid in the trees until they passed by."

"Smart."

"I have my moments."

Sean smirked and kept climbing.

At the top of the stairs, the men stopped and crouched low on the second to last step. A little over a hundred feet away, the big group was clumped together staring up at a massive five-story pagoda. Snow covered the top of it and most of the sloping, curved roofs below. Hideo was in the middle of the group, closest to the pagoda's base. The woman was next to him, bending at her knees to get a closer look at the small wooden door set into the wall.

"OK, general. We're here. Now what?"

"Honestly," Sean said, "I thought it would be a lot farther before we got here."

"How would that change anything?" Tommy asked. He kept his eyes forward and his voice low.

"It doesn't. We'll still execute the plan."

"Which is?"

"Cut the head off the snake."

Tommy finished his thought. "And the body dies. Yeah, but how do we get to Hideo? There are fifteen people between us and him."

"I'll flank him." Sean pointed to an area of forest to the left. "I'll go around and take him from the other side."

"Yeah, but they'll see you coming. You'll never make it."

Sean's eyes squinted with his grin. "That's why I'll need a diversion."

It took longer than he would have liked to circle around to the other side of the pagoda. Every time he could get a glimpse of the big group of gangsters huddling around it, Sean felt sure they could see him. But every one of them was staring at the giant structure as if trying to figure out a puzzle. Almost ten minutes later, after wading through a field of snow, Sean was on the other side of the sacred structure.

Tommy lost sight of his friend about halfway through Sean's journey. He'd been told to wait ten minutes and then get the gangsters' attention and to use whatever means necessary. He checked his watch. *Go time,* he thought. He stood up in full view of the group and waved a hand around, keeping the one holding his pistol behind his back.

"Oh, hey there, guys!" he shouted. "Mind if I crash this little party?"

Everyone in the group spun around, startled by the American's voice piercing the tranquil forest.

Hideo pointed at him and shouted something in Japanese. Tommy didn't need to speak the language to know what the words meant. He got the translation the next moment when the men spread out and started firing.

Tommy retreated down the steps for cover just as bullets zipped through the air over his head. Some clipped tree branches nearby while others splashed harmlessly into the snow near where he'd been standing.

"OK, Sean. I hope this works."

On the other side of the pagoda, Sean took off at a sluggish sprint from his hiding place. The snow was so deep it made the act of running nearly impossible. He pressed his leg muscles to their limit, going as fast as he could until he reached the clearing where the snow had been tamped down around the reliquary. He jumped up on the wooden platform at the base of the pagoda and slid around to the other side, his momentum carrying him all the way off the landing and onto the ground right behind Hideo. He popped up and pressed the muzzle of his gun to the back of the gangster's shaved head.

"Tell them to stop firing!"

The woman next to him spun around, but Sean jerked Hideo to the left in case she had any designs on taking out the American from the side. Using Hideo as a human shield, Sean wrapped his free arm around the man's neck and squeezed, keeping the gun muzzle jammed firmly against his head.

Some of the men turned at the sound of Sean's voice to see what was going on. Soon, all fourteen shooters had spun around and were facing Sean and Hideo. Every weapon was pointed at the two men.

"Tell them to drop their weapons."

"You cannot escape," Hideo answers. "Even if you take all of our guns, we will still get the sword. And you will die."

"Maybe. But I'm willing to take my chances. Do it." Sean mashed the gun harder into Hideo's temple.

The gangster winced and ordered his men to drop their weapons, barking out the Japanese words harshly as if angered to be caught in this situation. His men lowered their guns reluctantly, placing them on the packed snow at their feet. Sean motioned with his head to the left. "Tell them to go over there, away from the pagoda."

Again Hideo hesitated, so Sean gave him a little more encouragement through the pressure of cold metal against the man's head. Once more, the captive issued orders, and the men obeyed, stepping away from their weapons and over to the side of the clearing. The woman didn't move, standing still with a confused expression on her face.

Tommy appeared at the top of the steps, warily checking to make sure everything was OK. He was pleased to see all fourteen men moving to the side, completely disarmed. He quickly covered the distance between the stairs and the pagoda.

Before he could say anything, the woman took off her glasses and pulled back her hood. "Tommy, I'm so glad you're here. These men came and took me. It was awful. I think they may have killed a police officer." She was blabbering hysterically, ending her rant with "Thank you. Thank you. You saved me."

Sean stood there—still holding his prisoner—in stunned silence. He wasn't so shocked that he dropped the gun in his hand, but it was close. Feeling a little resistance from his prisoner immediately brought him back to full alert.

Shocked and suddenly relieved of a burden he didn't know he had, Tommy stepped toward her and reached out his arms. "How did they find you?"

"Yeah," Sean added. "I thought you took her someplace safe."

Sean had been a poker player for over ten years. He'd seen bluffs of every kind. His background in psychology combined with the keen ability to read body language gave him a huge advantage both at the table and away from it. As his friend moved toward the young woman, he stared at her eyes, watching them as a hunter watches his prey.

Then it happened. It was subtle, but Sean saw it. Unfortunately, his friend was moving in too fast for him to do anything about it. Keiko's eyes flashed to the gun in Tommy's hand, and then it all became clear. The gun lowered as Tommy wrapped his free hand around Keiko's waist.

"Tommy, wait!" Sean shouted. He spun Hideo to the ground and extended his pistol at the pair.

But it was too late. With swift precision, Keiko grasped the gun in Tommy's hand, twisted it sharply backward, and yanked it away. Before he could react, Tommy was twisted around with a gun muzzle jammed into the base of his skull.

In a matter of seconds, the situation had been reversed. Now Tommy was a human shield, and Keiko's little frame provided no clear shot for Sean to alleviate the problem.

"Keiko?" Tommy whined. "What are you doing?"

She didn't answer immediately, instead ordering the men to pick up their weapons. She snapped her head at the guns on the ground as she barked at them in Japanese.

The men moved quickly to reacquire their arms and surrounded the standoff, every one of them pointing their guns at Sean.

He'd had dozens of weapons trained on him before. But this was different. "Put the gun down, and no one gets hurt, Keiko." It was a desperate offer and one he didn't think would work. If he so much as twitched the wrong way, there wouldn't be much left of him when the gangsters were done unloading their magazines.

She shook her head. "You two are idiots. Do you know that?" Her voice was far more confident and commanding than before. It was as if she was a completely different person.

"Keiko?" Tommy continued to wallow in confusion. "We're on your side."

He struggled momentarily, but a quick jab in his lower back finally sent the right signal to his brain and he stood still.

"She's working with the Yakuza, buddy."

The realization was one Tommy didn't want to believe, but the pistol against the back of his skull underscored the truth. There was nothing he could do to avoid it. Keiko was Yakuza.

26

MOUNT HAGURO

Sean kept his weapon level, staring through Tommy at the woman behind him.

"Put the gun down, or I will kill him," Keiko said.

"You're going to kill us anyway. It's what your kind do."

"True. But you should cling to life as long as you can. And if you do as we say, you might get to see the Masamune before you die. It would be a great honor for you."

Tommy cut into the conversation. "You're Yakuza? Why? I don't understand."

"That's right, Tommy. She's Yakuza." He directed his next comments at her. "I knew something didn't feel right about all of this. The way your lackey here kept showing up everywhere, the easy escape we made from that factory. It all adds up. But I have to say I didn't really expect this. Not from you."

"We all have our secrets," she sneered.

"And yours is an underworld empire. Let me guess, Taka isn't the one in charge. It's you. Your story about how he killed your uncle is probably true. I believe that. You wouldn't do the dirty work yourself. Once he sent you the clue, you didn't need him anymore. So you had Taka throw him off a building."

Keiko smiled behind Tommy's back. "Very perceptive, Sean. I can see why my uncle trusted the two of you. But he was old, and the information he had could stand in our way. So yes, I had Taka eliminate a loose end. Regrettable, but it had to be done."

"You're in charge of the Yakuza?" Tommy couldn't believe it.

"That's right, buddy." Sean answered the question. "She's the one in charge. And if she gets that sword, she believes all the other clans will bow to her."

"They will," she said. "They won't have a choice."

"So you say."

"Enough talk, Sean," she barked. "Drop the gun now, or I will end your friend's life."

Sean sensed Hideo standing close by, ready to pounce as soon as Sean lowered his gun. There was nothing that could be done. It was checkmate. All they could do was surrender and see how things played out. Still, after all the games, all the misdirection, she'd allowed the two Americans to lead them to this point. That could only mean one thing: Keiko needed them. It wasn't yet clear why. But if Sean had to guess, he'd say it was for their expertise. There might still be a chance for them to get the upper hand. He would simply have to wait for that window of opportunity.

"OK," Sean said. He held up one hand and slowly lowered his weapon to the snow. His fingers released it, and a second later, Hideo lunged forward to grab it.

The gangster stepped back and pointed the pistol at Sean's head, eager to pull the trigger.

"Easy, my friend," Keiko said. "Everything is going according to plan. I'll let you kill them once we have the sword. But we may have need for these two until then."

Hideo didn't respond. Sean could sense the man's desire to pull the trigger. Even in the icy cold air, the tension was as hot as a sauna.

"Now," Keiko said shoving Tommy toward his friend. Sean caught him, and the two stood together facing the entire group of armed Yakuza. "Let's see what this thing is hiding." She waved her pistol toward the façade of the pagoda.

"What? You want us to go in there?" Sean pointed at the little wooden door. They'd have to crawl through. This time of year, he doubted there would be any spiders or other creatures he'd rather avoid; the cold made sure most of those were gone for the winter. That didn't make her request any more appealing.

"Not both of you. Tommy, you stay out here."

Tommy's eyes didn't leave her, but they'd certainly changed. No longer were they filled with confusion and hurt. Now the orbs flamed with anger and betrayal. He didn't say a word, instead saying everything with his death-like stare.

"Fine," Sean said. "Seems you hurt my friend's feelings." He took a slow step over to the timeworn door and investigated the seams to figure out how to open it. "You hurt him, you know. He liked you."

"He won't be the last, I'm sure. You American men like Asian girls. I've heard the rumors."

Sean shook his head and returned his attention to the task at hand. He spoke while he worked. "Not me. No offense, but I like Spanish women."

His fingers found a clasp on either side of the frame and with a little effort pushed them down. One more on the top, and the door nearly fell out of its housing. Sean caught it with his free hand amid a small poof of dust. Stale air escaped through the opening, filling his nostrils with the scent of time, wood, metal, and dirt: a distinct contrast from the fresh air, snow, and spruce that permeated the region.

Sean carefully placed the door to the right of the opening and looked back to Keiko for further instructions. "Now what, boss?" His tone was overly sarcastic, mostly because he didn't care at this point. And he had no intention of showing her any kind of respect.

Tommy hadn't moved an inch, and Sean was starting to get a little concerned about his friend's near-catatonic state. "You OK, buddy?" No response. After six or seven seconds, Sean said, "OK, great. You've really pissed him off. I've known this guy my whole life, and I don't know if I've ever seen him like this. Just saying he's like a boiling volcano right now."

"Shut up, and get inside," Keiko ordered, taking a step toward the pagoda's entrance.

"All righty then."

He crouched down low on all fours and crawled into the darkness. Keiko asked one of her men for his phone, and she turned on the bright LED light on the front of it before following Sean inside. It was a bold move to leave the security of her subordinates outside to enter the pagoda alone with the American. With the weapon in her hand, she didn't feel like there was any threat.

Tommy watched her disappear into the darkness, barely turning his head as she moved. Hideo followed close behind Keiko, stopping at the threshold of the opening to make sure Sean didn't try anything crazy.

"Move over to the far side," Keiko ordered and pushed herself up from the creaky wooden floorboards. She kept the weapon level, aimed straight at Sean's chest.

His hands hung by his sides as he stepped back to the far wall. A musty smell hung in the air, which was surprising considering how dry the air was. Streaks of pale sunlight leaked through narrow cracks in the wall on the left.

"Now what?" Sean asked. He kept his head still but let his eyes wander around the little room.

The interior of the pagoda was much less ornate than the exterior. Only a small shrine on the right stood out against the otherwise drab space. A single candle sat atop the miniature devotional altar. The object appeared to be made of stone but was covered in gold leaf.

Keiko looked down at the shrine. There was nothing written on it and no other items of note lying around in the room. Sean raised his eyebrows as if waiting for an explanation from her.

"Seems like maybe we're in the wrong place. Oh well." His tone didn't impress her.

Hideo crawled through the portal and moved over near the shrine. Keiko gave a nod, and he kicked the shrine over. There was nothing on the floor under it, which must have been her reasoning behind the order.

"It better not be the wrong place," Keiko said evenly. She took one step toward Sean and stopped. "Because if I think that you and your friend out there led us here, knowing all along that there was nothing to be found...well, that would be bad for you."

Sean took a long, slow breath of the stale air. "Yeah, you were the one who read that piece of Japanese on the underside of the stone lantern yesterday. So if we are in the wrong place, you've got no one to blame but yourself." He crossed his arms as if to emphatically end his comment.

Hideo was listening to the conversation, but he also scanned the room for anything that might resemble what they were looking for. Of course he had no idea what that might be, but he had no intention of letting his boss look like a fool. When he found nothing in the immediate area, his head slowly tilted up. His eyes adjusted to the darkness rapidly thanks to the slivers of light coming through the pagoda's walls.

Sean noticed him looking up and sighed. He'd already seen the object dangling from the center of the ceiling high above. And he'd noticed the notch in one of the four posts supporting the structure. It led to another board nailed to the first ceiling level about five feet up. There were several others, going all the way to the top like a sort of ladder. A very dangerous, old ladder.

Hideo pointed to the ceiling. "There," he said.

Keiko looked up and immediately saw it. A cylinder hung from a hook in the ceiling. It was attached to a frail-looking chain that connected to the tube at both ends. She lowered her gaze to Sean, and a wicked grin eased across her face. "You'll need to go get that for me."

His head moved back and forth as if he was watching the fastest tennis match ever. "Why can't he do it?" he asked, pointing at Hideo. "He's not doing anything constructive."

For a second, Keiko almost looked amused. "That's right. You have a fear of high places." She waved her pistol at the rickety first step. "Up you go. It's cold out. I'm sure your friend doesn't want to stand out there all day. And neither do my men."

Sean knew there was no getting around it. It was climb or get shot. Most of the time, he didn't mind climbing things like ladders or trees. But once he reached a point over twenty-five feet up, things started to get dicey pretty fast. This climb was definitely over twenty feet, and he wasn't going up something as secure as a ladder. He wasn't even sure how the little boards were held in place. As Sean stepped closer, he gripped the wood. The top ledge was narrow, not as wide as a two-by-four. He'd essentially be standing on his toes.

He pulled down on the board to test its durability. To his surprise, it didn't budge. Whatever means had been used to secure the piece of wood to the post, they were strong enough. At least for his arm. The real test would come when he hoisted himself up onto it. And that was the next problem. Fortunately, there was a beam going from one post to another. It looked sturdy enough to hold his weight, and he assumed it was the only way he could get up to a standing position on the narrow wooden ledge.

Sean turned one last time to Hideo, "You sure you don't want to—"

"*Now*," Keiko said, emphasizing her command by jabbing the pistol at him.

"OK. Fine." He looked up at the first support beam. *A ninja would have a hard time doing this,* he thought.

He bent both knees and jumped. His hands reached for the wooden beam, and a second later his fingers wrapped over the top of it with his palms pressed flat. Using his upward momentum, he pulled hard. His feet found the narrow ledge, and he relaxed for a moment to test the durability of the board with his arms slung over the higher beam. He drew in a breath and hauled his legs up, swinging them over the beam. Stopping in a straddling position, he let his feet dangle for a moment as he examined the step attached to the near post.

Sean checked it as he'd done with the first, making sure it was sturdy enough to support him before standing up and readying himself for the next jump. This one was more difficult because he had to balance on the eight-inch-wide beam. A wrong move here, and he'd probably twist an ankle, maybe bang his knee or elbows. Higher up, the danger would get increasingly worse.

He took a deep breath and jumped again, once more grabbing hold of the beam above, using the toes of his boots to stabilize his body and then eventually pulling himself to the next level. Sean straddled the beam as he'd done before and examined the next step. He was now at the point where his fear started to tap on his shoulder. People always told him not to look down when he was in a high place. He knew that was the best course of action, but human instinct often drove him to do the exact opposite. He couldn't help himself. Sean leaned over and looked below. *That's not too bad,* he thought, half trying to convince himself.

Pressing his palms against the beam, he shimmied closer to the post, and as he stood up, gripped it tighter than he'd done the two before. *Halfway home, Sean.* He kept his left hand against the pole to maintain his balance while he looked up at the next beam. His eyes drifted over to the cylinder hanging from the black chain in the middle of the ceiling. *How in the world did Iemasa do this?* He drew in another breath and jumped. Again, his fingers wrapped around the far edge of the next beam, and he brought his toes to the next step. His breathing picked up, and his heart rate quickened. For a second, he let his weight rest on his toes. Suddenly, his body shifted as the step under his feet broke free. Sean's arms had relaxed momentarily, and as a result he dropped a few terrifying inches before reacting and squeezing the beam tightly.

The narrow board tumbled to the floor below and smacked against the floorboards, narrowly missing Hideo as he stepped out of the way. There was no avoiding the forewarned look down now. Sean stared below for a long moment before hauling his legs up over the beam.

Stupid. He cursed himself for not checking that step. He'd gotten into the routine of the climb after just two levels. His head tilted back, and he gazed at the last beam. The cylinder was close now, looming over his head like a cookie jar on the top shelf to a seven-year-old.

"Be careful," Keiko said from below. There was no sincerity in her voice. She had plenty of other *volunteers* waiting outside who would likely be sent up the pagoda's dangerous climb should Sean fail.

He glanced down one more time. His mind played with him. Thoughts of shattered bones, falling headfirst, and breaking his neck pelted his brain like hail against a tin roof.

"Thanks," he muttered under his breath.

He double checked the step attached to the post, tugging on it hard with both hands in one direction and then the other. It seemed firm, but after what happened to the last one, Sean had already decided to pull himself up as fast as he could the second his fingers grasped the beam above.

"Don't look down," he told himself, this time taking the advice to heart and keeping his eyes locked on the wooden landing above.

He braced himself with a hand against the post and stood up. *Just like a Band-Aid,* he thought. *Just do it fast.*

Sean leaped higher than before, probably due to the adrenaline pumping through his body. He soared up to the next beam and grabbed on tight, planted his left foot on the step, and pushed while pulling with his arms. The move was his quickest so far, and he soon found himself straddling the top-tier beam. He breathed heavily, more from anxiety and fear than from the physical exertion, though the latter certainly added to it.

Only a few feet away from him, the cylinder dangled from a black iron chain, fastened with looped screws on both ends. He wrapped his right hand around the post to keep his balance and leaned out toward the cylinder. His fingers were close, but not close enough for him to grab it. He let his right hand slip a little to get closer, but it was still just out of his reach.

"Let go of the post," Keiko said from below. Her head was tilted back, and she was staring up at Sean as he stretched for the cylinder.

"You wanna come up here and do this? Be my guest!" he shouted back. In spite of the cold air, sweat trickled down the side of his forehead. "You let go," he mumbled.

She was right, though, and he knew it. He was going to have to release the post to be able to reach the tube. Sean swallowed hard and squeezed his thighs together as hard as he could against the beam. He leaned out again, this time only keeping his fingertips on the nearest edge of the post. The fingers on his left hand grasped the end of the cylinder, and he quickly flicked it up to free it from the hook in the ceiling. Thankfully, he got it loose on the first try and shifted his weight back to the right and the relative safety of the post in front of his torso.

Sean breathed heavily, and he relaxed as if a huge burden had been lifted from his shoulders. He looked down at the cylinder with curious eyes. It was made of wood, intricately carved to a near perfect shape. On one side was a symbol he'd recognized before. It was a Japanese character. Even though he didn't speak the language, he knew what it meant. It was the symbol for the Tokugawa clan.

He sighed, satisfied with the difficult task he'd just accomplished. Relief poured over him, and he sat in silence just staring at the tube. The relief was short lived, though, as a new problem presented itself.

How in the world am I going to get down?

27

MOUNT HAGURO

Getting down from the pagoda's fifth level had proved every bit as tenuous and difficult as getting up, though the downward climb was more physically taxing. Sean had resorted to the old rope climbing drill from high school. Most of the kids he hung out with couldn't climb the rope. Sean could, but he learned that getting down was just as difficult, and somewhat more terrifying. The biggest takeaway he gathered from that exercise was that he had to squeeze the rope hard and lower himself an inch at a time.

In the high reaches of the pagoda, Sean applied this same logic to the support post. While it was much thicker than a climbing rope, he simply used his arms and legs to squeeze it and lower himself a few inches at a time. He stuffed the cylinder into one of his coat pockets and buttoned it to keep the thing from falling. Then he began the descent.

Going up took less than five minutes. Getting down took almost twelve, simply because the going was much slower, and for the first two and a half levels, Sean was terrified. Once he arrived at the lowest beam, he hung from it with his hands and dropped to the floor. His heavy boots hit the wooden floorboards with a hollow thud, and he cushioned the landing with bent knees.

He swallowed and looked at Keiko, who still held Tommy's gun in her hand. The muscles in his back, arms, and legs were swollen and fatigued. They felt like heavy Jell-O.

She put her free hand out, palm up. "The cylinder."

Sean reached into his pocket and took out the object. His creative mind ran through three scenarios where he threw it into the air and attempted to take the gun away from either Keiko or Hideo, killed them both, and then ran outside to save Tommy. None of them were realistic options, and he knew that, which is why he simply handed the tube over to the young woman.

Her fingers curled around it, and she narrowed her eyes. "Back outside," she said and waved the pistol in the direction of the entrance.

"You're welcome," he said and turned away.

He hadn't realized how much warmer it was inside the pagoda until the cold mountain air hit his face again when he crawled out. Tommy was still standing rigidly with his hands by his sides, an odd mixture of being both forlorn and angry written all over his face.

"You OK, buddy?" Sean asked as he stood up and dusted the snow and dirt off his knees.

"I'm fine." His lips barely moved as he uttered the words. There was something distant about his tone and an even more distant look in his eyes.

Sean didn't express it, but he was worried about his friend. He'd never seen Tommy this way. Usually, he took everything in stride. And getting rejected by girls was something fairly commonplace, mostly because he didn't get out there and meet many and as a result didn't know how to interact well.

This was different from rejection, though. It was a betrayal. And apparently he thought there was a better chance with this one than with the others.

Sean didn't push the issue, instead standing silently next to his friend as Keiko and her assistant reappeared through the portal.

Once she was in the clear light, she motioned for the Americans to take a step back—she'd leave nothing to chance, especially after seeing what Sean was capable of firsthand.

Half of her men circled around the Americans, hemming them in a human corral full of pistols and submachine guns.

Keiko handed her weapon to Hideo and set to work opening the vial. It was small, maybe seven inches long and two inches in diameter. She recognized the symbol on the side of the tube immediately and smiled with satisfaction.

"You might want to be careful with that," Tommy blurted out. His voice was cold and uncaring in spite of the warning.

She looked up from her task with a scowl. "And why is that?"

He shrugged. "Sometimes those little things have the worst booby traps. Could be full of acid gas or something. You never know."

Her eyes narrowed as she searched his face for the truth. She only paused for a moment as she studied the caps on both ends. The chain dangled loosely from the cylinder. After a moment's thought, she squeezed one cap with her fingers and twisted.

To her relief, the end of the tube unscrewed easier than she'd expected. She'd figured it would be on much tighter for any number of reasons. With the cap off, she let it fall, hanging low near her shins since it was still attached to the other end.

Inside the vial was a delicate piece of parchment, rolled up into a tiny scroll. She turned the tube upside down and let the paper fall into her hands.

Tommy and Sean both winced at the reckless treatment of such a historic and fragile document. Tommy swallowed hard, hoping the thing wouldn't crumble in her gloved hand.

"Be careful with that," he said. "One wrong move, and that little piece of paper will fall apart."

He had no way of knowing that since he didn't truly know how old the document was, but Tommy always erred on the side of caution when it came to historic evidence.

She ignored him and unrolled the parchment, only being mildly cautious as she did so. Holding it at both ends, Keiko examined the surface of the sheet with curious and confused eyes. After a few minutes of failing to comprehend what she was looking at, she turned the scroll toward the two Americans and held it up for them to see.

"What is this?" she asked.

Two of her men stepped to the side to give them a better view.

"Looks like a map," Sean said.

"I know it's a map, idiot. But a map of what?"

"If I had to guess," Tommy jumped in, "I'd say it looks like a treasure map."

Keiko's eyes roared. She turned to the man closest to Sean and nodded. The gangster immediately raised his pistol and pointed it at Tommy's head.

"Jeez, you are impatient," Sean said. "Take it easy." He held both hands out in front of him. "If I had to guess, I'd say it looks like a cave map. Wouldn't you say that's about right, Tommy?"

Tommy responded with a slow nod. "Yep. Definitely looks like a subterranean drawing of some kind."

"How do you know that?" she demanded.

Tommy swallowed before answering. He pointed at the sheet. "You can tell because it isn't a two-dimensional drawing. The lines are in two dimensions, but there are up and down directions indicated by these dots. Of course that's just an assumption, but I'd say that means whoever made this was trying to tell whoever found it that this path isn't just two directions. You have to go down, up, left, and right. In our experience, that's usually a cave."

"And believe me," Sean added, "we've seen our share of caves. I'm kind of getting tired of them to be honest."

"Shut up," Keiko ordered. She turned her attention back to Tommy. "Where is this cave?"

Tommy leaned forward to get a better look at the parchment. His head went back and forth. "I have no idea. That's Japanese there on the side. You tell us what it says."

"It's a riddle," she answered. "It says, 'To the sky you have risen, and to the earth you descend.'"

"Sounds like a cave to me."

Sean's eyebrows furrowed. "It doesn't give a name of a cave, a tunnel, a mountain, any sort of location? Nothing?"

"No. It's just another riddle."

"Well, without knowing where to go next, I'd say that map is pretty much useless," Tommy said. He jabbed an irritated finger at the scroll. "There's only a few thousand caves here in Japan, and all kinds of treasure hunters from all over the world have scoured them in search of the Masamune. So good luck with that."

Hideo didn't need a signal from his boss. He raised his pistol and aimed it straight at Tommy's face. When he spoke, his tone was cold and matter-of-fact. "Then we have no further use for either of you."

Sean eased one foot in front of the other and stood between his friend and the barrel. He remained cool on the outside, even though his heart pounded deep in his chest. "You guys need to settle down with all the threats. That's, like, six times you all have pointed those guns at us in the last five minutes, not counting when we were inside the pagoda there. If you want to shoot us, go ahead and shoot us, but if you do, you won't find what you're looking for."

Keiko's eyes narrowed again. "So you know where this cave is?"

"I didn't say that. I'm not saying that."

"What are you saying?"

Hideo answered for Sean. "He's wasting our time, like a dog begging for one more treat, he's trying to stall to get in a few last breaths of life. This American doesn't know anything."

"Like a dog?" Sean tilted his head to the right. "Now see, that's just insulting and quite frankly unnecessary."

"Shut up! All of you!" Keiko raged. "Enough games, Sean. Tell me where the cave is. *Now.*"

Sean didn't say anything at first. He just stared back at the entryway of the pagoda. It was a hunch, really. He didn't know for sure if the cave entrance was there. But it was in keeping with the riddle and some of the other signs he'd noticed when they were inside: the dry air but musty smell, the hollow thud when his boots hit the floorboards as he dropped from above, and then the clue, "to the earth you descend." If the clue were talking about rising to the sky and descending to the earth, why would those two things have to happen in separate places? Sean saw a flicker of movement in the trees off to his left. Had anyone else noticed it? From their lack of reaction, the answer was a clear *no*. He shook his head slowly back and forth, signaling to whoever was out there. He had an idea who it might be, but there was no way to be sure. Sean found himself in an odd place, hoping it was Aoki's man hiding in the trees.

It took Keiko a moment before she realized what Sean was insinuating. When it hit her, she turned her head to follow the line of his gaze back into the dark interior of the pagoda.

Tommy glanced at his friend out of the corner of his eye. Part of him hoped Sean was right. Part of him didn't care if all of them went out in a blaze of glory right now with fists and bullets flying.

Hideo looked in the direction Keiko and Sean were looking, and more than a few of the other men did the same.

"If I had to guess," he said, "I'd say we were just standing right on top of it."

28

MOUNT HAGURO

The floorboards inside the pagoda didn't come up easily despite being held in place by very old wooden pegs. Finally, Sean had the idea of breaking through the boards instead of pulling them up. He and Tommy cringed at the idea of wrecking a historic national monument, but from the looks of it not many people went inside. And when the next monk finally did come for a visit, he'd likely think the floor rotted away.

Sean stared at the floor. "We need a big rock. As big a rock as three or four of your men can carry."

Keiko gave the order, and four of her men disappeared into the woods. Several minutes later they returned with a huge stone that probably weighed 150 pounds. It was covered in mud and snow.

Tommy wondered how they'd dug it out of the ground, but it was a pointless question to ask.

"They'll need to take it inside. If I were to guess, I'd say dropping it dead center would be best. It should be the weakest point, and that rock will go right through."

"You hope," Tommy said.

"Well, it's not perfect. Might take a couple of tries. But I'm pretty sure there's an empty space under that floor."

"And if you're wrong?"

Sean shrugged and smiled at his friend. "It's been a good one."

Tommy sighed. "I wish I could be so laid back about it."

Sean glanced over at his friend with a smug expression. "The cave is there. What you need to be thinking about is how we're going to get out of this mess once we find whatever's down there."

"Isn't that usually your department?"

"I'll be pondering it too. Just keep your eyes open."

Keiko's men set the stone down on the floor just outside the doorway. Two of them squatted behind it and shoved the rock, moving it back and forth to work it over the threshold. Once it was far enough through, the same two men crawled inside while a third continued to push from the outside. After another few seconds of work, he joined the other two on the inside, and the three men hefted the heavy object off the ground once more. They heaved and grunted, raising it up to about chest level, and then when one gave the signal they simultaneously released the rock.

The thing crashed through the floor, splintering the aged boards as if it were made of toothpicks. Keiko's three men all jumped back to avoid the debris. A massive cloud of dust erupted from the damaged floor and rolled out of the reliquary's entrance.

Hideo and Keiko both took several steps back to avoid inhaling the dirty air or being covered in dust. All eyes focused on the darkened doorway until the dust settled a few minutes later.

After a dramatically long wait that seemed to last an eternity, one of the men inside shouted. His words came out in a frantic rush. Sean and Tommy didn't know exactly what he was saying, but from his excitement they figured there was something of interest under the pagoda's floor.

Keiko turned to the two Americans with a slightly impressed look on her face. "It would seem you were correct. There's a hole in the floor that drops down into the mountain. He says it's not man-made."

Sean's know-it-all expression beamed. "You should know better than to doubt me."

Keiko's eyes closed slowly and reopened. "Perhaps. But if there is nothing down there and this proves to be a waste of time, you will suffer."

"Way ahead of you, sister," Tommy chimed in.

Sean made an offer he knew wouldn't work. "Tell you what. Let us go down there and check it out. If everything is safe and there's something worth seeing, we'll come back and get you."

She laughed in his face. "My man says there are grooves cut into the rock; a ladder of sorts. We'll all go down there together. I suggest you don't try anything foolish."

"Foolish? That doesn't sound like us."

Keiko turned and started snapping out orders to her men. The three inside the reliquary took phones out of their coat pockets and turned on the LED lights. Two stood near the hole while the third hovered over the opening. He lowered himself through the shattered boards and disappeared into the cave as the other two watched. A moment later, the man in the hole shouted something back up to the others.

"He says there's a tunnel," Keiko translated. She ordered the other two men into the cave and then turned back to the Americans. "You're going in next."

Back inside the reliquary, Sean and Tommy stared into the cavity at their feet. The cave definitely was a natural occurrence, about six feet in diameter with jagged edges of rock jutting toward the middle from every side. The first three men to enter waited below, their phones shining a bright corona of light onto the ladder cut into the stone. The steps were cut about four to five inches deep, and nearly that high, to make climbing up or down easier. This time of year, the air was much drier than normal, so getting up and down wouldn't be a problem. However, in the wetter seasons, Sean had experienced his own problems with caves that had vertical entrances.

As he climbed down the steps, Sean noted the raised bump along the edge of each step. Whoever had carved the rock ladder had possessed the foresight to include a lip to make gripping with fingers easier. *Smart.*

He stepped off the ladder and eased his way toward the three men standing in the dark with their lights and guns pointed at him. His hands remained palms out by his sides to make sure they didn't think he was going to try anything. Even so, the three took a collective step backward just to be safe.

Tommy made his way quickly down the ladder and stood next to Sean, staring at the three men. "What do you think? We take them right now?"

The three guys looked at them suspiciously. They obviously didn't speak English, which Tommy assumed to be the case.

Sean snorted. "Yeah, if we had a diversion, absolutely. As it is, pretty sure we'd be dead."

"I dunno. They don't look so tough to me." Tommy eyed them with disdain.

"Step back," Keiko's voice came from behind on the stairs.

Sean looked over his shoulder at her and complied, moving forward two steps to keep out of her way. Hideo came down next, and after a few minutes all but two of the Yakuza had joined them in the cave tunnel. Sean didn't need to ask where the other two were or why they weren't coming down. He assumed Keiko had left them up in the reliquary to keep watch in case someone else showed up. He hoped if someone did, that it wasn't a pilgrim showing up to worship. Then Sean's mind snapped back to the person in the trees. If it was Aoki's guy, he might be able to overpower the two guards above. Of course, the young Yakuza hadn't been difficult for Sean to overpower, so maybe he was stretching his hopes a bit.

Keiko cut off his thoughts. "Move, gentlemen. I'd prefer to get out of here before it gets dark."

The three in front went ahead, shining their lights into the darkness. Sean and Tommy didn't dare make a move for their phones. They knew better. Doing something like that would look suspicious and they'd been in enough sticky situations to know what actions to avoid.

"Another cave," Sean muttered to his friend.

"Most of the lost relics and artifacts in the world are found in caves. They make for great hiding places."

The tunnel bent to the left and then back to the right, descending down at a gentle slope. The walls were wet, and the rock floor was slick from water trickling down from the ceiling. At first, the corridor was narrow, only four or five feet wide. As the group continued, though, they found that it opened wider. More and more natural cave formations began appearing. Stalactites and stalagmites dripped from the ceiling or grew from the floor next to the walls in their seemingly infinite journey to the opposite.

The passageway suddenly opened up into a large room, full of the calcified formations. And for the first time upon entering the cave, a problem presented itself to the gangsters. There were two new tunnels imbedded in the far wall.

"So," Sean piped up, "which way should we go?" He unzipped his coat and stretched his neck to the left and right.

One thing he'd learned a long time ago was that the temperature in caves was much more consistent than above ground. Sure, it was cool, usually in the high 50s Fahrenheit, but in this case it was much warmer than where they'd been.

Keiko pulled the scroll out of her coat pocket and examined it. Uncertain about what to think, she passed it to Tommy, all the while keeping her gun pointed at him. "Tell me. Which way do we go?"

Sean could tell his friend wanted to tell her where to shove that map, but he resisted, instead taking it reluctantly from her fingers and prying it open. He was much more careful with the document than she'd been. The respect and care for a historic document was imbedded in him.

He and Sean eyed the sheet. Sean traced a finger along the drawing from where he assumed they'd begun and then stopped where two lines forked out away from the first.

With a huge layer of sarcasm, he spoke up. "Well, looks to me like this tunnel goes in two directions from here."

Tommy couldn't hold back the snort of laughter as his friend overstated the obvious.

"Before you go pointing that gun at me again," Sean stopped her, "I'd guess we have to make a difficult decision at this point."

"What do you mean?" she asked. Her eyes were slits, concealing the irritation behind them.

"Well, you see," Sean pointed at the line to the right, "this one represents what I think will be a difficult journey. That is illustrated by the jagged drawing. Usually in history when a line is jagged, say, on a cave drawing or an ancient scroll of some kind, it means there are tough times ahead. Whereas this line is smoother, but it appears that taking it will cost us quite a bit more time." He pointed at the other one that was smoother but looked like it went up and down with dots and circled around to where the lines joined again.

She drew in a breath and sighed, pondering the options.

"Which will it be, boss lady?" Tommy asked. "Short and tough or slow and easy?"

Keiko looked up after a long moment of silent thought. "You decide." She aimed her weapon at his forehead. "Which way would you go?"

"I like things to be nice and easy, usually," he answered. "Although most of my paths in life seem to be fairly difficult. It depends on what the trouble might be if we take the shortcut. There could be any number of dangers, even traps of some kind."

"But?"

He shrugged. "But in the interest of saving time, it might be the best thing to do. You said you want to get back up to top level before it gets dark. Time goes by pretty fast down here, so saving as much as we can is probably for the best."

He could tell she was assessing his answer.

"For the record," Sean chimed in again, "I agree with him. We should take the shortcut."

His reason for the comment was less about saving time and more about hoping they could find a way to use whatever danger the path provided, against the Yakuza.

"Very well. We will go that way." She nodded at the three men who'd been leading the way, and they took off toward the tunnel on the right. She peered at the Americans through wary eyes. "But if you're thinking of leading us into some kind of trap—"

"Yeah, yeah, we're gonna pay. We get it," Sean finished her sentence, which only served to irritate her further. Without saying anything else, she spun around and motioned for them to go ahead of her.

The tunnel narrowed considerably just a few feet beyond the entrance. And the ground was much wetter, with pockets of mud and silt here and there. They were fortunate to be wearing boots suitable for snow; otherwise normal shoes would be completely ruined in the filth. The passage cut to the left, then right, down, and then back up until the group reached a wall about five minutes into their journey. A piece of the ceiling had collapsed in front of it and provided a step up to a shelf atop the barrier. The first three men clambered up and over the edge. Two of them went ahead while the third waited for the Americans, shining a light on the surface so they could see. He also made sure to keep his gun trained on them.

Sean hopped up onto the landing and then pulled himself up to where the gangster was waiting. The man cautiously took a step back as Sean joined him. Tommy followed immediately and waited atop the plateau for further instructions.

Keiko said some words to the man watching the two Americans. Whatever it was, he relayed it to the others who'd already gone over the other side. For a moment there was no answer. Sean and Tommy glanced at each other with curious expressions.

"Where'd they go?" Tommy whispered.

"Down there," Sean pointed into the darkness. "I guess they decided to scout ahead."

The lights the men had been using were gone, replaced by a complete void. Then the sound of water splashing echoed through the pitch black and reverberated up to the shelf where the Americans were standing.

"Was that water?" Sean asked.

"Sounds like it. I have a bad feeling about this."

"Quiet!" Keiko shouted and then said something in Japanese to the guy with the Americans.

The man chirped back a reply and glanced over the far edge to see if there was any sign of the other two. A second later, lights began dancing off the walls of the narrow passage. The first of the two appeared with a forlorn look on his face. The other followed shortly behind with a similarly distraught expression.

The first shook his head and said something quickly to the middle man, who relayed the information to Keiko. She frowned at what she'd heard. Then she turned to Hideo and asked him something. Her right-hand man shrugged and pointed at the Americans.

"Have them check it out," he said in English.

"Have us check out what?" Tommy asked. He didn't like the sound of that. Usually, when a bad guy wanted to send one of the good guys in to do something, it was because they weren't sure the situation was safe. Better to lose expendable strangers.

"It appears there is an underground river just beyond a turn in the tunnel ahead. The ceiling drops down into the water so the only way to get through is to swim. One of you is going to go through and see what's on the other side."

Both Americans balked at the idea.

Sean spoke up first. "That water has to be way too cold. Even if we make it to the other side and back, we'll die of hypothermia. You need special gear to do a job like that, preferably a dry suit."

"Yeah, not a good call," Tommy said. "Not to mention we don't know how far it is to the other side, and once we get there we won't be able to see what's there."

Hideo fished a flashlight out of his coat pocket and tossed it up to Tommy, who fumbled it for a second before securing it out of the air.

He turned his head and glanced questioningly at Sean.

Before he could say anything, Sean turned his attention back to Keiko. "Why don't we take the other route? That way no one has to die. Say I make it to the other side of the wall down there. OK, great. Now what, you're all going to come through? Not a chance. Some of your men will drown. And those who don't will freeze to death. Including you," he jabbed a finger at her. "Might be a good idea if we turn back and take the long way."

She started to object, but he cut her off. "I know you want to save time, so you may as well start marching because the longer we stand here and debate about it, the darker it's going to be when we get back topside."

Keiko stared at him for a long moment, assessing his statement.

"If it makes you feel better," Sean added, "Tommy and I can run ahead of the rest of you and check it out. You know, make sure everything's clear."

She sneered at him and started barking out orders for the others. The men in the rear spun around and started trudging back the way they'd come. The one with Sean and Tommy on the shelf jabbed Sean in the back with his gun.

"OK, OK. I got ya. We're heading the other way." He looked down at Keiko, who was steaming like a cup of hot tea on a cold winter morning. "I don't know why you look so angry. You're making a good decision here."

He could tell she couldn't wait to kill him. He'd seen that look before when his sarcastic wit started to rub to the bone. He'd gone beyond that, grating on every last nerve she had. In some cultures, sarcasm didn't translate so well from English to another language. In the case of Keiko, she knew enough to understand fully.

Sean hopped down from the plateau and marched ahead. Tommy followed behind, passing the female gang leader and her henchmen to catch up with his friend. When he did, he whispered to Sean in a tone only the two of them could hear.

"Nice work getting us out of that. I guess you bought us some time."

"Yeah," Sean said. He glanced over his shoulder and then diverted his eyes straight ahead. "I just wish I knew how much."

29

MOUNT HAGURO

After making their way back up to the fork in the cave, the group turned right and filed into the other passage. Like the other corridor, it was narrow and descended downward —at a much steeper angle at first—before sloping up again. The tunnel then bent to the left, taking them farther away from where they assumed their destination would be, at least based on their previous direction.

Sean considered jumping the guy in front of him, bashing the man's skull against the jagged rock wall, taking his gun, and blasting his way out. He immediately discounted the notion. By the time he'd wrested the gun from the unconscious gangster, Tommy—behind him—would have been shot dead, followed shortly by Sean. As much as he hated waiting, Sean was good at it. He had a fisherman's patience, which probably came from years of fishing with his Uncle Ben when he was younger.

The first time he'd ever gone out with his bushy-bearded uncle, the biggest lesson young Sean learned was patience. They'd stood there for hours on the banks of a small lake in the mountains of East Tennessee. The day had grown long, and dusk was approaching, as were a legion of dark, roiling clouds. Of course, Ben had been catching fish all day. Brim and largemouth bass were champing at the bit to get a taste of what he offered on his line. Meanwhile, Sean barely had a nibble. The raindrops started pecking away at the rippling water at first—a sprinkled warning of what was about to come. Sean turned to Ben and asked if they should go, but his uncle shook his head. The words his uncle said to him at that moment carried with Sean all his life, and likely always would.

"Just give it a little more time. If you're patient, your chance will come."

As if said by a prophet from the Bible, mere minutes later Sean saw the bobber on his fishing line dive beneath the surface. He was so excited, it was all he could do to not panic and jerk the rod back. But he didn't. Remembering what Uncle Ben had told him before, he suppressed the adrenaline and calmly twisted the rod's tip to the right and began reeling it in.

Sean's parents had already left the camping area to head home. But as his uncle guided the jeep down the mountain in a deluge that would have impressed even Noah, there was nothing that could squelch the pride on Sean's face.

He recalled the event as the group continued their march through the cave's eerie darkness. *Just give it a little more time,* he recited Ben's words in his head. *Your chance will come.*

The path started to curve back to the right but again veered left, sending the group back off course. After fifteen minutes of hiking, Keiko yelled out an order for the men in front to stop.

Sean and Tommy turned around, wondering what the problem could be.

"What now?" Sean asked.

"We are going the wrong way," Keiko answered.

"This is the only way. Unless you want to go back and risk drowning or freezing to death."

She shook her head. "The direction we were going before was far away from this."

Sean risked getting shot and took a step toward her. "Give me the map," he said, holding out his hand.

Keiko hesitated for a moment. She deliberated and then finally passed it over to him. Sean held it up and pointed to the line representing the path they were on. "See here?" he asked. "This thing circles all the way around. I told you it would take longer to go this way. But we'll get there."

He analyzed the drawing and then said, "It looks like we are close to here," he tapped the paper. "Which means we don't have far to go. OK?" He shoved the scroll back into her hand and turned around to start marching again.

Keiko said nothing but motioned for her men in front to once again begin moving. The path wound its way back to the right after another three minutes of walking. Both the Americans were surprised at how smooth the floor was. It had bumps, crevices, and cracked spots, but for the most part it was an easy walk. Most of the mud had been closer to the cave entrance, leaving them an easier task of navigating the damp rock underfoot.

Eventually, the tunnel opened up into another room. At first it was difficult to see how large the space was. The darkness engulfed the tiny phone lights like a sea monster swallowing a rowboat. The LEDs did little to penetrate the black air, only brushing the nearest walls a few dozen feet away. When everyone had arrived in the middle of the room, the combined power of the lights made seeing the surroundings easier, but still their beams didn't touch the farthest reaches of the enormous cavern.

The room was an huge natural formation. More stalactites and stalagmites surrounded the group on all sides, these much longer and taller than those they'd seen previously. A musty scent of old water and ancient rock filled the air. It was a smell all caves seemed to possess, at least in Sean's experience. The faint sound of rushing water filled the room, a signal that the other tunnel was somewhere nearby. Sean couldn't help but wonder how much shorter the other route was. In spite of his curiosity, he hoped he and his friend didn't get to find out.

Keiko's men fanned out to investigate the area while she and Hideo kept a close eye on the two Americans. The men continued to spread out, inspecting the walls and corners of the room. One of them shouted something back at Keiko.

"He says this room just keeps going," she translated for Tommy and Sean.

She stared wide eyed at the incredible work of nature. It was obvious that being from the city, she'd probably never seen anything like this in her life. Most of the men probably hadn't either.

"What's that?" Tommy blurted. He pointed to something in the far left corner of the room.

A second later, the man closest to it turned around and shouted back.

Sean's heart pounded a little faster. It always did whenever he and Tommy found something of historical significance, especially something that had been hidden from the world for a long time.

Keiko turned to Hideo. "Watch these two," she said.

He nodded, and she trotted over to where the anomaly had been spotted. Her man was standing over something with a glittering surface, staring down at it. She slowed to a stop next to him and shone her light at the object.

She looked back at Hideo and ordered him to bring the Americans over to her.

"You heard her," Hideo said. He wagged his pistol to reiterate the command.

The two friends walked slowly toward her as several of the other gangsters were starting to hover around the area as well.

"It's a shrine," she said, pointing down.

The shrine was diminutive, only a few feet tall. It consisted of a torii with faded greenish beams supporting a red one over top of the gate. Underneath the crossbeam, a golden Buddha statue sat smiling at the first light it had probably seen in over seventy years.

"Yep, it's a shrine all right," Tommy agreed. "Now what?"

"You tell me," Keiko demanded. "Where is the sword?"

"If I may venture a guess," Sean piped in, "I'd say it's not here. But before you get all huffy and puffy, maybe we should take a look."

He took a step forward with all eyes on him and knelt down at the little place of prayer. A half-burned candle was positioned next to the idol. It likely hadn't been burned since the person who placed it there had visited.

"It's another shrine to the god of the mountain," Tommy said. "Common in these parts of the country, as we discussed before. Although I've never heard of one being placed in a cave like this, I'm sure it's not the first." He scratched his chin. "Kind of poetic, actually, that they would place it here."

"What do you mean?" she asked.

"Whoever placed this here wanted to put it close to the heart of the mountain. If there is or was something here, it must have been extremely important."

"The Honjo Masamune," she whispered.

"Maybe," Sean interrupted. "Or maybe it's just another clue."

He tilted the base of the little statue back by pinching the head and pushing. Underneath it, a new object came into view in the sterile glow of the phone lights. He reached out and picked up the golden disk.

"What is that?" Keiko asked, instantly curious.

"It's a coin of some kind." Sean knew she was going to take it from him so he took as many mental photos as he could.

The golden disk was about an inch in diameter and maybe an eighth of an inch thick. On one side, a picture of a building was engraved into the surface. It was framed by another torii, as if the artist was standing in the perfect position to create that view. The other side featured a short sequence of characters that Sean couldn't read. In spite of that fact, he was awed by the incredibly intricate craftsmanship of the engraver. Every character was perfect and all of equal size.

"Give it to me," Keiko interrupted Sean's moment of admiration.

He pressed the coin into her palm and took a step back. Two men were behind him against the wall. The rest were surrounding Keiko and Tommy. *Right about now would be a good time for a diversion.* He wished he had one of those flash bang disks from his friend at

DARPA, but the few he'd brought along on the trip were up in the reliquary.

"There's some stuff on the back I couldn't read, obviously," Sean said.

Keiko went over the lines and then translated. "Find the master, and recite the prayer of power."

Sean and Tommy twisted their heads toward each other. Their faces mirrored an expression of sarcastic curiosity with lips puckered and eyes wide.

Sean looked back at Keiko. Her face was almost ghost-like in the creepy darkness. "Well, what do you know? Another riddle. That's interesting." He laid the sarcasm on thick. Based on the bewildered, drawn expression on her face, Sean could tell that coin had just bought them some more time. Keiko had no idea what it meant.

Again, she pointed her weapon at Sean. "Where is this place, the one on the coin? What is it?"

"Looks like a shrine. Could be any of them. Your country's got, like, a thousand or something crazy. So who knows?"

Keiko's facial muscles relaxed, and she cocked her head to the side. "Well, I guess we won't need you anymore."

Her finger tensed on the trigger. Sean could see it start to pull back, and he readied himself for the blast.

"No, wait," Tommy stepped between the two. "We can figure it out." He held his hands up at shoulder level. "If you kill us, you'll never get the sword. We just need some time. And you're going to have to let us contact our research team back in Atlanta."

She shook her head. "Not a chance. You must think I'm stupid."

Tommy tilted his head to the side and started to say, "Well..." but he refrained. Sean listened to his friend as he pled their case.

"Maybe our friends in Atlanta can figure this out for us. But only they can do it. They have access to software that can cross-reference every known shrine in the area with the image on that coin. But we're going to have to call them." He paused for a second and added, "And we're going to need a computer to send them an image of the coin."

Keiko considered the proposal. The Americans knew it was a long shot. Any number of things could go haywire if they were permitted to call anyone. All it would take was a word and wherever they were would be crawling with police. While Keiko had a good number of the police in Tokyo on her payroll, out here in the northwest her resources were limited.

She passed the coin over to Hideo. "Do you recognize this place?" Keiko asked. She kept her eyes on the Americans, staring at them with a gaze that told them if her second in command did know, they would both die right here in the cave.

Hideo analyzed it carefully as one of the other men held a light over it to give him a better view. He flipped it back and forth, inspecting the image and the writing. The seconds ticked by like a sledgehammer on an anvil. Sean and Tommy both prayed silently that the gangster had no clue what he was looking at. The smug expression of confidence on Keiko's face didn't exactly give them a great deal of hope.

Finally, after what seemed like days, Hideo passed the disk back to his boss and shook his head. "Sorry, madame. I don't know where that is. I've seen several shrines, but I don't recall that one."

The Americans didn't sigh, instead keeping their feelings hidden. But inside, they were flooded with relief.

Keiko's face drooped with disappointment. "Shame," she said. "I was hoping to get rid of this excess baggage right here. Looks like you two will have a little more time to live. But don't worry, you'll meet your end soon enough. We will return to the city. When we get there, you will call your team in the United States. If you utter a single word that is suspicious, or doesn't have anything to do with the image on this coin or the writing on it, you will die. If you mention anything about needing help, calling the police, or any words other than getting the location of this shrine, I will kill you myself. Are we clear?" Her voice echoed through the massive chamber and faded off into the abyss.

The two friends nodded slowly.

"Good. Now move. I'm growing tired of this ridiculous puzzle."

She said a few words to the men in the rear, and they immediately spun around and started back toward the tunnel. Sean and Tommy simultaneously turned their heads toward each other and exchanged relieved yet questioning glances, as if to say, "What do we do now?"

As the big group made their way back through the pitch-black passage, Sean continued to wonder where the person was that he'd seen in the forest. If it was Aoki's guy, why hadn't he done anything yet? Maybe he was waiting for the perfect moment. If he kept waiting, the moment would never come. But after the group reached the rock ladder, climbed back up to the reliquary, and were back out in the cold, dry air, no rescue had come. The two guards left at the pagoda were clearly tired of being in the frigid air, but they reported seeing nothing out of the ordinary.

They trudged through the snow, back down the trail to the parking area, and still Sean saw no sign of the mysterious figure. His head turned back and forth as he searched the trees but found nothing.

Tommy noticed what his friend was doing. He could tell Sean was looking for something but what it was, he didn't know. "What are you looking for?" he whispered as they descended the final steps to where the first vehicle was parked.

Sean shook his head. "Nothing." He was bewildered but kept his composure. "Just hoping for a miracle."

30

SENDAI

The Americans weren't surprised to discover that the hotel Keiko's men were in was only a few blocks away from where they'd been originally staying. When the convoy of Yakuza vehicles arrived back in the city, they filed their way into the rear parking area, which was a six-story garage filled with cars. The first men out swept the area to make sure no random people were milling about and then returned to give the all-clear.

Entering the building was quick and efficient. No one seemed to pay any notice to the group, and if they did, they probably knew better than to draw any attention to themselves.

Keiko left the majority of her men in the SUVs, choosing to only bring Hideo and two others into the hotel for additional security. It wouldn't make much sense to bring more than a dozen people into the building. If no one was suspicious before, they certainly would be if they saw a group that size enter.

For as innocent as she'd played during her little ruse, Keiko had turned out to be a cunning villain. She didn't make many mistakes, which was beginning to concern Sean.

Once they were in the hotel, she nodded at Hideo and ordered him to set up a laptop. The shaved-headed man nodded curtly and stepped over to a corner near the window where a black bag sat on the floor. He picked it up and pulled out the computer, set it on the desk, and flipped it open. The screen flickered to life, and after he entered the access password he stepped off to the side.

Until that moment, Keiko had concealed her weapon inside her coat. She brandished it again as one of her men helped her remove her outer layers since there was no need for winter wear in the warmth of the hotel room. She was wearing a tight T-shirt with a skull on the front. For the first time, the Americans noticed the top portions of her gang tattoos peeking out from under the shirt's collar. It was the telltale sign of the Yakuza. While they had room for personal expression, there was a uniformity to all the body art the gang required of its members.

Tommy noted the splotches of ink on her skin but said nothing. He was disgusted now more than anything, though anger still boiled inside of him. Part of it was due to the fact that he'd been so blind. But Sean had been fooled too, and that was no easy task. He consoled himself with that reminder, telling himself that if Sean couldn't see it coming, no one could.

She nodded at Tommy. "Well?"

He shrugged. "Well, what?"

"Call your friends. But remember what I said. If you try anything, say anything I don't approve of, I will kill you right here."

Tommy snorted and called her bluff. "You're not going to fire that thing in this room. Everyone on this entire floor would hear it. The place would be crawling with cops within five minutes."

She raised her eyebrows as if to say, "Really?" Her free hand reached out to the side with palm up. One of the other henchmen reached into his coat pocket and produced a suppressor. He placed it in her hand, and within twenty seconds the silencer was fitted into place. Her face tightened with menace. "No one will hear a thing," she said.

Tommy pursed his lips and nodded. "Right."

He slid into the chair and checked out the computer. Then he turned back to her. "I'm going to need my phone. They may not answer if they don't recognize the number. But if they see it's me, they will pick up right away."

The gangsters had taken the Americans' phones earlier as a safety precaution before loading them into the SUVs at Mount Haguro. Keiko drew in a long irritated breath and then turned to one of the men and gave him an approving nod. She said something in Japanese, which must have meant, "Give him his phone," because the guy reached into an inner pocket and pulled it out.

Tommy eyed her suspiciously as he tapped the contact for the laboratory in Atlanta. He didn't even think to consider what time it was back on the East Coast. They would be nearly a day behind, so he figured Tara and Alex would be in the building, as they almost always were.

Tommy put the device on speaker to alleviate Keiko's suspicions during the conversation. The phone only rang twice before Tara picked up.

She answered in her usually perky voice. "Hey, Tommy, what's up?"

"Hey, Trouble, Sean and I are doing fine over here. We just needed to ask you a question about something we found."

Tara paused for a second and then responded. "OK, what can we do for you?"

"I'll just cut through the chase since I know you're busy and we'd really like to figure this out quickly."

Keiko's eyes narrowed, but she said nothing.

Tommy continued. "We found a golden disk in a cave out in the northwestern mountains here in Japan."

"A golden disk?"

"Yeah. It's a coin of some type, but we've never seen anything like it."

They could hear her pecking away at her keyboard through the speaker. "And you say you found it in a cave?"

"Yep. It has some writing on the back that we've already translated, but the image on the surface is a little confusing. We think it's a clue as to where we're supposed to go next, but we have no idea where it is."

"OK. What's the image?"

"I'm going to take a picture of it and send it to you. Give me a second."

"Okeydokey. I'm ready."

Tommy looked up at Keiko and put out his hand, demanding the coin. She glared at him, surprised by what seemed like a sudden change of plans. He was insistent with his tone. "I have to send them a picture, or none of this works," he whispered.

"What was that?" Tara asked.

"Nothing, just talking to myself. I have the coin here somewhere. Just trying to remember which pocket."

Sean watched the entire thing transpire. His friend was handling himself well under the circumstances. And Sean continued to keep an eye open for a chance to take the weapon from Hideo, who stood only a few feet away with eyes locked on him.

Keiko relented and withdrew the coin from her pants pocket. She handed to him cautiously, like a zookeeper tossing a T-bone to a lion, and then stepped back.

Tommy nodded graciously, opened up the photo app on his phone, and snapped a quick picture. A few taps of the screen later, and the image zipped away to Tara's email.

"I just sent it to your email," he said.

A ding came through from the other end of the line, telling everyone that the email had arrived.

"Got it," she said.

The keyboard clicked several times again before she spoke up. "Wow. That is incredible. You've got that thing right now?"

"Yeah. Pretty amazing craftsmanship, right?"

"Definitely. Though I'd say it doesn't look very old."

"It's not. Less than a hundred years."

"That makes sense." She went silent for a moment, and the sound of a mouse clicking and more keys being pecked came through the speaker once more. "I'm scanning the image now and cross-referencing it with images from the Internet. Should only take a minute."

The IAA computers were some of the best on the planet. And Tommy made sure his team's equipment was updated every six months to keep ahead of the curve. With top-of-the-line quantum processors, Tara and Alex could find answers to things that would take a normal computer hours of searching—maybe even days.

Within forty-five seconds, Tara spoke up. "Looks like we have a match."

"Gimme what you got."

"I'm double checking this image with the one the computer pulled off the web. Give me one second." The mouse clicked two more times, and then she came back on. "Yeah, I'd say this is definitely it. Looks like a perfect duplicate."

Tommy tried to remain patient, as much as he could with a gun pointed at his head. "Where is it?"

"This is the Fushimi Inari-taisha Shrine. It's almost dead center of mainland Japan, in Kyoto. Where are you guys right now?"

"Sendai, in the north."

"Oh, yeah. OK. It's going to be south and west of where you are. Need me to send you directions?"

Tommy could tell she was half kidding. She knew he could find his way around almost anywhere in the world, especially now with the benefit of GPS. He laughed uncomfortably. "No, I'm good."

"Is there anything I can do for you?"

"No, I think that's all," he said. "We just needed to know where to go next. Thanks for your help. We appreciate it."

"No problem. Always happy to assist."

He ended the call and turned to the laptop. Tommy's fingers flew across the keyboard as he typed in the name of the shrine. It took him a few guesses to get the spelling correct, but eventually the search engine helped him get it right.

"What are you doing now?" Keiko asked. She moved an inch closer to make sure he wasn't doing anything suspicious.

"Relax. I'm looking up this shrine."

He clicked the first result on the search page, and dozens of images filled the screen: red toriis, trails, and a massive structure with sloping roofs just beyond one of the crimson gates. In most of the images, hundreds of people were gathered around the structure, some tourists, some probably parishioners there to worship. Either way, both Americans knew that could be a logistical issue for the gangsters.

"Looks like an awful lot of people visit that place," Sean voiced the concern he knew Keiko might have been considering. "Will be difficult to get in there with all your men and guns."

She remained stoic. "Leave that to me." She turned to Hideo and said, "We leave for Kyoto at once. Take these two back out to the cars. I want to arrive before midnight."

Hideo gave a curt nod and waved his gun, signaling the Americans to get moving. Tommy stood up and stepped to the side. No one noticed as his left hand brushed over his phone and picked it up, concealing it in his palm as his hand disappeared into his coat sleeve. It was a pickpocket trick he'd learned a long time ago. Typically, he only used it for fun to mess with friends. On this occasion, it proved to be useful. The other two opened the door, and one stepped out and stood guard as the little procession made its way back out into the hall. Keiko lingered behind for a moment to put her coat back on.

As Sean crossed the threshold of the room, she stopped them. "Wait."

He spun around and looked back at her. She stepped toward them with her pistol leveled. She directed her question at Tommy. "Did you really think I didn't see what you just did?"

Tommy's eyebrows lowered. "What do you mean?"

She put her hand out. "Give me your phone."

He sighed. "You saw that, huh? And here I thought I was getting pretty good at that sort of thing." He reluctantly tossed her the device.

Keiko snatched it out of the air and put it back in her pocket. Her eyes opened wide, and she pushed her head forward. "Get moving. We don't have all night."

The group made their way back to the rear parking lot and

stepped out of the elevator onto the fifth floor. A cold gust of wind blasted through the openings at the end of the garage, sending a chill down everyone's spine. The SUVs were only sixty feet away from the elevator doors. As they started to walk over to the vehicles, the sound of tires screeching on concrete reverberated through the area. It drew closer and closer, approaching in what must have been a hurried pace. The noise was accompanied by that of multiple engines revving, causing the six to stop in place.

Suddenly, a black Mercedes sedan appeared around the bend in the driveway at the other end of the lot. Another came into view just after it, followed by three others. The first car sped across the concrete until the driver slammed on the brakes thirty feet away from Sean and Tommy's position.

The two Americans looked at each other with questioning eyes. Keiko swallowed hard, but her two captives didn't notice. They did, however, see Hideo take an exaggerated step to the side, which told Sean all he needed to know. Whoever was in the car wasn't with Keiko.´

The driver's side door of the front car opened first, followed immediately by the rear door on the same side. A man with a buzz cut stepped out from behind the wheel and waited for the person in the back. The other cars were lined up in single file behind the lead sedan, and every one of them emptied quickly, spewing forth men in sunglasses, white shirts, and black jackets. They all produced guns, mostly H&K submachine guns and Glock 9mm pistols, aiming them at the six people near the elevators. Sean was fairly certain he'd never seen a cloned human being, but these guys were the next best thing.

Dramatically, a black Italian leather shoe stepped out of the lead car's rear door. It was shined to a perfect gloss and was followed by a second. The man attached to the shoes exited the vehicle and stood up straight behind the door and its darkly tinted window. His hair was thick and matched the color of his suit and shoes. He was probably in his mid- to late forties, if Sean had to guess.

Surveying the area, Sean didn't see the man who claimed to work for Aoki. A sickening feeling crept into his gut as he realized the man he was looking for was nowhere to be found. That meant these new guys weren't working for Aoki. They were something else entirely.

The guy in the suit crossed his arms and stared at Keiko. "How is the search for my sword going, Keiko? Are you making progress?"

"Taka," she stuttered. "What are you doing here?" Her voice trembled as she asked the question. "I was going to call you to inform you of our progress. We just learned the location of the sword and were about to go to retrieve it."

"For me?" he asked. His eyes searched her for the truth that it appeared he already knew.

Her head half nodded, half shook back and forth. "Yes. Of course for you. It is in a shrine in Kyoto. We were just about to—"

"About to go retrieve it for me? Yes, I know. You just said that."

Taka took a few slow, tense steps forward.

Sean realized what was going on as soon as Keiko had said the man's name. She'd lied to them, again. Keiko wasn't running the operation. And Taka didn't work for her. She was using all of them to get the sword for herself. To what end, Sean didn't know for sure, but if he had to guess he'd say it was a power play on her part.

"I'm wondering," Taka said. "What was your plan once you acquired the Honjo Masamune? Were you going to try to kill me and take over my position?"

She shook her head quickly, defensively. "No. Of course not."

He stopped walking twenty feet away from the group and put his hands behind his back. "I think you're lying, Keiko. And you're playing me for a fool. If there's one thing I won't tolerate in my organization, it's dishonesty."

Sean and Tommy felt the urge to comment on the irony of the man's statement, considering he ran an organized crime syndicate, but they thought better of it and kept quiet.

Sean did take note of the two henchmen to his right and Tommy's left. All of their focus was on Taka and his men. He shifted one of his feet back a little, a centimeter at a time so that the guy closest to him wouldn't notice.

Keiko's voice was starting to sound desperate. "I know you're not a fool, Taka. I swear. I would never betray you. I gave you my uncle. It was I who brought this information to you. It will make you an unstoppable force in the Yakuza underworld. Your rule will be unquestioned." Her pleas were a stark contrast to the domineering confidence she'd expressed just moments before in the hotel, and in the cave earlier.

Taka clicked his tongue and held up a warning finger. "I know all that, my dear. And I appreciate your help. It *was* your idea to find the sword. And I appreciate your help in getting the information from your uncle. But Hideo here has told me everything." He motioned at the shaved-headed man who had stepped clear of the line of fire. "Did you really think my friend of all these years would betray me for you?"

"Taka, please," she begged. "You're making a big mistake."

"*Silence!*" he roared. "I've heard enough of your lies. I brought you in. I made you Yakuza. I shared everything with you. And this is how you repay me?" His voice bounced off the concrete walls and ceiling, filling the air with his rage.

He calmed himself for a moment and straightened his jacket in an attempt to look dignified. "Now, where are you going with these two? Where is the sword?"

Keiko swallowed. She was about to answer but paused. Sean noticed movement near one of the cars close to the end of Taka's convoy. "Yes," she said. "I used you and your resources to help me find the sword. Yes, I am going to overthrow you. The Yakuza will kneel before me, their new queen. And no one will be able to stop me." The confession was bold. And Sean knew why.

"Buddy?" he whispered.

"I see them," Tommy answered.

"Time to find cover."

31

SENDAI

A gun popped at the end of the line of sedans, and one of Taka's men dropped to the ground. In a second, he and the others instinctively spun around to see where the attack had come from.

The gangsters next to Tommy and Sean raised their weapons to fire at the Yakuza leader, but the Americans lunged at them, both planting shoulders into the would-be shooters before they could pull the triggers. The tandem crashed to the concrete as Keiko turned to Hideo, her pistol at waist level. Hideo already had his gun aimed at her, and he would have shot her dead at point-blank range if not for a freak occurrence.

As Sean drove his opponent into the ground, the man's trigger finger twitched. Just before the guy's head smacked against the hard surface, the muzzle erupted with a bang and sent the chambered round into Hideo's knee.

Hideo howled in pain, reaching down with his free hand to grasp the destroyed kneecap. The hand with the pistol wavered and gave Keiko the chance she needed to eliminate him. She fired twice from the hip, planting a bullet in Hideo's chest and stomach. Then she raised the gun and finished him with a shot to the head.

He collapsed to the ground, bent in half at the knees as he fell over backward.

Taka had already turned and started running back to his car. Gunfire boomed through the garage. The constant popping was amplified by the surrounding concrete and steel. Taka's men were firing on the rest of Keiko's troops who had exited their SUVs and flanked the unsuspecting newcomers. Four of Taka's men were already dead, and the situation wasn't getting any better. He ran past his driver and dove into the back seat as the man continued firing toward the rear of the convoy.

Keiko stalked toward the front car with big strides. Her pistol was outstretched as she took aim at the Yakuza leader. She squeezed the trigger over and over again, but her jarring movements caused her volley to be inaccurate. One of the stray rounds struck Taka's driver in the back of the neck, and he fell forward against the open rear door just as his boss disappeared into the back seat. For a long moment, the driver clutched the top of the window with both hands. As his strength waned, his fingers loosened, and he slid down to the ground, leaving a dark streak of crimson on the glass and paint.

Tommy hadn't had the good fortune Sean did when he struck the man closest to him. While Sean's had been knocked out cold, Tommy's target landed on his shoulder and immediately twisted his arms and torso to point the gun in the American's direction.

Tommy grabbed both wrists and squeezed hard as he pushed and pulled, desperately trying to keep the gun's barrel from lining up with his face. The gangster grunted and tightened his muscles in an attempt to steady his aim, but Tommy was much larger and considerably stronger. Even so, with Tommy straddling him, the guy put up an unrelenting fight. The man's arms started to shake from the exertion. His muscles would give out soon, and Tommy knew the gangster was getting desperate. His arms flailed wildly back and forth to try to throw the American off him. The fight had gone on long enough, and Tommy reverted to the only move he could use in such a stalemate. He leaned back, pulling the man off the ground and then lurched forward.

The American's forehead drove hard into the gangster's nose, shattering it in several places and driving part of the bone back into his face. Blood spurted out of the nostrils, and the man instantly dropped the gun and grabbed for his broken appendage. The dark red liquid seeped through the cracks between his fingers, and he yelped in agony. Tommy reached back with a tight fist and plowed it into the man's jaw, knocking him out with a single blow.

He stood up, panting for breath as he stared at the guy to make sure he was out cold, then grabbed the pistol lying on the ground a foot away from a limp hand.

Sean rushed over to his friend and looked down at the unconscious gangster. "Nice work," he said.

Tommy was still breathing heavily. "Thanks. What took you so long?"

"I was about to ask you the same thing."

A stray bullet zipped between the two and struck the elevator door behind them with a thud.

"Over there," Sean said, pointing at a car parked against the wall nearby. Hideo lay motionless near the bumper, his eyes fixed on a random point in the ceiling.

The two Americans sprinted over to the car and dove behind it for cover as the hailstorm of bullets continued to fly through the air.

Sean risked a peek around the rear bumper of their hiding place and saw Keiko stalking toward the open rear door of car number one. He raised the weapon he'd picked up from his guard and squeezed the trigger. The shot missed, and the round pinged into the front quarter panel. Keiko somehow heard the recoil amid the sound of dozens of weapons. Or maybe she heard the bullet hit the car. Whatever the reason, she spun around and saw Sean taking aim at her. She whipped her pistol around and fired three rounds at his position, sending him ducking for cover behind the car once more.

Keiko turned her attention back to Taka. She arrived at the door and swerved around it with the weapon extended. He was sitting across the back seat and holding a huge hand cannon at arm's length. Taka squeezed the trigger as she came into view, but she kept moving, spinning out of the way. The blast sounded like a massive explosion coming from the confines of the car. He shot twice, but with his target gone was forced to wait for her to reappear.

She slid around the back of the car, keeping her eyes on the gun battle blazing between Taka's men and her own. She was pleased to see that his troops were losing; only four remained while she'd only lost three. Creeping low around the back quarter panel, Keiko reached the rear door and was about to open it, hoping it would send Taka spilling onto the ground. But the door opened from the inside instead.

Taka had anticipated her move and as soon as he saw her through the bottom edge of the side mirror, he opened the door and pointed his pistol through the gap. She rolled out of the way, and he missed twice more.

Now he only had two shots left in the big revolver. It was one of the reasons she never liked those weapons: They didn't hold enough ammunition. Even so, a single hit from a gun like that would be devastating.

She rolled all the way to the front tire and stopped with her arms extended, aiming her weapon at the rear door. Keiko kept her breathing steady so she wouldn't waver. It was a chess match now. What did Taka think she would try next? Go through the other side again or come back to the door she just tried? That's what he'd assume. He'd figure she was going in for the point-blank kill shot. What he didn't anticipate was her attacking from the front.

The car shifted once and then again. He was probably inside moving back and forth, checking both sides.

Keiko's eyes narrowed, and she shimmied back to the front bumper, keeping low as she did so. The car continued to wobble. She knew Taka was getting paranoid now. He must have been panicking, switching from one side to the other, wondering which side she would come from next.

She pushed herself up off the ground and calmly extended the pistol, aiming through the windshield at the back seat. It wouldn't be bulletproof. She knew that much. Taka was too full of himself to think he needed such protection. His ego wouldn't allow it. Plus bulletproofing everything made vehicles too heavy, almost impractical to drive. Keiko knew of no Yakuza members who took those measures simply because it was impractical.

She closed one eye and lined up her gun's sights with the man in the back seat. He was looking out one side when he caught sight of her with his peripheral vision. His reaction was much too slow. When his shoulder jerked to the left to bring his big gun around, she'd already started to pull the trigger.

The muzzle flashed over and over again, faster and faster, peppering the windshield until the whole thing was a tangled mess of spiderweb cracks stretching from one side to the other. The epicenter was a collection of bullet holes, all tightly grouped between the driver and passenger seats. She lowered the weapon, its muzzle seeping hazy smoke and its magazine empty.

All movement in the car ceased, and she paused for a moment to stare at the carnage. Then she stepped around to the back of the car and looked inside. Taka was lying across the seat. His right hand hung out of the door, loosely clutching his big shiny gun. His eyes were vacant, staring blankly out at nothing. A little trickle of blood oozed from the corner of his mouth. His chest and shoulders had taken the brunt of her barrage. At least one or two rounds had pierced his heart, ending his life instantly.

It was an oddly serene moment as she stared down at her lifeless rival, the man who'd brought her into this world she now controlled. Guns popping from farther down the line brought her back to the fight at hand. There were only two men left from Taka's crew, and she still had nine. They were moving in to pin down the last two standing, flanking them by using the cars in the convoy for cover.

Keiko watched with grim satisfaction as one of Taka's men ran out of ammunition. He turned and started to run for the rear drive of the garage but was cut down after only five steps.

The last guy saw his comrade fall, taking multiple shots in the back. He knew there was no way out, no way to win. Determined and desperate, he stood up from his hiding spot and started firing at will, taking aim at every target he could. One of Keiko's men took a round to the shoulder and spun to the ground in pain. But the others opened fire, tearing the last of Taka's troops apart. His body shuddered from round after round as it ripped through his muscles and organs. Eventually, he dropped to the ground and gurgled his last breath.

Keiko stepped away from the car and walked quickly toward her men. "Magazine," she ordered the one nearest her. He reached into his jacket and produced what she wanted. With the press of a button, Keiko ejected the empty one from her weapon and slid the new one in with a click. She pulled back the slide and turned toward the elevators.

"Sean? Tommy? Are you still here?" She paused for a second and let her words echo through the garage. The acrid scent of burned gunpowder loomed in the air amid a cloud of bluish-gray smoke. She didn't wait for them to answer. "I know you are. I can see your feet underneath that car. Throw down your weapons, and come out. Maybe I'll let you live."

Sean and Tommy stayed in their hiding spot, crouching low to keep cover.

"What now?" Tommy whispered. "They have us cornered."

"Yeah. But we have the element of surprise."

Tommy was staring ahead at the side of the car when he heard Sean's comment. His head turned slowly toward his friend and he glared at him as if he was crazy. "What? Element of surprise? What are you talking about?"

Sean giggled. "They'd never expect us to just come out with guns blazing."

"Yeah, I'm with them on that. I don't expect us to do that either," he hissed.

"I was kidding."

"You're an idiot. Seriously, what are we going to do?"

Keiko's voice interrupted them again. "You are outnumbered, boys. There is no way out of this alive if you don't surrender. I am in charge of the Yakuza now. I might even decide to let you work for me, as slaves of course, but it would be better than death."

"No it wouldn't," Tommy said under his breath.

Sean answered her offer. "Without us, there is no way you'll get that sword. You throw down your weapons, and maybe we'll let you tag along."

He knew it was a ridiculous thing to say, but he was trying to buy time to figure a way out of the pickle they were in.

The Americans didn't see Keiko make a motion with her hand for one of her men to move down the wall toward their position. He would have them pinned down at point-blank range in a matter of thirty seconds. Then there would be no escape.

"I like you, Sean. You're funny. Perhaps I have a better use for you."

Tommy's nostrils flared, and he stood up from his hiding place with gun drawn. He took aim at her and fired. He yelled in full rage as his finger squeezed the trigger six times. While he didn't hit Keiko or her minions, he did send them sprawling for cover before Sean grabbed his friend's jacket and pulled him back to safety.

"Have it your way!" Keiko shouted. "We will find the sword with or without you!"

Guns started popping from near the location of her voice, and soon the car they were using for cover started taking the brunt of the onslaught. Windows shattered, doors thunked, and the rear left tire spewed air from a fresh bullet hole.

"Good one, buddy," Sean said. He shook his head. "Now what are we gonna do?"

Tommy breathed angrily through his nose as he leaned against the car door. He said nothing.

Suddenly, like a banshee screeching in the night, the sound of tires squealing on concrete mingled with the gunfire. An engine revved from the driveway just beyond the elevators. A moment later, a black BMW appeared around the curve and whipped around with the front passenger-side door open.

Behind the wheel, Aoki's observer stared at the two Americans.

"Get in." He was ducked down behind the dashboard to keep from being hit by any bullets directed his way.

Sean and Tommy didn't need a second invitation. They launched off the ground, keeping low as they ran hard to the car. The two dove into the front seat, landing on each other in an awkward pile with feet dangling out of the door. The driver didn't wait for them to get sorted. Keiko and her men had already taken aim at the intruder and started peppering the hood, windshield and grille with bullets. He stepped on the gas, and the wide tires squealed again as he jerked the steering wheel back to the left, fishtailing the sedan into the driveway and around the curve.

The Americans pulled themselves into the car the rest of the way. The door closed itself from the force of going around and around in the circular driveway.

Tommy sprawled to get off Sean and climbed into the back seat. When he was sitting upright, he swallowed hard while catching his breath. "Who's this guy?"

Sean clambered up into the front seat and fastened his seatbelt. "He works for one of the rival gangs. It's OK. He's a good guy."

Tommy's eyebrows knit together, and he shook his head. His voice was full of confusion. "Wait. You just said he's in a rival gang, but he's a good guy? Those two don't go together."

"He just got us out of there," Sean said and jerked his thumb toward the rear window. "I'd say we should give him the benefit of the doubt."

The driver was focused intently on the narrow driveway ahead. They reached the bottom floor, and he punched the accelerator again, speeding the sedan out onto the main road.

"I guess," Tommy said.

Sean looked back in the side mirror to make sure no one was following them. The driver yanked the wheel to the right and sped down a quiet side street. After a few blocks, he turned again, back onto one of the main roads that stretched out toward the south.

"Do you have the sword?" he asked. He'd been silent since the

Americans got in the car. Now his question seemed blunt and awkward.

"Does it look like we have the sword?" Tommy blurted out. "Oh wait. Let me check up my butt and see if I hid it there."

Sean snorted a short laugh. And took over the conversation. "No. We haven't found it yet. But we know where to look next. And we're going to need a ride there since our car is unavailable." Sean thought about the rental they'd left in the mountains. Eventually, the police would locate it and return it to the company. That was the least of his worries.

The driver ignored Tommy's comment and spoke to Sean. "Do they know where it is?"

Sean nodded. "Yeah. So we're going to need to hurry to beat them to it. Keiko said something about getting there before midnight." He momentarily switched subjects. "Hey, if you're going to drive us for the next several hours, you mind telling us your name?"

"Hiroki."

"OK, Hiroki. Thanks for getting us out of that mess back there."

The younger man kept his eyes locked on the road, steering by a few slower vehicles and then merging back into the right lane.

"You're welcome. But I didn't do it for you."

"I know. You did it for your boss."

Tommy's mouth was wide open as he listened to the conversation. "Hello? Wait a minute. How do you know this...Hiroki...guy again? And why are you cavorting with the Yakuza?"

"It's a long story," Sean answered. "But don't worry. His boss doesn't want the sword. He just doesn't want Taka to have it."

"Well, here's the good news. Taka's dead! So he's the least of your worries."

Hiroki's expression changed for the first time since they'd gotten in the car with him. His head twisted slightly, and he looked at Sean for confirmation. "Taka is dead?"

Sean nodded. "Afraid so. Turns out Keiko was the mastermind behind all of this. She engineered the whole thing, even the execution of her own uncle. She and her men just took out at least a dozen of Taka's guys. And she killed Taka herself. It was Keiko's idea to find the Masamune. She wants to be the head of all the Yakuza in Japan."

Hiroki frowned at the new information. "I will have to inform Aoki of this matter."

"Well, let's get to where we're headed first, and then you can tell him all about it."

The driver thought for a second and then asked, "Where are we going?"

Sean looked out the window at the buildings and pedestrians passing by.

"Kyoto."

32

KYOTO, JAPAN

The drive from Sendai to Kyoto took longer than expected. Fortunately, Hiroki knew exactly where he was going, and as they were making the journey at night, it eliminated much of the usual traffic they would have experienced during the day.

For the first hour of the drive, all three men in the car kept a close watch on the road behind them to make sure they weren't being followed. Their getaway from the shootout in the parking garage had put them a step ahead of Keiko, but there was always the chance she'd catch up or had someone waiting outside in case something crazy happened. With no sign of trouble for over an hour, Sean and Tommy relaxed a little, though Hiroki seemed to be on edge the entire drive.

They found a hotel on the outskirts of town and holed up for the night since venturing out to the site in the darkness wasn't an option. The Americans banked on the fact that Keiko would have the same problem. The glaring problem was that the head start they'd achieved would be wiped away.

Hiroki wasn't sure about letting Tommy pay for his room, but the American insisted: an apology for his initial reaction in the car, and as a way of saying thank you.

"If it weren't for you," Tommy said, "we'd be dead in a parking lot right now."

Hiroki reluctantly allowed him to pay, and he retired to his room for the night.

The conversation between Sean and his friend had been minimal. They were both exhausted, and even though Sean wanted to address the elephant in the room regarding Keiko, he decided to leave it for another day.

The two friends woke up the next morning and went next door to wake up Hiroki. At first, the young gangster didn't answer the door when Sean knocked. After a third knock, the Americans were starting to get concerned that their new friend had bailed. As Sean was about to knock a fourth time, the door swung open. Hiroki was standing in the doorway, rubbing a towel behind one ear.

"Oh, sorry," Tommy said. "We thought you'd already be up."

"You're ready to go?" Hiroki asked. "I'll get my things."

Tommy turned to Sean. "I like this guy. He just snaps to it. Maybe he should come work for me."

Sean guffawed. "This from the guy who, just a few hours ago, was incensed that I would be associating with a gang member."

"Maybe I was too quick to judge. He seems solid enough."

"Well, just remember that he has probably committed any number of crimes. I'd suggest doing a background check before you bring him on with IAA."

Hiroki appeared again at the doorway, apparently unaware of the conversation between the two. Tommy grinned awkwardly at him as if trying to convey everything was normal.

The morning greeted them with a dense fog that hung in the air like thick miso soup. Hiroki made sure to drive a little slower to be safe. And because of the heavily restricted visibility, both Americans appreciated their driver's caution.

The trip from the hotel to the grounds of the Fushimi Inari-taisha Shrine only took about twenty minutes. With every precious second that passed, Sean and Tommy felt a greater and greater sense of urgency to get where they were going. It was still early in the morning when Hiroki parked the car at the base of the mountain where a sparse but growing crowd of people had started gathering.

They shut the doors to the BMW and started walking toward a trailhead underneath a red torii gate. Sean glanced back at the sedan and noticed the bullet holes in the hood and one of the headlights.

"Lucky none of those hit any vital engine parts," he commented and pointed at the damage.

Hiroki nodded. "Or any of us," he added.

"True."

The three made their way over to the red gate and looked up. What they saw was unlike anything they'd ever imagined. The steep path forged its way up the mountain under the cover of hundreds and hundreds of torii gates. It was like a tunnel of red poles and beams.

"This is incredible," Tommy said. He marveled at the spectacle. "Imagine how many man hours went into this."

"Yeah, it's pretty awesome," Sean agreed. He looked around the parking area, surveying it to make sure there were no suspicious onlookers.

Satisfied they were in the clear, he passed through the gate and started up the trail.

"I've been thinking about the riddle from the coin," Tommy said as the group passed under the seemingly endless red beams. "It said something about a prayer of power or something."

In spite of the fact they'd only been walking for a minute or two, Sean was surprised his friend wasn't already gasping for air. He nodded, acknowledging Tommy's comment, but kept his head on a swivel and his eyes wide open. Through the narrow gaps between each torii, he could make out the snowy ground beyond, layered like melted marshmallow among the endless stands of evergreen trees. He wasn't admiring nature, though. Something in his gut told him they'd not seen the last of Keiko.

"You know?" Tommy urged.

Sean snapped out of his focused daze and answered. "Yeah, sorry. The prayer of power."

They reached a bend in the trail and kept moving at a steady pace. Sean tried to make sure they weren't moving so fast that his friend would wear out too quickly.

"Well, what do you think about it? We're here. And if we get to meet this master or whoever the guy is, according to that coin, we're going to have to say some kind of prayer."

Sean breathed evenly. He could feel his heart rate increasing, pumping blood through his extremities as they continued the climb. He could smell the snow and spruce in the air. The touch of the cold brushed over his skin like a frigid feather.

When he spoke, his voice remained steady. "I don't know," he said. "I guess maybe there will be another clue. Or maybe we'll just have to figure it out when we get there."

The trail bent back to the left and evened out for a short patch before sloping up the hill once more. Tommy was breathing heavier now, and when he spoke his sentences were more fragmented than before.

"I just think we should have a game plan before we go walking into a monastery, that's all."

Sean smiled and stared at the path ahead. "Sometimes the best plan is to just feel it out and go with the groove. You know, take what's given to you and work with it as best you can."

Tommy frowned. He was trailing behind Sean by a few feet with Hiroki next to him. "I guess. I'm just worried that one of these days your little method of shooting from the hip is going to catch up to you. And I'd rather not be there when it happens."

Sean feigned offense. "So you don't want to hang out anymore? Oh, I see how it is."

"You know what I mean."

Hiroki had remained silent for the entire hike, listening into the conversation between the two but not completely sure what they were talking about. Finally, he interrupted. "How long have you two known each other?" he asked innocently.

Tommy answered first, joking. "Long enough to almost get killed plenty of times."

"All our lives," Sean corrected. "We've only been almost killed a handful of times."

"A handful is more than most people experience in their entire lifespan."

Sean shrugged. "Hey, you called me for this little expedition. Remember?"

Tommy recalled the coffee spill that covered the floor and counter at Sean's house and snorted. "Good point. That coffee really was everywhere."

It was Hiroki's turn to frown. He had no idea what the two Americans were talking about.

Sean diverted the conversation to involve their new companion. "So what's your story, Hiroki?"

The young Japanese man's confusion grew. "Story?"

"Yeah. You speak great English. And you don't strike me as the criminal type. Throw in the fact that you saved our necks back there, and the idea of you being in the Yakuza seems a little far-fetched. So what's the deal?"

Hiroki hung his head for a second before answering. "My parents were killed in a fire when I was young. I was in and out of different homes, orphanages, all sorts of places. The Yakuza took me in. They became my family." His words hung in the cold air for a second and then vanished through the cracks in the red beams overhead.

"Sorry to hear about your family," Tommy said. Their companion's story was a sobering reminder of his own loss years ago.

Hiroki gave a short nod.

Sean still didn't feel as if they had all the pieces yet. "OK, so you joined the gang, but there's something you're not telling us. I don't think you want to be with them. Maybe you're too scared to leave, or maybe you don't want to. But if I had to put my money on it, I'd say you don't approve of the Yakuza's actions."

Hiroki stopped on the trail. His face scrunched with a hint of anger. "Aoki took me in when no one else would. He became my family. He fed me, gave me a place to sleep. Maybe I don't approve of the things I have to do for him, but it is a duty of honor for me to serve him."

Sean and Tommy had stopped and turned to listen to the younger man.

"Sounds like quite the conundrum," Sean said. "You know that what you do for Aoki is wrong, but at the same time you feel a strong sense of responsibility to do his bidding. Weird. But I get it."

"Weird?"

Sean turned around and started walking again. He did not intend to let their conversation slow them down. "Yeah. Weird."

The other two hurried to catch up.

"Why weird?" Hiroki pressed.

"You know why. It's what bothers you deep down inside. There is no honor in committing crimes against innocent people."

"I leave the innocent alone. I've never done anything to anyone who didn't have it coming."

"Based on your own thorough investigations? Or based on what your boss told you?"

The question sank in deep and left Hiroki speechless for a few moments.

While he was thinking, Tommy jumped back in. "What he's saying is, it's great that Aoki took you in when no one else would. He gave you a shot in life. But eventually, the gang is going to get you killed. Or when they run out of uses for you, they'll just take you out themselves."

"Once someone is in, there is no getting out," Hiroki answered. "I saw what they did to a man who wanted to leave the Yakuza. They peeled the skin from his face before they cut off his hands and feet. Then they threw him into the river. He was never seen again. There is no getting out of the Yakuza."

"Well," Sean said. "If you ever change your mind, I have connections that can make that happen. I'm sure there are places in the world where the Yakuza's arm doesn't reach."

"Not in this country."

Tommy chuckled. "Then maybe you need to get out of this country."

"I wouldn't know how to start. And getting into America—it's not the welcoming country it used to be."

"It is if you know the right people," Tommy said. "We help people who help us. If you want out, we could use a good man like you in IAA. Just a thought."

"IAA?"

Sean shook his head. "We'll tell you all about it when this is over. Tommy's got a whole recruitment speech on the topic." He turned back to his friend. "I didn't realize you guys were hiring again."

"Pay no attention to this cynic, Hiroki. We're always looking for promising young talent. The question is, have you ever had an interest in history?"

Hiroki's eyebrows stitched together. "History? No. Science was something that always fascinated me, though."

Tommy gave a shrug. "Well, that's something I can work with."

In another thirty seconds the path leveled off, curved around to the left, right, and back again, winding its way up the mountain until it came to a stop where the tunnel of toriis ended at a single massive gate. The three stopped and stared through the tall red posts at the green-roofed shrine beyond. Ornately designed and decorated, the main building of the shrine was only two stories tall, maybe three. It was hard to tell due to the massive open door on the main floor. A veranda wrapped around the second floor with a short railing accompanying it. Bright reds offset the gold and dark green trim of the windows, posts, shutters, and walls.

"This is it," Tommy said. "It's the view engraved on that coin."

Sean nodded. "Sure looks like it." He also noted the absence of the many people they were expecting, with only a few loitering around a circular pool of water off to the left of the entrance. "Let's see if we can find this master the coin mentioned."

"Yeah, the sooner, the better."

The three walked through the main gate, across the courtyard, and up the steps to the entrance. Tommy started to go in, but Hiroki grabbed his shoulder and stopped him. He pointed at Tommy's shoes.

"You must remove these before going in." He demonstrated by taking off his own shoes and walking softly into the building.

"But it's cold out," Tommy said to Sean, who was already removing his shoes.

"I know. But it's bad juju if you don't. It's part of their culture. Who are we to argue with that?"

Tommy rolled his eyes and untied his shoelaces.

Once they were inside, the group was greeted by a large bell with lettering engraved all over it. "A prayer bell," Sean said.

"Yep," Tommy nodded, admiring the simple beauty of the object. "Wanna ring it?"

Sean shook his head. "Maybe some other time. Probably best if we don't draw too much attention."

Just as he finished his sentence, a man in flowing white robes appeared from behind a partition at the rear of the bell and smiled at them. His head was clean shaven, and he had a peaceful, welcoming look about him. He said something to the group in Japanese, to which Sean and Tommy looked to Hiroki for translation.

Hiroki replied to the monk's question, which produced a broad smile on his face.

"Ah, so you are visitors from America?" he asked.

Sean bowed low to show respect to the monk and then answered. "Yes. And we are here on a quest." He waited for a second and drew in a quick breath. No sense in beating around the bush. "We were told to seek the master."

The monk's eyebrows raised halfway up his forehead, and he stared at the two with wide-eyed curiosity. "You were told to seek the master? Pertaining to what?"

Sean glanced over at his friend and then back to the monk. Once more, he chose to forego mincing words. "The Honjo Masamune."

Puzzled, the monk cocked his head to the side, but his expression never changed save for his mouth opening in a tight circle as he spoke. "Oh?"

Tommy stepped in. "Hello, sir, my name is Tommy Schultz. I'm an archaeologist and a historian." He waved both hands as if the introduction wasn't important. "Anyway, we found some evidence that suggests the Masamune might be located here, in this shrine." He pointed to the floor. "Or if it isn't, there might be some more information here as to its whereabouts."

Sean took over again as the monk listened to the explanation with a stoic curiosity. "We discovered a coin on Mount Haguro. On one side it had a picture of this place." He motioned to their surroundings. "The other side said to find the master. We assume it meant the master of this monastery." His eyes pled with the monk. "Is there such a person here?"

The three visitors waited for several long seconds as the monk assessed them. His eyes went from one to the other until he finally spoke. "Come with me."

33

KYOTO

The monk's robes fluttered behind him as he seemingly floated down a short corridor and then turned left. The next hallway extended out away from the main building. Sounds of chanting and prayers echoed throughout, reverberating off the wooden walls and ceiling.

As the group continued, the noise grew louder until they reached another smaller building and the doorway inside. The chants were obviously coming from the room just beyond the door.

"What are they saying?" Tommy whispered. "Just curious."

The monk smiled. "They are praying."

"It's beautiful," Tommy said. "I wish I knew the words."

Their guide continued to smile. "The words are not what is important. To them, the words are just a way to connect with their feelings. The feelings the words produce are the true prayer."

Sean was interested in what the monk was saying. He'd always considered himself to be a sort of philosophical and spiritual person. But this was something new. "The feelings are the prayer?"

The monk nodded. "Yes. Words themselves have no power. But feelings invoke belief deep inside. And belief is the most powerful form of prayer. Many great religious masters have taught this."

Sean recalled a story he'd learned from the Bible as a child. In it, Jesus sent the disciples to cast out demons and heal the sick, but when they returned, they claimed to be unable to perform the miracles. Jesus told them that it was their unbelief that kept them from being able to perform the miraculous events. Now this monk was sort of telling him and Tommy the same thing.

"What feeling are they trying to invoke?" he asked.

The monk's smile broadened by an inch. "Appreciation."

Sean nodded and stowed that away for the moment.

The monk turned and slowly opened the door. The volume of the chanting increased fivefold. Inside, dozens of monks were chanting in long drones. Some leaned forward and back in a slow, trancelike movement. "We must go through here to reach the man you seek. He is in his personal quarters at the moment."

Uncertain about walking through the prayer room in the middle of a big session, the three visitors lingered at the threshold. They looked at each other, wondering what the other was thinking before deciding they should follow the monk through the chamber instead of standing there looking like idiots. The monk never looked back and didn't see the three scrambling to catch up as he reached the far side of the room and started ascending a set of steps to another door.

Once they were through the door, they found themselves in another shorter hallway. This one contained no windows to let in outside light and was only illuminated by dozens of candles lining the walls in a number of sconces. The monk closed the door behind them and motioned with his hand for them to follow him down the passage. At the end of the hallway, another sliding paper door waited. Yellowish candlelight danced on the white paper from the other side.

The monk once more twisted around to face the visitors. His face no longer carried the smile it had before, which was replaced by a drawn, somber expression. "The master is through this door. It is highly irregular for him to see unannounced visitors. You must wait here while I tell him you are here and what you want."

Sean bowed his head to thank the monk before the man opened

the door and sidled through the opening. The door closed behind him, leaving the two Americans and their companion waiting in the hall.

Tommy looked over at his friend. "I hope this works."

"Why wouldn't it?"

"I don't know. Maybe because we still don't know what the whole power prayer thing is. Or maybe because this master guy has probably had to deal with the issue of treasure hunters coming here before."

Sean frowned, dubious about Tommy's concerns. "Come on. No one has found that coin before. If they had, they wouldn't have left it in the cave. I seriously doubt many people have come by bothering this dude about the sword."

Hiroki watched the interaction between the two but said nothing.

"It's been well documented how several treasure hunters believe the Masamune is in a shrine just like this one. There was even a television series about one guy's search for it. He came to a place not unlike this and bugged the monks about it."

"I'm guessing he didn't find it," Sean joked in a hushed tone.

"That isn't the point," Tommy hissed.

Hiroki pointed at the paper door, and the Americans noted the silhouette moving against the white surface. A second later, the door slid open, and the smiling monk reappeared.

"He will see you. Please come in."

He pulled the door wide open and stepped back, extending his hand with palm up to make way for the visitors. Tommy and Sean bowed awkwardly in thanks and stepped through the opening into the room.

Inside, they were greeted by an incredible sight. Hundreds of candles lined the floors and walls. The floor itself was tiered, with three steps leading to a lower central floor. Candle wax had piled up on the wooden floorboards over what appeared to be years. Off to one side of the room, a little prayer altar was placed against the wall. An old man with a face full of wrinkles sat atop a white pillow in the middle of the low point in the floor. He wore a robe that matched the one in the visitors' guide, with one distinct difference: it had a golden ribbon sewn into the collar.

He was staring straight ahead at a random point on the far wall when they entered the room. The door closed behind the three visitors and startled them. The two Americans turned and realized their guide had left them alone with the man known as the master.

They exchanged wondering glances as the man in the room's center continued to stare ahead. Sean shrugged as if to say, *What do we do next?* But neither man said anything.

Finally, after the awkward wait, the master's head twisted slightly to the right, and he looked at them with a calm, peaceful gaze. He extended a hand out before him to three pillows positioned a few feet away from his.

The visitors shuffled down the steps and made their way to the pillows and sat down, mimicking the way the old monk was sitting. No one said a word, instead thinking it best that the master speak first, though they weren't exactly sure about the customary way to proceed.

He looked at each one of them individually for several seconds before switching to the next. When the old man spoke, it was with a voice that could soothe a raging tempest.

"So you are here seeking the great sword?"

The two Americans nodded simultaneously. "Yes, sir."

"And what makes you think it is here?"

Tommy and Sean glanced at each other. Tommy gave him a nod, preferring to let his friend do the talking.

"We found the cipher of the last Tokugawa who possessed it. That riddle led us here. We have faced many trials on our journey. A coin we found in a cave on Mount Haguro said that we should seek the master of this place. And so we sit before you."

The old man's head tilted back as he appraised Sean's explanation. "And you seek this weapon for the fame and fortune it will bring?"

"No, sir," Tommy interjected. "We are historians—well, I am. He's retired." He jerked a thumb at Sean. "But we seek to restore something to the Japanese people that has important cultural significance. It should be put in a museum for all of Japan, and the world, to appreciate."

The master drew in a deep breath and sighed. "Many people have come looking for the great sword. I have entertained many audiences with treasure hunters from all over the world."

Tommy shot Sean an *I told you so* glare and then returned his attention to the old man as he continued speaking.

"It is a noble thing you say, that you would like to return the blade to the people. But the sword will only be revealed to the right person, to someone who is of pure heart and who fights for honor."

"So it *is* here?" Tommy asked. His voice was suddenly full of hope.

The old monk smiled and held out a finger. "I did not say that. I merely said the Honjo Masamune would reveal itself to the right person."

Sean was confused now. "So it isn't here?" he asked.

"I did not say that either."

More riddles, Sean thought.

Before he could ask another question, the master continued. "The warrior who fights for honor and the cause of justice must also know peace. He must know the true source of power in its purest form. Only then will that warrior be permitted to hold the great sword."

There it was, a reference to the part of the riddle regarding the prayer of power. Sean recognized it, and he was pretty sure Tommy did too.

Sean spoke to this effect first. "The coin we discovered, it said that we should pray a prayer of power. Is this where we do that?"

It was a tenuous question, and Tommy wasn't sure if it was the right thing to ask. Then again, he had no idea what to ask next.

The monk nodded. "Yes. This is a place of prayer."

The two Americans glanced at each other. Hiroki, who sat to Sean's left, simply watched, unclear as to what was going to happen next.

Finally, Sean faced the monk and stood up. He walked back up the steps and over to the little altar behind the master's seating position. He reverently took a place on another floor pillow and crossed his legs. Sean had meditated before, usually as a means of dealing with stress. Now he wasn't going to meditate. He had to think of which words to say.

Sean's mind raced through a million ideas. He knew his friend was watching him from the middle of the room, probably wondering what the heck he was about to do. Out of the barrage of words, thoughts, and prayers that came to mind, only one made any sense. It was something he'd gleaned from their guide's comments on the way into the monastery. Just before entering the big prayer room, he'd said that the monks were trying to evoke feelings of appreciation, and that that sort of feeling was the most powerful form of prayer. Sean closed his eyes and internally crossed his fingers that his assessment was correct.

He drew in a deep breath and then spoke two words loud enough for the other three people in the room to hear. "Thank you."

He kept his eyes closed, sealing them off from the flickering light of the many candles. His focus was entirely on feeling grateful for something, anything, good in his life. For the fact that he'd lived as many years as he had, for his home, for his car, for his motorcycles. The more he thought about it, the more the appreciation in his heart grew. He'd lived a blessed life. Sure, he'd nearly been killed more times than he could count. But he'd survived and served his country and mankind dutifully. And he had friendship. Tommy was as loyal a friend as anyone could hope for. His thoughts soon drifted to Adriana. He couldn't wait to see her again. Love and appreciation for her flowed from his body and coursed through his heart.

Suddenly, his thoughts were interrupted by a set of fingers pressing on his shoulder. Sean opened his eyes and looked up to find the old monk standing over him. The man's wrinkled face stared down at him with a beaming smile.

The old monk spoke kindly. "Did you mean what you said about the sword? That you do not desire it for personal gain?"

Sean nodded slowly. "Yes, sir. We aren't treasure hunters. We just want to make sure it ends up in the right hands. It would be awful if the wrong people found it."

The master gave a single nod. "Then follow me."

34

KYOTO

The master led the three visitors through a side door and into a dark antechamber. The room was only ten feet wide and about that long. A humble cot sat against the near wall with plain white sheets and a matching roll pillow. By the residual light coming from his main quarters, the old monk was able to find a match and light a single candle that was sitting on a plain wooden table in the corner.

Hiroki and the two Americans watched the old monk as he turned his attention to a woven burlap rug in the far corner. He moved over to the rug, bent down, and yanked it away from the wall. In the wooden floor was a trapdoor with an old iron latch. The master stood up and smiled energetically.

"I have waited a long time to reveal this to someone. Two masters before me protected this secret. And now, finally, I am the one honored to reveal it." He paused to think for a moment and scratched his chin. His eyes had a mischievous flare about them. "I have to admit, though. I did not expect the ones to solve the riddle would be Americans."

He leaned over and pulled on the circular latch. With a good heave, the trapdoor came loose and tilted up. The rusty hinges creaked loudly, and a cloud of dust tumbled up and out of the opening. The old monk laid the door down on its back and clapped his hands together as if cleaning them of debris.

"It seems destiny is not without a sense of irony."

Hiroki didn't know the story of the sword, so he had to ask, "Irony? What do you mean?"

The master reached over and patted Hiroki's shoulder. "Americans. It was the Americans who took Japan's weapons, including all the swords they could find. The last Tokugawa wouldn't allow it, and so he hid it here. Now, after all this time, Americans have come to return it to its people. And *that* is ironic."

Hiroki nodded, finally understanding.

"I apologize I do not have more candles. I assume you have phones?"

Sean shook his head.

The master almost looked impressed. "Oh. Well, then. Stay close. I would not want you to stumble. And it is quite dark down here."

As the old monk descended into the cavity, the light from his candle cast upon a set of ancient-looking wooden steps, much like an attic ladder.

"Go ahead," Sean said to Tommy, and as his friend disappeared into the hole he motioned for Hiroki to follow him. Warily, he took a last look around the cell before climbing down the ladder and pulling the trapdoor closed.

The interior of the tunnel was cramped. Its breadth was only three feet wide. The hewn walls were smooth to the touch, carved out of the rock with a machine-like precision. Sean and Tommy figured they'd been done by hand, though. It was unlikely the monks had allowed any kind of machinery to do the task, although it would have made more sense.

The master scurried along the passage and into the dark. His candle cast an eerie corona around him. At various points, he stopped and wiped down some cobwebs. Spiders, it seemed, had been making quite the home for themselves in the tunnel. Sean's spine tingled. He hoped that the cold had driven most of the arach nids away for the winter. While heights were his biggest fear, spiders and snakes were a close second. The old monk, however, seemed unaffected. Sean stole a glance behind into the pitch black, more out of habit than from cause. Nothing was there, but he kept repeating the paranoid gesture anyway.

The group had only been walking in the tunnel for two or three minutes when they arrived in a square room cut entirely out of the mountain rock. In the center, the candlelight helped display a wooden box sitting atop a stone plinth. The container was covered in decades of dust and debris. A few chunks of rock from the ceiling had fallen down and lay on top of it. A circular metal clasp was on the top, much like the latch on the trapdoor. The object appeared to still be in good condition but hardly seemed like the appropriate container for the greatest sword ever made.

There was a singular Japanese character on the side, burned into the wood.

Sean and Tommy stared for a long moment at the box, until the master cleared his throat and stirred them from their trance.

"Are you going to open it?"

The two Americans nodded and stepped closer. They looked at each other, silently asking the question: *Who should open it?*

"Go ahead," Sean nodded.

Tommy didn't wait to be told twice. He lifted the clasp and pulled up on the lid. The layers of dust shook free and hung in the air for several seconds, but the light from the old monk's candle pierced through and shone onto the long, slender object within the container. The outer shell of the box had taken the brunt of age's punch, keeping out the dust and moisture to preserve the black scabbard in pristine condition, showing off a dim gloss even after all the years of being underground. The sword's handle was perfectly wrapped in black fabric, capped with a golden hand guard that hadn't lost its shiny luster through the decades.

The two Americans swallowed hard as Tommy reached out to the weapon with both hands. He eased his palms under it in two places and carefully, inch by inch, lifted it off the two holders. His breath came heavily but steady as he brought the sword away from the box and close to his chest. He stared down at it for a moment; they all did, seizing the chance to pay homage to the gravity of their find.

"In your hands," the master cut the silence, "is the greatest sword ever created by man. It is a masterpiece by the ultimate master."

Tommy and Sean glanced over at him and nodded. They knew how important it was. People had spent their lives trying to locate the Honjo Masamune. Fortunes had been lost in their vain pursuits. Now, at last, the Masamune would see light once more.

Tommy turned to his friend, holding the sword out to him as if he were a king presenting a weapon to a knight long ago.

In turn, Sean looked to the master. "You have protected this secret all these years, but you've never laid eyes on it?"

He shook his head. "No. I have only been in this room one time when the master before me brought me here to see the box. But you are the first to open it since Iemasa Tokugawa."

Tommy knew where his friend was going with the question. "Then you should be the first to unsheathe it."

"Yeah," Sean agreed. "That's only right."

The old monk was overcome by the kind generosity of the two Americans. He bowed low and smiled. "You truly are the right ones to have found this. I thank you."

He set down the candle next to the box, reached out his hands, and grasped the sword's scabbard. The three visitors expected him to draw the blade out slowly but instead, they were startled when the old monk yanked it out as if going into battle.

The steel slid easily from its housing, ringing at a high pitch in the chamber of rock. The old monk smiled at the elegant beauty of the craftsmanship. The steel still shone brightly, glimmering in the candlelight. He held his hand back to keep the blade close, as if ready to attack an invisible enemy, and stared at the sharp edge.

"Still perfect after all these years," he said. "Truly a magnificent weapon. Its balance is unparalleled." He twisted to the right and then to the left, feigning a few easy strokes but careful of his tight quarters.

Then after only a minute or so of testing out the sword, he bowed, put it back in its sheath, and passed it back to Tommy.

"I thank you again," the master said. "I am greatly honored."

Tommy handed it to Sean. "You have to feel this thing."

Sean let a childish grin escape as he took the sword. Holding it in both hands, he slid the blade out much more cautiously than the old monk had done. He held it out at arm's length, inspecting it by twisting it to the right and then the left.

"The balance is remarkable," he said.

The monk nodded.

Sean handed it to Tommy, who took the handle and kept the blade low. He let it rise and fall a few times to test the weight before shaking his head. "It's absolutely incredible."

Hiroki had been silently watching the scene unfold. Tommy could tell the younger man was curious, so he held the weapon out for Hiroki to take. Uncertain at first, Hiroki deliberated until he could see Tommy wasn't going to let him get away without at least touching it.

"It's OK. Feel it. Once we take it to the proper authorities, you'll never get another chance."

Hiroki reached out and grasped the end of the handle. He waved the tip of the sword back and forth in short arcs, testing the weight and balance for himself. Then he put his other hand on the long grip and twisted his torso to the side in an attacking stance, holding the sword at an angle like someone who'd done it a thousand times.

"This is a fine weapon," he said.

Tommy and Sean suddenly didn't like the sound in Hiroki's voice.

"And you should not have given it to me. Americans. Always so trusting."

A sickening feeling crept up into Tommy's gut. Sean's initial reaction was to reach for the weapon tucked away inside his coat. But he refrained. Not because of any danger; he could draw the pistol and take out the kid in less than two seconds. He had a feeling Hiroki was messing with them.

His suspicions were confirmed when a wicked grin creased across the younger man's face. He lowered the weapon and held it back out for Tommy to take.

Tommy, relieved and a little pale, smiled uneasily and grabbed the end of the handle. "You really had me going there for a second."

"I know," Hiroki said amid a round of chuckles.

The old monk joined in the laughter, and soon all four men were nearly roaring. When things settled down again, Tommy put the blade back in its scabbard and handed it to Sean.

"Mind carrying it?"

Sean shook his head. "Nope."

He slung the strap over his shoulder and looked back at the old monk. "Sir, it has been a pleasure. We thank you for your help. But we must be going. This sword tends to have a good bit of trouble chasing after it, and we'd rather not bring any of that to your peaceful monastery."

Something in the master's eyes told Sean he understood, even though the man wasn't entirely sure what Sean was talking about. He nodded at the three visitors, picked up his candle, and started back toward the tunnel entrance. Five minutes later, the group had returned to the master's main room and were once again surrounded by the warmth of the candlelight.

"Have a safe journey," the old man said. "Take good care of that sword."

Sean nodded. "Don't worry. We will."

The master smiled. "I never worry. I am a monk."

"Right."

"Thank you," Tommy said. "We appreciate your help, especially considering we are foreigners."

"Goodness knows no nationality."

The three turned and walked to the sliding door. Tommy and Hiroki went through first. Sean lingered for a second and looked back. The old monk had already returned to his meditative position in the middle of the recessed floor. His eyes were closed, and his hands rested palms up atop his knees.

Sean closed the paper door behind him and started down the hall after his companions. The guide who had met them at the door was standing just outside the main prayer room. He smiled at the group as they returned and noted the sword strapped to Sean's back.

"I see you received what you came for."

"Yep. Thanks to the master. We appreciate your help."

The monk bowed low. "And we appreciate you carrying this burden to where it belongs."

"We will," Tommy said. "We'll make sure it's well taken care of."

The guide led the way back through the prayer room where dozens of monks were still focused on their chanting. As soon as the visitors had exited through the paper door on the far side, their guide bid them farewell and went back in with the others.

The three hurried back to the front door where their shoes were still sitting by the frame. They slipped them on quickly, wishing to waste no time in getting back to the car.

"We should probably get out of here fast," Sean said. "There's no telling when Keiko and her crew will show up."

"That's a good idea," a familiar feminine voice said from around the corner of the entrance. "It would be a shame if they arrived before you could get away."

Sean grimaced. Tommy felt his heart drop into his gut. Neither of them knew what Hiroki was feeling, but it couldn't have been positive.

Keiko stepped around the edge of the building, followed by several of her men. They poured into the front room and surrounded the group of three before the Americans could react. Guns were aimed at them from every angle. Keiko simply stood in the doorway with her arms crossed. There was no escaping this time.

35

KYOTO

"I see you found my sword," Keiko leered. Then she took a dramatic step forward and stopped a few feet from Sean. "Give it to me. Slowly."

Sean reached back and took hold of the strap. He pulled it up over his head as carefully as he could and then held it out with both hands to Keiko. She took one more step toward him as if approaching a coiled rattlesnake, aware that any sudden move might bring terrible consequences. Once her fingers were wrapped around the black sheath, however, she snatched it away and jumped back in case the snake tried to bite her.

Sean stiffened but didn't make a move. He couldn't with so many guns pointed in his direction. Tommy was frozen in place, but that didn't keep the fire from blazing in his eyes.

"Thank you," Keiko said, inspecting the scabbard.

She took hold of the sword's handle and jerked it out. Once more the steel rang its high-pitched siren's sound up to the ceiling and out the door. Her eyes went from the hilt to the tip and back again as she admired the ancient weapon. In the light of day, it was even more magnificent.

The two Americans doubted she appreciated the historical significance of the Masamune. To her, it was a means to an end. She would be the unchallenged queen of the underworld in Japan. And her reach would extend far beyond the country's borders to wherever the Yakuza presence lurked.

Her wrist flicked to the left, and the blade sliced through the air, the tip stopping right at the base of Sean's jaw. She gently pressed the sharp steel into his neck, the edge easily cutting through the skin. Blood started to ooze out of the tiny wound. A little of it smeared onto the blade.

"I could end your life right now," she said.

He stood undaunted. "Go ahead, then. Or maybe you don't have what it takes."

She snorted cynically. "I guess you didn't see how I executed Taka in the parking garage yesterday."

"No, we saw it. But shooting a man from a distance and killing them with your hands up close are two completely different things."

She raised her eyebrows as if accepting the challenge. "Very well, Sean. I will kill you. But not in here."

"What's the matter?" he asked. "Suddenly have a conscious about doing evil deeds in a place of worship?"

Keiko tilted her head to the side. "Let's just say I'd rather not tempt fate." She turned to the men on her left and ordered them to bring the prisoners outside.

Three men grabbed Sean and dragged him out the door and down the steps. Four others split the duties of getting Tommy and Hiroki. The gangsters threw the three companions to the snow and stood over them like bullies in a schoolyard.

Keiko descended the stairs and walked around in front of the three men. "On your knees."

Hiroki obeyed, but the two Americans were less eager to oblige. She motioned to one of her men, who kicked Sean in the stomach and then pulled him up by the back of his hair until he was in a kneeling position. The gangster kept a firm grip on Sean's scalp, exposing his already bloodstained neck.

"You were a worthy adversary," Keiko said. "Unfortunately, there is no parting gift like you Americans love so much. All you will receive is a swift death, which, honestly, is far too easy, but I don't have time to torture you. I have an empire to build."

A million clever responses ran through Sean's mind, but he didn't voice a single one. Instead, his eyes stayed locked on a spot far behind Keiko's back. He'd been staring at it since they were brought outside.

"What are you waiting for?" he yelled.

Keiko looked almost impressed. "My, you *are* eager to die."

She twisted her body and raised the sword high over her shoulder.

"Take the shot!" Sean shouted.

The moment passed like sap running down the side of a maple tree in the middle of winter. One second, Keiko's arm was tensing, ready to strike. The next, a shot rang out from somewhere far behind her, near the edge of the woods.

A splash of blood and tissue erupted from her shoulder, and the next instant, the sword fell from her hand and onto the snow. She screamed, clutched the wound, and dropped to one knee. The man holding Sean's hair looked up into the woods to find where the shot had come from, but it was already too late. Another blast sent a round through his chest, sending him five feet back, where he crashed into a fence and collapsed to the ground.

The rest of the gangsters panicked. Their leader was down, another man dead, and they had no idea where the shooter was. They fanned out, instinctively looking for cover, but another one was cut down before he could find a hiding place.

Sean lunged forward and grabbed the sword's handle from amid several red splotches in the perfectly white powder. The gangsters had started to return fire, most of them aiming at random places among the trees. Branches snapped from the trunks, and bark flew through the air. If the shooter was in the woods, the gangsters didn't see him.

Sean ran at the nearest one who was hiding behind a barrel and launched at him with the sword. He cut through the man's arm as he turned to protect himself a moment too late. The severed limb dropped to the ground amid the man's howls. Sean cut the screaming short by spinning him around and running the tip of the blade through his abdomen. He yanked it out and kicked the gangster back to let him die on the ground next to his fallen limb.

Tommy pulled the gun out of his jacket and fired at two men on the left. He hit the first one in the back and the second one in the leg, but he and Hiroki were exposed at the front of the shrine. As the wounded gangster turned to respond, Tommy grabbed Hiroki and charged up the steps to take up a position behind the railing. Wood splintered along the rails going up the stairs. The corner of a post shattered into a dozen jagged pieces. Tommy knew the rails weren't enough, so he dragged Hiroki back into the interior of the shrine's entrance.

He poked his weapon around the corner and fired twice. There was little chance he would hit the target, but scaring the enemy could be just as useful in a frantic situation such as this. The wounded guy scurried clear of the volley and hopped on one foot over to a tree on the courtyard's edge where two other men were busy shooting into the woods.

Only seconds after the wounded man made it to the others, they turned their attention to the shrine's entrance. Their strategy was immediately apparent. One was going to run around to a side entrance, and the other would take the front. The guy with the bullet in his leg would remain by the tree and cover them.

Tommy pressed the release button on his weapon and freed the magazine. A quick check on the back told him he only had one shot left. He'd forgotten to account for those he'd used prior to the journey to the shrine. Now it looked like it would prove to be a costly mistake.

He turned to Hiroki. "They're going to come after us. I only have one shot left. I'll try to take out the guy coming in the front. Then we can fight the other one by hand."

Hiroki nodded. "Sounds good."

Tommy spun around the corner of the giant door frame and lined up the gangster who was swiftly sneaking across the courtyard with his knees bent in a crouch. He positioned himself just behind the stone basin at the edge of the steps and waited to attack.

Forty feet away, Sean lunged after another gangster. He swung the sword wildly, the edge zipping through the air with a low whir. The tip tore through the man's coat but missed flesh, and he immediately reacted with a counter, kicking high at the American and striking him in the cheek with his boot. The foot moved so fast, Sean barely had time to see it, much less defend the blow. He stumbled sideways, momentarily disoriented, and had to widen his stance to gather his balance. By then, the enemy was upon him, striking out with a sharp jab, another, and then a right hook. Sean was barely able to turn his head to absorb the first punch; the second glanced off his cheek. But the right hook landed squarely on his chin and rocked him backward. He staggered several feet, the chaos around him suddenly sent into a blurry tailspin.

A dark figure charged toward him. Sean blinked rapidly to regain his bearings, but his body felt heavy. He fought to keep standing, but gravity and the onset of dizziness were winning easily. The dark figure screamed and launched through the air. Sean felt the weight of the sword in his hand. He knew if he fell, the attacker would seize it and end things swiftly. He dug deep inside to muster the strength to lift the blade, and just as the gangster's boot was only a foot from Sean's face, he thrust the tip of the sword up through the man's groin and into his torso.

The boot struck Sean in the jaw and sent him to the ground, but the wound he'd inflicted on the enemy was mortal. Sean rolled around for a moment in the cold snow. The sting of the icy ground helped steady his senses and stabilize him. He could hear the other man groaning, but at first couldn't see him. Seconds passed into almost a minute before the world around Sean began to steady. He pushed himself up from the ground and stumbled over to the dying man who was trying in vain to pull the blade out of his body.

Sean obliged him and jerked it out. He looked out across the courtyard. His jaw and chin throbbed, and the dizziness hadn't completely dissipated. But he could see someone running toward the woods behind the shrine. *Keiko.*

She was clutching her shoulder as she jogged through the knee-deep snow. Sean started after her, but she'd already opened up a huge gap between them.

Inside the shrine, Tommy was focused on the man behind the stone basin. He kept aim with his pistol and felt the trigger give way under his finger's pressure. At the very moment he pulled, the wounded gangster by the tree fired. The round smacked into the wooden door frame, but it startled Tommy enough to cause his hand to twitch to the right. His finger was already in the act of pulling the trigger, and the gun blasted the round harmlessly into the snow fifteen feet beyond the target.

He ducked back inside the building and looked at Hiroki.

"Did you get him?" the younger man asked.

Tommy stalled for second. "No, not exactly."

"What does that mean? Not exactly? Either you did, or you didn't."

"I didn't, OK? Someone nearly shot me."

In the cloudy sky above, a break in the cover sent sunlight streaking through the area. And with it, Tommy and Hiroki saw the shadow of someone approaching through the front entrance. Around to the side, another door was opening. They were coming in.

"Take that one. I'll take this one," Tommy said and rushed around the corner.

As Tommy charged into the opening, he saw the approaching gangster. He was creeping up with a pistol held close to his cheek, trying to sneak in. His face turned from sinister to shocked as the American's big body flew at him.

There was nothing the enemy could do to stop him. His reactions were too slow, and by the time he even thought about firing his weapon, Tommy's shoulder plowed into his chest and drove him back down the stairs in a tumbling mass of arms and legs.

They rolled to a stop on the snow where the struggle continued. The gangster fought desperately to line up the gun barrel with

Tommy's face, but the American was bigger and stronger. Tommy smashed the guy's hand into the packed snow over and over again until the gun finally jogged loose. It was a short-lived victory.

Seeing his weapon fall free, the gangster swung his other fist around and landed it squarely on Tommy's right cheek.

It did not have the effect he thought it would.

The brutish American's head twisted to the side for a moment, and then he looked down at the man pinned beneath him. Tommy roared like a ravenous bear and started pummeling his opponent in a reckless rage. He gave no thought to technique or style, instead using his fists like hammers, pounding the man's face until it was a swollen, bloody mess.

Tommy's muscles grew heavy, and the blows came slower until he realized the man was unconscious. His chest heaved, and it took a moment to catch his breath. Then he reached out past his opponent's limp hand and grabbed the pistol. He glanced over at the guy behind the tree, but he'd left his position and taken off into the woods, hoping desperately to get away from the American madman. Tommy fired one shot at him to make sure he kept running and then turned his mind to his companions. He quickly surveyed the courtyard but found no sign of Sean and, equally as concerning, no sign of Keiko. A loud thump from inside the shrine brought his attention back to Hiroki.

"Crap," he said and rushed back up the steps. "Hiroki!"

He ran through the big doorway and slowed to a staggered stop. The sight before his eyes was unexpected to say the least.

Hiroki was standing there with his arms crossed and a devious grin stretched across his face. On the floor at his feet was the other gangster who'd tried to come into the building.

Tommy wiped a sleeve across his face where he'd taken the punch and continued to breathe heavily. "OK, good. You're OK."

Hiroki nodded. "What took you so long?"

Tommy coughed a short laugh. "Why does everybody always ask me that?"

36

KYOTO

S ean reached the edge of the woods and stared into the seemingly endless array of trees. He'd seen Keiko disappear into the forest. Where the field ended, the mountain dropped off, sloping down toward the valley below. Once she'd passed beyond that lip, Sean couldn't see where she went. She was wounded, though, and there was no way for her to cover her tracks in the snow.

He looked down and noted crimson drops of blood mixed into the path she'd forged in the white powder. The Masamune was still clutched tightly in his fingers. His face ached in multiple places, but the dizziness he'd experienced was mostly gone, replaced by a dull pain in his skull. It was likely a concussion, but he'd have to deal with that later.

A branch snapped somewhere in the woods beyond Keiko's tracks, and his mind snapped back to the moment. The gunfire back at the shrine had come to a stop, and now he was thrown back into the serene forest silence. Thick clouds rolled across the sky once more, ending the momentary glare of sunlight that had graced the area.

Sean took off down the hill. He moved fast, planting his boots in Keiko's path so he could move faster. He paid no attention to how loud he was being. She was on the run, and Sean had to catch her. If she got away, they may never get another chance at bringing her to justice.

A gunshot popped loudly from below, and one of the tree branches a few feet away snapped off. Instantly, he changed direction in mid-stride and dove to the right behind a big fir tree. He scanned the area the shot had come from but saw nothing. Sean's eyes narrowed as he searched every inch of the forest for any sign of Keiko. He could have sworn she wasn't armed, but then he remembered when she'd fallen, no one had bothered to check.

Another shot fired and exploded in a burst of white powder several feet away. His head twitched in the direction the sound had come from, but again he saw nothing. Sean crouched behind the tree trunk, keeping his left shoulder pressed against it to give her as small a target as possible. A few feet away, he saw a fallen branch in the snow. It was about three inches thick and had broken in half at some point. Flurries began fluttering through the treetops as he cautiously reached out and grabbed the stick. He expected another bullet to whizz by, but none did.

Sean stood up, keeping his back to the tree trunk. He switched the sword to his left hand and the branch to his right, then stepped out and heaved it through the air. He immediately ducked behind his hiding position as the stick tumbled end over end down the hill. It struck several branches on a spruce forty feet away, causing a significant amount of noise in the otherwise perfectly silent forest.

The gun fired again, this time taking aim in the direction of his diversionary stick. Now he knew where she was. Sixty feet away, in an outcropping of larger trees that anchored that part of the forest. She must have known that there was no escape unless Sean was dead.

Using the diversion, he crept from his hiding place and moved back over to where Keiko's tracks carved a trail through the snow. He found another smaller branch on the ground near the path and threw it down the hill, far to the left of where he knew she was holed up.

Sure enough, as soon as the stick clacked against another limb, a flash popped from behind one of the trees straight ahead. In the cold, windless air, smoke lingered in a gray haze against the dark outline of the evergreen trees below. If Keiko was trying to hide, she wasn't doing a very good job of it. This was her last stand.

He veered out of her tracks and into the powder, finding that the fresh snow crunched less than the stuff that had already been packed down. He waded forward, keeping the sword in a ready position, just in case. She was close now, and he could smell traces of the burned gunpowder lingering in the air. The pistol in her hand came into view, and Sean shifted to the left. She was moving it back and forth. His diversion had caused her to panic, and now Keiko had no idea where the attack would come from.

Sean wished he still had a pistol with him, but it had fallen out of his coat pocket in the courtyard struggle. He neared the first of the larger trees and stopped next to it. She was less than twenty feet away now. He could hear her breathing, her feet shifting uneasily in the snow as she swept the area for the imminent attack. As soon as Sean stepped around the tree, he'd be an easy target at point-blank range. He thought for a second and looked around at the ground for another stick. But all he could manage were a few twigs. Then he realized what he had to do.

Sean loosened his grip on the sword and held it by the handle's end. His lips parted, and he drew in a long, slow breath through his mouth and nose. He could feel his heart pounding in his chest as the tension built. There would only be one shot at this, and if he missed he would likely end up dead. His muscles felt the weight of the sword as he tensed and twisted his torso to the right.

The world stood still for that moment. Snowflakes seemed to hang in midair as he stepped out from behind the tree, reached back, and flung the blade at the target. The sword flew through the air like a gymnast tumbling head over heels off a pommel horse.

Keiko saw the movement out of the corner of her eye and whirled around to fire. Her reaction was a second too late, and the sword's handle struck her cheek just below the right eye. Her weapon fired, but the sword had knocked her sideways, and the bullet dove into the snow, coming nowhere close to her target. Sean hurried forward, knowing that since his plan had only partially worked, she would recover in a second, and then the advantage would be hers.

She took a step backward and planted her foot in the snow to steady herself. Then she noticed Sean running at her and tried to whip the gun around in his direction. He dove through the air with a loud yell and crashed into her as the gun blasted loudly. The bullet ripped through his coat and grazed his side, instantly sending a fresh twinge of pain through his body, but it wasn't enough to stop him.

His shoulder drove hard into her abdomen and sent the two of them falling down the hill. They rolled ten feet until they came to a stop with Keiko straddling Sean. She squeezed both legs and attempted to point the gun at his face, but he grabbed her wrist and, using a move he'd learned from his government training, twisted it down and back, snapping the bone easily. Keiko screamed in agony, and the pistol fell, disappearing into the powder.

Sean tossed her off him and stood up, clutching her coat. Despite the pain from her broken wrist, Keiko mustered enough strength to attempt a quick jab, but he dipped to the side and threw a right hook that landed on the rim of her jaw. With her eyes blank and her legs suddenly limp, she wavered for a moment before collapsing to the snow.

The vigorous activity caught up with Sean now, and he panted for air. He put his hands on his hips and stared down at the unconscious woman. "Dad always told me never to hit a woman." He shook his head. "Pretty sure in this case he'd make an exception."

A familiar voice echoed down from the top of the hill. "Sean!" Tommy yelled. "*You OK?*"

Sean stepped into view and saw his friend standing next to Hiroki at the lip of the slope. He nodded. "Yeah. I'm good." He looked back at Keiko still lying on the ground. "I knocked out your girlfriend, though."

Tommy shook his head, laughing. "She's definitely not my girlfriend. After all this, I think it's fair to say I've moved on."

Sean nodded. "That's probably a good idea, buddy. I don't think she's the girl for you."

The two Americans dragged Keiko back up the hill and across the field to the shrine. Seeing the bodies of the Yakuza gang strewn about the usually peaceful setting, the white-robed monks had gathered in bewilderment. One of the monks was examining the guy on the ground that Sean had run through with the sword. The Masamune was back in its scabbard, strapped to his back as they approached the scene.

Amid the confusion and the men in robes, the Americans noticed a few faces that stood out in the crowd. Standing over by the large torii, Tara and Alex were standing together. Alex had a backpack slung over his shoulder, while Tara had what appeared to be a hunting rifle.

Sean and Tommy noticed them at the same time and waved.

The two newcomers walked toward them, and they met in the middle of the courtyard.

"Boy am I glad to see you two," Sean said. "But how did you know we were in trouble?"

Tara beamed. "Well, when Tommy phoned in, he called me Trouble. He told me that if he ever called me by that name, he needed help. Alex and I figured this was where you'd be headed, so we chartered a flight and came straightaway."

"You're going to need to reimburse us for that, by the way," Alex added. "Turns out that chartering a last-minute flight to Japan from Atlanta isn't exactly cheap."

Tommy snorted. "I'll write you a check."

Tara pointed at the unconscious girl draped across the Sean's shoulders. "Who's this?"

"This," Sean said, "was the source of our trouble. But she's taking a little nap right now, so I don't think she'll be a problem."

Alex looked across the chaos. "So this is what you two do when you're not at the lab?"

Tommy rolled his shoulders. "More or less."

37

TOKYO, ONE MONTH LATER

Giving an explanation to the master of the shrine had been a delicate matter, especially to a monk who'd spent most of his life in pursuit of nonviolence. It hadn't taken a lot of persuasion for him to understand what was going on and that Keiko and her minions were the bad guys. The authorities required a little more convincing. A call from a friend in the White House, however, went a long way to clearing the air. After all, the president owed Sean a favor.

Sean looked out at the scene. The Japanese government had spared no expense. He and his friends sat atop a stage overlooking the palace grounds in Tokyo. All of Japan's heads of state were in attendance, as were many of the top historians from all around the world.

The prime minister—who'd been speaking for the last five minutes—finished what he was saying at the podium and then called Tommy over to make the presentation.

Cameras flashed from the hundreds of guests and several members of the press who were huddled around the front row. Tommy stood up and strolled over to the podium. He shook the prime minister's hand and then bowed to him first, then to the crowd. The people applauded, clapping their hands vigorously. When the applause slowed to a halt, Tommy looked out over the audience and smiled.

"For many years, the Honjo Masamune has been sought by trea-sure hunters, historians, archaeologists, and anyone else you can think of." He looked down to his right at a stand with a drape over it. "This weapon has now been returned to its rightful place, to the Japanese people, and to the original home of the Tokugawa clan."

The crowd roared again, applauding even louder than before.

Tommy waited once more for it to die down before speaking again. "I've been doing this kind of work for a long time. Sometimes it's fun. Sometimes it's dangerous. But it is always satisfying to discover a piece of lost history and bring it back to the world, espe-cially when it is something as important as the Honjo Masamune. This sword represents the enduring spirit of Japan, the toughness and resilience of its people, and the ability to adapt to whatever destiny throws your way."

The people whipped into a frenzy, and Sean smiled broadly. He'd never seen his friend play to a crowd so well before. Even the prime minister seemed impressed, perhaps even a tad upstaged.

"And so, without further delay, I present to you, Mr. Prime Minis-ter," he nodded at the leader, "and to you, your highness," he bowed to the emperor sitting off to the left, "the greatest sword ever made. The Honjo Masamune."

With dramatic showmanship, Tommy reached down and yanked away the drape. A rectangular glass case gleamed in the light. Contained inside was the black scabbard holding the slender blade.

The crowd gasped at first, and then the cameras started flashing again. People snapped dozens of photos with their phones, anxious to be the first to share them on social media.

Tommy's face beamed with pride as he stared out at the crowd, his head slowly turning one way and then the other.

Sean scanned the crowd. Adriana sat in the front row, smiling at him with her usual sly grin. She'd been permitted to be a guest of honor at Sean's request and had flown in from Spain to see the presentation. He couldn't wait to spend some alone time with her. He needed the rest and a little time in a nice hot tub to sooth his aching muscles.

His eyes drifted past her, across the rows of curious onlookers. Suddenly, his gaze stopped on a familiar face, one he'd not expected to find here. He blinked several times before he realized he wasn't hallucinating. It was Aoki. How had the gangster gotten through security? Sean instinctively reached into his jacket but then remembered no weapons were permitted at the gathering.

He tensed for a second, sensing the threat. Then Aoki smiled at him and bowed his head slowly, as if to say thank you. Hiroki was sitting next to Sean on the stage and had seen the wordless interaction between the two. He leaned close to Sean and put his hand on the American's shoulder.

"The boss says to tell you thank you. You have done a great favor to the Yakuza and are always welcome in his home."

Keiko had been arrested, though first she required a trip to the hospital to treat her broken wrist and a minor gunshot wound. She would no longer be a threat, at least as far as anyone knew. Her connections in the underworld had been rooted out, mostly by the police, but Sean had a feeling that there were some other things happening as well that were not of a legal nature. It was only a matter of time until the bodies of the men who had sworn loyalty to her would start turning up in random places.

Nonetheless, Sean relaxed, relieved that Aoki was not a threat to him or anyone else in attendance. At least not now, anyway. His lips stretched to the right in a sideways grin. "Tell him I said thank you. But between you and me, I don't think I'll be taking him up on that offer anytime soon."

"That is probably for the best."

Sean looked back over at his friend who was stepping aside to allow the emperor to take the stage. He nodded at him and gave a thumbs-up to let Tommy know he'd done a good job.

As the emperor began to speak, Sean's mind wandered to past

adventures. There was no escaping it. This was what he did. And he was good at it. *Might as well stop fighting it,* he thought as he glanced at his friend again. *We are who we are. And this is what we do.*

THANK YOU

I just wanted to take a second to say thanks for reading my book. You could have chosen to spend your time with a million other stories and you chose mine. For that I am honored.

If you are new to my stories, swing over to ernestdempsey.net to get a free book in the Sean Wyatt series. All you have to do is enter your email to join the free VIP group. You'll also get exclusive content like video interviews, free unedited chapters, and much more!

Once again, thanks for reading this story. Please take the time to leave an honest review on your retailer of choice. Those reviews are helpful to other readers and to authors too.

Have a great day!

Ernest

It is important to note that some of the geographical locations and terrain were altered slightly for this story. However, many of the places I mention in this book can be visited during the warmer months of the year.

The mountainous Dewa region is a spectacular setting, full of abundant wildlife and natural resources. The shrines and the pagoda mentioned in the story are all very real places. The caves and secret locations mentioned in the story were a figment of my imagination... as far as I can tell. They are, however, entirely plausible.

One of the pieces of fiction is where the sword was found in the story. No one knows where the great Honjo Masamune sword is hiding, though several Masamune blades are owned by wealthy collectors. Historians and treasure hunters alike are still on the hunt for the fabled weapon.

The Yakuza are real and extremely dangerous.

We may never know the true fate of the Honjo Masamune. It is sought after because it was created by the greatest sword maker of all time. Masamune's techniques were revered by all, and to own a blade made by him was considered an incredible honor.

If the sword was not destroyed by the allies at the end of the war, it is likely hidden away somewhere safe, protected by those who will never reveal its location.

OTHER BOOKS BY ERNEST DEMPSEY

The Adventure Guild:

The Caesar Secret: Books 1-3

The Carolina Caper

Beta Force:

Operation Zulu

London Calling

The Relic Runner:

Out of the Fire

Paranormal Archaeology Division:

Hell's Gate

For my friend Kimura Lea Zunich. You are missed.

ACKNOWLEDGMENTS

As always, I would like to thank my terrific editors for their hard work. What they do makes my stories so much better for readers all over the world. Anne Storer and Jason Whited are the best editorial team a writer could hope for and I appreciate everything they do.

I also want to thank Elena at Lᴛ Graphics for her tremendous work on my book covers and for always overdelivering. Elena definitely rocks.

Last but not least, I need to thank all my wonderful fans and especially the advance reader team. Their feedback and reviews are always so helpful and I can't say enough good things about all of them.

Made in the USA
Coppell, TX
03 June 2021